PENGUIN CRIME FICTION

DEAD ON THE STICK

Robert Upton divides his time between New York City and South-
ampton, New York, and spends too much of it on the golf course.
He is the author of three previous novels, including two Amos
McGuffin mysteries, *Who'd Want to Kill Old George?* and *Fade
Out* (available in Penguin Books). He has also written for the
screen and stage.

Dear Allan,

Happy Valentines!

Hope this book brings
further light into
the game of golf.

A

PENGUIN BOOKS
Viking Penguin Inc., 40 West 23rd Street,
New York, New York 10010, U.S.A.
Penguin Books Ltd, Harmondsworth,
Middlesex, England
Penguin Books Australia Ltd, Ringwood,
Victoria, Australia
Penguin Books Canada Limited, 2801 John Street,
Markham, Ontario, Canada L3R 1B4
Penguin Books (N.Z.) Ltd, 182–190 Wairau Road,
Auckland 10, New Zealand

First published in the United States of America by
Viking Penguin Inc. 1986
Published in Penguin Books 1987

LIBRARY OF CONGRESS CATALOGING IN PUBLICATION DATA
Upton, Robert.
  Dead on the stick.
  (Penguin crime fiction)
  I. Title.
PS3571.P5D3   1987   813'.54   86-21232
ISBN 0 14 00.7601 8

Printed in the United States of America by
Offset Paperback Mfrs., Inc., Dallas, Pennsylvania
Set in Linotron Caledonia

DEAD ON THE STICK

AN AMOS McGUFFIN MYSTERY

ROBERT UPTON

PENGUIN BOOKS

This book is dedicated to all those hackers, hookers, slicers, shankers, yippers, whiffers, scruffers, muffers, flubbers, sclaffers, dubbers, and chili-dippers out there—and especially to my golfing partner, Chuck Verrill, witness to all the above.

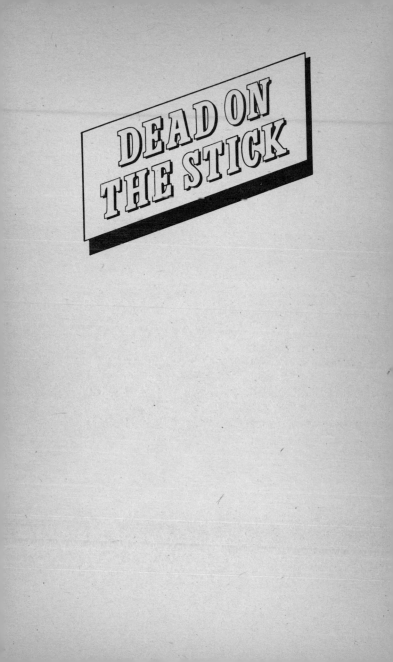

DEAD ON
THE STICK

1

It was the week of the Crosby Clambake and anybody in San Francisco who was anybody was in Pebble Beach, watching the golf pros and their celebrity partners by day and making the rounds of the gala house parties by night. Amos McGuffin, though, was in Goody's, watching the tournament on television from a stool midway down the bar. Golf wasn't nearly as popular as football among the lawyers, judges, cops, and assorted politicos who patronized Goody's, a saloon nearly as old as Troon, lying no more than a good mashie niblick away from the former site of the old Hall of Justice, but McGuffin liked it well enough. Golf or football, it didn't make much difference when you were half drunk—and McGuffin was at least that.

The only man present who was drunker than McGuffin was Danny the Drunk, who was asleep at one of the scarred oak card tables that lined the wall opposite the bar. When Jack Nicklaus reached the eighteenth green in two, a great roar went up from the gallery, which woke Danny. He sat up, rubbed his eyes, and stared uncomprehendingly at the television, then got up and made his way slowly to the bar.

"Amos, who's playin'?" Danny asked.

"Jesus, you want me to name them all?" McGuffin complained.

"Just give me the teams," Danny said, squinting at the television.

"The football season's over. This is golf," McGuffin informed him.

Danny blinked. "You mean I missed the Super Bowl?"

"You were here for the Super Bowl," McGuffin explained patiently, as he watched Nicklaus stride onto the eighteenth green with his familiar grin and a wave of his putter.

"I was?" Danny asked, regarding McGuffin suspiciously.

"You sat right there," McGuffin said, pointing to the stool next to him while keeping his eyes on the golf.

"Thank God," Danny spoke softly. He started for his table, then stopped and turned back to McGuffin. "By the way, who won?"

"I forget," McGuffin answered.

"Some sports fan you are," Danny muttered, going back to his nap.

Danny was right. Team sports didn't much interest McGuffin. He had played them in high school because it had been expected of him, but he preferred the individual sports, especially golf, having played a great deal as a kid while working as a caddie at the Olympic Club. It probably had something to do with his becoming a private eye and not a corporate team player, he guessed, but he wouldn't give it any more thought than that. Right now he was preoccupied with the seemingly inextricable realities of unemployment and demon rum—or in his case, Paddy's Irish whiskey. For although McGuffin never drank while on a case—it was one of an ever dwindling number of principles to which he still adhered—his gargantuan thirst during periods of unemployment was the stuff of legend in San Francisco saloon society. It had been almost a month since his last case, and since then he had not had so much as a hint of a new assignment. He was only at the bar to find a job, he told himself, as he drained the last of his whiskey from the glass.

Part saloon and part employment center to the lawyers and private investigators who gathered there, Goody's Bar held a strange fascination for a certain class of drinkers who could plainly afford a better joint. Goody's was a man's bar, with a floor of black and white octagonal tile, the sort seen in old bathrooms, and several battered tables and dented spittoons scattered about, but women had begun frequenting the place lately, mostly lawyers and secretaries, some looking for referrals, others for dates.

Although McGuffin, since his divorce, had a couple of times come up with a date in Goody's, his primary reason for being there was always the same—to find a case. Lawyers and insurance people were his best source of employment, but the police reporters and homicide detectives who frequented the place were occasionally good for a productive lead as well. It was that kind of business and Goody's was that kind of place. You could never tell what might turn up.

At the moment there were very few people in the bar, but in a little while, after the offices closed, they'd begin pressing in like cattle in a pen. They'd throw down their drinks as if the Russian rockets were coming, while the cigar smoke thickened and the volume rose steadily to a blurred cacophony. They'd talk of careers and politics (often the same here), the economy, sports, local history, screwed-up kids, greedy ex-wives, girlfriends and mistresses (wives were never mentioned except when they phoned looking for their husbands, who had always "just left"), and sundry topics of varying gravity. Some of it would be rumor, much of it gossip, and most of it bullshit. But to the trained ear, such as McGuffin's, there might well be one valuable kernel among the husks.

"Goody!" he called to the gorilla-shaped barkeep who was drawing a draft at the end of the bar.

Goody looked up and snarled, and McGuffin knew he would not get another drink for a while. Bartender though he was, Goody was also something of a Jewish mother. When he felt that certain of his charges were abusing the grape, he would lecture them harshly or in some cases cut them off entirely. Because Danny the Drunk was beyond help, and would only get mugged or hit by a car if he were eighty-sixed, Goody allowed him to drink and nod off at the table, as a reminder to the regulars, perhaps, of the fate that awaited those who spurned his advice. Goody had not yet given up on McGuffin, but he was becoming impatient. He had not spoken a word to the detective since he had entered the place, more than an hour before.

McGuffin pretended indifference to Goody's rebuff, as he idly studied his reflection in the yellowing mirror behind the bar. That was no longer a youthful blush on those swollen cheeks, but the flush of Paddy's, he realized, as he turned his face from side to side. And that girdle of flesh that hung from his ribs was not going away either. But he was not out of control. Everything would be all right, he just needed a job.

"Goody!" he called again.

"What do you want?" Goody shouted, coming at McGuffin like a wounded rhinoceros.

"Another drink," McGuffin answered.

"No more," Goody said, snatching McGuffin's empty glass in a broken-knuckled fist and splashing it in the sink. "I'm amazed you even have the audacity to show up here after what happened last night."

"What do you mean?" McGuffin asked.

"You don't remember a thing, do you?"

"Of course I remember," McGuffin answered, drawing himself erect on the bar stool. "We just seem to differ concerning my behavior."

"Cut the bullshit," Goody ordered. "You remember Sullivan being here last night?"

"Sullivan the cop?" McGuffin asked, trying to remember.

"What other Sullivan comes in here?" Goody replied impatiently.

McGuffin knew him. Sober, he was a loud, irreverent, foulmouthed wild man, whom McGuffin rather liked. Drunk, he was a weepy, repentant, evangelizing born-again Christian, and extremely sensitive to criticism.

"Yeah, I remember Sullivan being here, sort of," McGuffin qualified.

"And you know that when Sullivan is undergoing one of his religious experiences, he's not to be messed with?"

"I do."

"So when he proposed a toast to his saintly sister the nun, why did you say, 'And to all the holy priests she's servicing'?"

"I didn't say that," McGuffin said, shaking the blood from his face.

"I was standing right here," Goody insisted. "I managed to come over the bar before he could get to his gun."

"Jesus, was I that drunk?" McGuffin mumbled, running his hand through his hair.

"I'm warning you, Amos, you gotta slow down. It's no longer cute. You're not a college kid up for the big weekend. You're a guy pushing forty who's getting deep into the sauce. You think you can keep climbing out, but one day you won't, and then you'll be a stewbum like Danny, sleeping on the card table. Now, you can do that if you want, but I don't want to be around to see it, so you can either cut down or cut out. Do you get me?"

"Come on—" McGuffin began to protest weakly as Goody turned and walked off.

Even Danny the Drunk was staring, but McGuffin managed a careless smile that returned the drinkers to their conversation, or the golf match. He had heard Goody's temperance lecture many times before, but this was the first time the barkeep had turned his back on him, walked away without even listening to his excuse. Goody was exaggerating, McGuffin told himself. He could quit drinking whenever he liked. All he needed was a case.

Sitting at the bar without a drink in front of him, McGuffin began to feel awkward, but he would not cut and run. He wouldn't give Goody the satisfaction. Instead he feigned absorption in the golf tournament, watching Fuzzy Zoeller in slow motion as Ken Venturi analyzed his swing. "Not pretty, but he gets the job done," Venturi concluded. He could be talking about me, McGuffin thought.

Then, like a specter, Danny the Drunk appeared in the mirror beside him. Their eyes caught and held, and, it seemed to McGuffin, a flash of recognition passed between them.

"Don't worry, I'll get you a drink," Danny said, pulling a thick roll of bills from his pocket.

McGuffin watched as Danny swayed and fumbled at the bills, before peeling off a twenty. Danny had inherited enough money a few years ago to ensure that he would never again have to work. Until then he had been a good trial lawyer who drank a little too much but managed to keep on top of things, like so many of Goody's customers. Lately he had begun talking about giving up alcohol and going back to work, but McGuffin knew it would come to nothing. It was no wonder Goody had grown tired of excuses.

"What're ya drinkin'?" Danny asked, slapping the twenty on the bar. He clutched the bar with one hand and looked at his shoes, as if he might throw up.

"Nothing," McGuffin answered. "I've quit drinking."

Danny looked up and blinked quizzically as his mouth twisted into a grotesque smile. "Don't gimme that," he said, as McGuffin slid off the bar stool. "You'll never quit drinkin'," he called as McGuffin walked to the door.

McGuffin knew better. He was no alcoholic. He could quit whenever he wanted to, and he would quit now. The crowd at the bar cheered as McGuffin pushed the door open and stepped out onto the sidewalk. Nicklaus had just made a birdie putt.

2

Across the United States, at an exclusive golf club on a small island off the east coast of Florida, a golf event of a different order was taking place—the inauguration of new officers of the Palm Isle Golf Club. Men in black tie gathered about the circular bar in the main dining room to congratulate their new president and reigning club champion, Lyle Boone, the self-made millionaire who, in the less egalitarian days of "the Palm," could not have so much as gained membership in that august body, let alone elective office. But change was often cruel, and although the Palm had been a Roaring Twenties creation of men to the manor born, the advent of the income tax forced an unconscionable choice upon these gentlemen of wealth and breeding. They could either admit to membership those arrivistes who, without the advantages of birth, had risen to positions of great power and wealth by dint of energy and intelligence, or they could sell part of their island to a hotel chain and share their golf course with the hotel "guests." Being for the most part practical men, they generously agreed to welcome a limited number of well-heeled though lowborn men who would pay dearly for the privilege of mixing with their betters.

No wonder then that Lyle Boone was beaming, as representatives of the oldest and most distinguished families in America crowded around to pound his broad back and shake his beefy hand. The son of an Oklahoma sharecropper, he had grown rich purchasing oil and gas leases for next to nothing in his home state, then turning them into some of the richest oil and gas fields outside Texas. Already a millionaire by his thirtieth birthday, he then invested a few million in a Silicon Valley computer-chip company and quickly became a multi-millionaire. His future assured, Lyle moved to Los Angeles, married a horsefaced though penniless debutante, and set himself to the task of becoming a gentleman.

For Lyle this proved a far more formidable task than acquiring great wealth. Although he managed to lose his Oklahoma accent, thanks to the patient tutelage of Hollywood's top voice coach, and bought his clothes only at the most *au courant* Rodeo Drive boutiques, he still seemed to Angeleno aristocrats to be dripping with oil, not money.

"You can't blame them for disliking you," Francis Knight, his socially prominent lawyer, had explained when Lyle's application for membership in the Bel Air Country Club was rejected. Francis was a San Franciscan, the attorney for Lyle's Silicon Valley company, and no admirer of Los Angeles. "Many of these Los Angeles socialites are the descendants of refugees from the Dust Bowl, Okies and such. Your people stayed on and you eventually made millions on the very land their forebears had deserted."

Whatever the reason, Lyle was forever hardened to Los Angeles society. Unable to crack the Bel Air Country Club, he was forced to join Riviera, less prestigious but possessing a more challenging golf course. Still smarting from the rejection, Lyle decided to become a top player, the captain of the Riviera team that would one day travel across town like an invading army, to do battle with the best of Bel Air. And when they glimpsed his swing, silky and fluid as a mountain stream over smooth stones, they would realize, too late, their great mistake. The stage would be set, or the pins would be placed, for a devastation that would be total. He would leave the Bel Air team a pitiful rabble of shanking, slicing, yipping hackers.

Lyle applied himself to this task with a fervid intensity that disturbed and alarmed even some of the most hardened of golf addicts. Scotty, the old pro who had observed the horrible effects of the golf bug many times before, watched sadly from the pro shop atop the hill as Lyle beat balls on the practice range from dawn till noon, in preparation for their playing lesson in the afternoon. No good would come of this, the old pro was sure, other than a substantial increase in his own income. And he was right.

Within just a few weeks, the first signs of hopeless addiction began to appear. Lyle could not pass his reflection in a glass without stopping to practice and observe his golf swing; an umbrella, or similar familiar object, existed only to be swung, even in a storm; and conferences dealing with matters of life and death became nothing more than occasions to mentally replay a particularly good round, while carefully analyzing those few shots that went astray. Sometimes at a dinner party, or in a crowded elevator, or in church, he would suddenly blurt inexplicable commands, such as "Slow it down, stupid," which caused the nongolfers in the vicinity to fidget nervously, while the initiated only smiled knowingly.

When it became too dark to play (rain didn't stop him), Lyle retired to his study to devour the great books by Palmer, Nicklaus, Snead, Sarazen, Vardon, Jones, Cotton, Farnie, Tillinghast, Haultain, and all the others, going as far back as the Dutch originators of the game. The game of golf, it seemed, spawned more prose, sometimes even poetry, than all the other games combined. And everything written, it quickly became apparent, was contradicted by something else. It was a monkish novitiate, leaving no time for wife and family, but Lyle was a faithful and dedicated servant of his new god.

During the first year of his apprenticeship he played golf for 365 days, and on the last day he shot an eighty-nine. It would not qualify him for the U.S. Open, but—even the old pro had to agree—it was a remarkable achievement. One more year, Lyle decided, and he would shoot a seventy-nine. Then he would gather his warriors and lay siege to that bastion of privilege across town, the Bel Air Country Club. Ah, sweet vengeance.

But things happened in that second year that were to change Lyle Boone's life dramatically. He was playing with

Scotty one day, standing over a short par putt on the tenth green after a forty-four on the front side (missing two putts he should have made), when a man in a dark suit approached him on a golf cart.

"Mr. Boone?" the man asked, as Lyle bent over his putt.

Annoyed, Lyle stepped back from his putt and glared at the man. Obviously a nongolfer, the man in the dark suit walked brazenly across the green and handed Lyle an envelope.

"What the hell is this?" Lyle demanded, continuing to glare at the man. He had a crooked nose and several scars on his face.

"A summons. Your wife is suing you for divorce," the process server informed him, backing out of the defendant's reach. He quick-stepped across the green, jumped on his cart, and raced for the clubhouse.

Scotty shook his head sadly. He had known it was coming, even if his student hadn't. Divorce among golf addicts was as common as silicosis among textile workers, but far more expensive.

"Hold this, will you?" Lyle asked, handing the envelope to the old pro. He took a practice stroke, addressed the putt, and calmly knocked it in.

A radiant smile creased Scotty's sunburned face. It was only a four-footer, but now he knew—Lyle Boone had the makings of a champion.

Because there was a child, of whom Lyle was only dimly aware, the divorce was complicated. But Francis Knight, his San Francisco attorney, handled it extremely well, causing Lyle to lose half his fortune but only half a day of golf on the afternoon of the hearing. To show his gratitude, Lyle added an additional hundred thousand dollars to the lawyer's fee. And Francis, to show his gratitude, invited Lyle for a weekend of golf at his own club. Always eager to test himself over a new layout, Lyle was delighted to accept the lawyer's invitation.

"Bring black tie," his attorney said.

"Black tie? Where is this club?" Lyle asked.

"In the Bahamas," the lawyer answered.

At the end of the following week they boarded a plane in Los Angeles bound for Miami, where they were met by the club's private plane and flown to Palm Isle. They arrived after dark and were driven directly to the sumptuous main dining room of the clubhouse, where a reception was already in progress. Lyle recognized a few celebrity faces at the circular bar in the center of the dining room, but Francis ignored these as he led his guest across the carpet to meet a few of his friends. Although most of these faces were unfamiliar, the names were familiar to any student of American history or *The Wall Street Journal*. Lyle followed in stunned disbelief as Francis calmly introduced him, one after the other, to many of the most important people in America, most of whom seemed genuinely pleased to meet him. And they were. For although Lyle didn't know it, he was being courted by the dignified and affluent members of the Palm Isle Golf Club, whose governing board had recently decided to bring in a single new member, rather than assess themselves one and a half million dollars for a new underground watering system.

"All these famous people belongin' to the same golf club and I never even heard of it!" Lyle exclaimed later, when he and Francis were alone.

"The Palm is the best golf club the world has never heard of," Francis answered.

The next day, after Lyle had played eighteen holes over the most beautiful golf course he had ever seen, accompanied by Francis, a Supreme Court justice, and a famous entertainer, Lyle was ready to be plucked. That evening, after dinner and a few drinks, he was taken down to the Founders' Room by a group of his new friends, now including a former President of the United States, where they sat in deep leather chairs, smoked Cuban cigars, and obliquely discussed the making of a Palm man. Lyle agreed that while a two-million-dollar initiation fee might be considered expensive by some, these were hardly the sort of people the Palm should be interested in.

"Then it's decided!" the former President said, slapping his hands on his knees.

"Sir—?" Lyle asked. He seemed to be the only one who didn't know what had been decided.

"You tell him," the entertainer said to Francis.

"Well, Lyle, to put it simply—Palm men are given to the unadorned phrase—we'd like you to join us:"

Remembering his earlier rejection by a lesser club, Lyle regarded them suspiciously. "You mean you want me to join the Palm Isle Golf Club?" he asked hesitantly.

"That's exactly what we mean," the former President assured him.

Lyle was speechless.

"Lyle will be pleased to join us," his lawyer said.

They rose as one and began pumping Lyle's hand and congratulating him. Lyle stood with an uncertain smile on his face. Then he was ushered out of the Founders' Room and through a long corridor lined with photographs of men in plus fours, all of whom seemed to be scowling. They entered the locker room and walked past the rows of green lockers to an archway at the far end of the room that Lyle had not noticed before. This was a smaller locker room, Lyle saw when he followed his new friends through the arch, with no more than a dozen lockers in a line down the middle of the room. They positioned Lyle in front of the lockers and waited for his reaction. All the lockers looked the same to Lyle, except that one had a polished gold nameplate.

Then he saw the name—Gen. Dwight D. Eisenhower—etched on the gold plate, and under the locker, the General's spiked shoes.

"Ike," Lyle whispered.

After a few moments of reverential silence, they left the locker room and climbed the stairs to the main dining room, joking and laughing easily all the way. Lyle couldn't feel his feet on the steps, but he was slowly beginning to realize that this was where he belonged. He was a Palm man.

Back at the bar, an international financier tinkled an empty brandy glass with a mixing spoon until he had the attention of all his fellow members. Then, quite simply, he placed a hand on Lyle's shoulder and announced: "I would like to introduce our new member, Lyle Boone."

If the applause was restrained, it was only because of the dignity of the group. And if some of the members were not applauding at all, Lyle was too starry-eyed to notice. He was quickly assigned an account number so he could order a round of drinks for everybody, which was quickly followed by another. Later in the evening, when Dr. Byron Kilty, the famous heart transplant surgeon, suggested a toast to the Lyle Boone underground watering system, Lyle laughed heartily with his fellow members, even though he didn't get the joke.

Now, standing in the same place only three years later— the newly inaugurated club president and reigning club golf champion—Lyle Boone was even happier than he had been then. And when the beautiful blonde at his side kissed him and said, "Congratulations, darling," his joy increased. For this gorgeous woman, scarcely half his age, who until her marriage a year ago tonight had been one of the top models in San Francisco, was the new Mrs. Lyle Boone. This was indeed the American dream, and Lyle was living it to the fullest.

"Thank you, darling," Lyle said, his lips seeking hers for yet a second kiss. For although they were still on their honeymoon, Lyle didn't see his new bride nearly as much as he would like. Marian Boone was a shopper, not a golfer, so she spent most of her time aboard their yacht in Palm Beach, which was anchored conveniently close to the shops of Worth Avenue. Much as he missed her at night, he wasn't entirely displeased with the arrangement, as it left him free to play golf during the day. Despite Lyle's social successes, golf was still the ruling passion of his life. Being the defending champion, he had set a harsh regimen for himself—up at six for a three-mile run on the beach, two hours on the practice tee followed by thirty-six holes, then another session on the practice tee. Even when Marian was there, Lyle was often too tired to make love. But she, unlike his first wife, understood how important his golf was to him.

"After I've defended my crown, we'll have us a real orgy," he promised, on one of those nights he disappointed.

Marian was delighted, even though he had fallen asleep while she was describing the things she would like him to do to her. Tonight, she realized, would almost certainly be a disappointment. For although Lyle drank hardly at all while in training for the club championship, this night celebrating both his inauguration and their wedding anniversary offered more than sufficient reason to break training. In fact he was drunker tonight than anyone had ever before seen him.

When Dr. Kilty proposed still another drink to the new president, Lyle countered with the toast "To the underground watering system!"—which never failed to get a laugh, although he still didn't understand why. Then, like the old wildcatter that he once was, Lyle tossed his bourbon back with a smart snap and pushed his glass across the bar for a refill.

"Darling, don't you think you've had enough?" Marian asked, coiling a sleek, suntanned arm around her husband's generous middle.

"Don't you worry, honey," he said, stooping to whisper in her ear. "A little red-eye only makes it bigger."

Although she knew better, she grinned and gave him a squeeze. Then, as if her embrace had set off a powerful electrical shock in her husband, she was suddenly jolted away and slammed against the bar by a convulsive thrust of his body. He stood rigidly with his back to the bar, supported by one elbow, gasping, his face quickly turning dark and suffused, then changing to a hideous grin. When he brought one hand to his chest and began sliding to the floor, Dr. Kilty caught him and lowered him onto his back. Marian watched, horrified, as Lyle stared wildly at her with that same fixed grin, and the deep gasps gave way suddenly to convulsive shudders.

"He's having a heart attack!" Dr. Kilty said, dropping to his knees beside Lyle.

Marian's view was partially blocked when Dr. Kilty went to work on her husband, but she could see that his body had become arched in an inhuman way, only the heels and the back of his head touching the floor. His lips still bore a rigid, deathlike grin when, after a last violent spasm, his body collapsed on the floor and lay still. Dr. Kilty continued to work on him for several minutes, but Lyle's heart would not respond. Lyle Boone, president and club champion of the Palm Isle Golf Club, had died on the happiest day of his life.

3

Despite his pledge of the day before, McGuffin awakened late the next morning with a throbbing head and little recollection of the evening's events. He remembered leaving Goody's and stopping off at the Washington Square Bar for one last drink, just to celebrate the taking of the pledge, but after that things became a bit blurred. He vaguely remembered being driven to the *Oakland Queen*, the converted ferry boat on the Embarcadero which he called home and office, but couldn't remember if it was in his own car or someone else's. Lying stiffly in the narrow wheelhouse bunk, McGuffin silently renewed his pledge of sobriety, then pulled himself up and across the deck to a small refrigerator.

Usually after four Alka-Seltzer tablets in half a glass of beer, followed by a long shower, some of the events of the night before would begin to take shape in his mind, like a pointillist painting that requires only proper distancing. But today, even after hanging from the shower nozzle for some time, he could still see nothing but dots. He would have to get a job and get one quickly, or he would either drink himself to death or starve to death, he realized, as he dropped the towel on the deck and stepped back into the wheelhouse.

He had been almost a month without a job, and his checking account was eroding faster than Malibu Beach. Still, I don't have to worry about being evicted for nonpayment of rent, he reminded himself, as he selected a clean shirt from one of the narrow chart drawers against the starboard bulkhead. Elmo, the architect who had converted the ferry boat to offices, insisted that all the original marine equipment remain in the wheelhouse, which made the living a bit clumsy. McGuffin hadn't been too concerned with the accommodations when he first moved in, because the arrangement, whereby he was to serve as security officer aboard the boat in exchange for free rent, would be brief, lasting only until he made a killing and moved into a proper apartment and office. That was more than five years ago, during which time he had staggered from one financial crisis to another. But one of these days, if he held on long enough, he could feel it, he would be rewarded with one of the plums of private investigation— bodyguard to a shiek, or industrial espionage—something clean and safe instead of the knocked-down, beat-up, shot-at real thing. Until then, however, insulting though it might be to a top detective like himself, he would have to remain aboard the *Oakland Queen* as security officer.

As McGuffin was standing in front of the locker, trying to decide on his least stained tie, the phone rang. Sensing work, he pounced on it in the middle of the second ring and, despite his hangover, answered cheerily:

"Amos McGuffin, confidential investigations."

"Well, aren't we getting fancy. Whatever happened to 'Yeah, whattaya want?'"

"Shit," McGuffin said softly. It was Mrs. Begelman, his answering service, calling no doubt to find out where her check was. "If it's about the check, Mrs. Begelman—" he began.

"What check? I got the check," she answered. "Though the way it was stained and scrawled, I'm not surprised you don't remember. And if you don't mind, Mr. McGuffin, I wish you would not mutter obscenities into the phone when I call with important messages. Do you know what happened last night?"

"Of course," McGuffin answered reflexively. Then, realizing he was talking to his answering service and not his bartender, he asked: "What?"

"I didn't think so. You got a call from Mr. Francis Knight, that's what happened."

"Francis Knight?" he questioned. Knight was the whitest of

the white-shoe lawyers—adviser to Republican Presidents, a former ambassador, past president of the American Bar Association, as well as the exclusive (though ironically named) Bohemian Club—and not at all the sort of person most likely to be calling a gumshoe like McGuffin. "What did he want?"

"What, am I nosy? All I know is he said you should call first thing this morning, so I been calling since eight-thirty. What, have you been out?"

"Sort of," McGuffin said, glancing at the ship's clock beside the barometer. It was eleven-thirty, scarcely first thing in the morning. "Give me his number."

McGuffin scratched the number hurriedly on a pad, thanked her and hung up, then quickly phoned Knight's office.

"Mr. Knight has been waiting for your call," a woman with a British accent informed him, perhaps peevishly, after McGuffin had identified himself.

A moment later Francis Knight came on the line. He spoke with the calm, unhurried assurance of a man who needed nothing from anyone. "I don't know if you remember, Mr. McGovern, but you and I once shared a client."

McGuffin remembered. Poor old George. He had unfortunately been killed shortly after hiring the detective. "I remember very well. And it's McGuffin, not McGovern," he informed the lawyer.

"Of course. Are you at liberty at this time, Mr. McGuffin?"

"I'm always available to take an interesting case," McGuffin informed him, his standard reply, even when out of work.

"I was afraid you might be busy," the lawyer remarked—pointedly, it seemed to McGuffin.

"I was just finishing something up," McGuffin answered.

"Are you quite finished with it?"

"Quite."

"This assignment requires that you be free to travel," he warned.

"I'm free to travel," McGuffin fairly exclaimed. This was beginning to sound more and more promising.

"How soon can you be at my office?" the lawyer asked.

"Within the hour," McGuffin assured him.

Hell, I can be there in fifteen minutes, he said to himself as he hung the phone up. This was it, easy work in a clean, well-lighted place. Pinkerton territory. And it called for his best suit, the brown one just back from the cleaners. Although he had never intended it, all of his suits were for some reason brown. And his only clean, unwrinkled tie was blue. Because McGuffin was slightly color-blind, he had memorized the rules of sartorial color combinations, and knew that blue and brown did not mix, which explained the pristine condition of the blue tie. He did not even remember where it had come from. Not to worry, he said to himself, slipping into his brown jacket sans tie. There was plenty of time to stop at a clothing store on the way to the lawyer's office.

McGuffin locked the door of the wheelhouse after him and hurried downstairs to the main passageway, gleaming with refurbished teak and mahogany. Behind the glass walls bordering the passageway, architects and designers were huddled over their drawing boards, plotting ugly buildings. He pushed through the glass doors and out onto the aft deck, then made his way down the canopied gangway to the Embarcadero. He could usually find a cab in front of the World Trade Club, but because it was still too early for the lunch crowd, he threaded his way across the Embarcadero and made for California Street. He would pick up the tie at a clothing store only a few blocks away, then take a cab to Knight's office.

He found the store all right and quickly selected a tan silk tie with black and gold regimental stripes.

"I'll take it," he said, reaching into his pocket. "Shit!" he exclaimed.

"Sir—?"

"I forgot my money."

"A check or credit card will be fine," the clerk suggested.

McGuffin frisked himself, knowing already what to expect. "I forgot my wallet too."

"Oh, I am sorry," the clerk said, lifting the tie from McGuffin's hand.

"Listen, I've got a very important business meeting in a few

minutes. I need a tie. If you let me have it, I promise I'll come
back with the money in a couple of hours," McGuffin pleaded.

"I'm sorry, sir," the clerk said, carefully folding the tie.

McGuffin glanced at his watch. He had less than ten minutes to get to Knight's office. "I've got to have that tie!" he
said, grasping suddenly at the trailing end.

McGuffin was quick, but so was the clerk. He held one end
of the tie as tightly as he could while McGuffin pulled on the
other end.

"Sir!" the clerk said through clenched teeth, as he felt the
tie slipping from his grasp.

"It'll just be a couple of hours," McGuffin explained, backing toward the door. Then he spied the uniformed guard coming quickly toward him from the back of the store. "Oh, shit,"
McGuffin said, then turned and started running.

"Police, stop him!" the guard shouted as McGuffin pushed
through the door and out into the street.

McGuffin turned in the direction of Montgomery Street
and started running, followed by the shouting guard. He was
a beefy middle-aged guy, and McGuffin was sure he would
lose him by the time he got to the corner. Frightened pedes-
trians stepped aside as McGuffin jostled through, followed by
the guard, now somehow blowing a police whistle as he ran.
Surprisingly, the guard had gained on McGuffin by the time
he reached the corner.

All for one lousy necktie, McGuffin thought, deciding to
turn up a less congested side street where he could really
open up and leave that guard in his tracks. He leaned on the
wind and began pumping his knees. He could hear the wind
in his ears and feel the tears welling up in his eyes. But by the
time he reached the next corner, the sonofabitch was still on
his heels. All for one lousy necktie.

Dodging horn-blowing motorists, he ran across the street
on a red light and turned down Clay Street in the direction of
the Maritime Plaza, where he knew he could lose the bastard.

But it wasn't to be. When he got halfway down the block,
lengthening his lead now, a police car appeared at the corner,
stopped for a second, then turned against traffic and came for
him.

McGuffin froze. Faced with a choice between the cops and the puffing guard drawing up from behind, he would take the cops. He knew most of them—a lot of them hung around Goody's, and he was always careful to see that their glasses were filled.

But as soon as he got a look at the red-faced cop who jumped out of the car, gun drawn, McGuffin knew he had made a bad choice.

"Sullivan!" McGuffin said.

"What the hell are you up to now, McGuffin?" the cop demanded, waving his gun menacingly in the air.

"He stole that tie!" the security guard shouted, coming up from behind.

"I told him I'd bring the money later," McGuffin began. Then, "Ah, the hell with it," he said, extending his wrists for the cuffs. He knew he had no chance with Sullivan after the remark about his sister, but damned if he would beg. "Go ahead, book me."

Sullivan stared incredulously at him as he holstered his gun. "For stealing a tie? What, are you nuts, Amos? How much is the tie worth?"

"I don't know—he stole it," the guard panted.

"Eighteen ninety-five," McGuffin answered.

Amazed, McGuffin watched as the cop dug into his pocket and came out with a roll of bills. He peeled off a twenty and handed it to the guard.

"I don't want the money, I want him arrested," the guard said, nevertheless pocketing the money.

"Don't worry, I'll take care of him," Sullivan assured the guard, as he took McGuffin by the elbow and steered him to the car.

Yeah, that's more like it, McGuffin said to himself as he slid into the back seat. No doubt Sullivan had something particularly unpleasant in mind for anyone who would insult his saintly sister. Sullivan slammed the back door, then wedged his large body under the steering wheel. While the guard watched, not entirely satisfied, Sullivan backed the car around in a screeching turn and headed down Clay Street in the proper direction.

"What the fuck are you drinkin', Amos, Sterno or somethin'?" the cop asked.

"I haven't had anything to drink," McGuffin said.

"You've done some wacko things—but stealin' a tie! Jesus," he said, shaking his head. "You're just lucky it was me and not some fuckin' cowboy comin' by. Where you wanna go?" he asked, turning right at the corner.

"What—?" McGuffin asked.

"I said, where you wanna go?" he repeated, shaking his head impatiently.

"The Mills Tower," McGuffin answered dully.

When Sullivan turned right at the next corner and headed toward Montgomery Street, McGuffin leaned forward on the seat. "Listen, Sully, I really appreciate this," he began.

"What appreciate? You owe me twenty bucks."

"I mean you not even bringing up that remark I made about your sister. For which I apologize," McGuffin added quickly.

Sullivan braked suddenly near the corner of Sacramento and Montgomery streets and turned to face McGuffin. "What remark?" he demanded.

"What remark?"

"What, has the alcohol affected your hearing? I gotta say everything twice? What was the remark about my sister for which you're apologizing?"

"Nothing, it was nothing," McGuffin said, trying the door. It was locked, and only Sullivan could open it. "All I said was, I thought she should get married and have kids."

"Married and have kids—?" the cop repeated, staring curiously at McGuffin. "She can't get married and have kids. She's a nun."

"I know, I know," McGuffin answered. "That's why I'm apologizing."

"Jesus," he muttered, shaking his head. "When you're in your cups you say a lot of things you oughta apologize for, but that sure as hell ain't one of them. Don't you think I been after her to quit the order and get married?"

"I didn't know that—"

"The last time I seen her I told her: 'If you don't use it it's gonna dry up and you're gonna get cancer, that's a medical fact!' And you know what she says? She says: 'Jesus is all the lover I need.' You ever heard such bullshit?"

"Never," McGuffin replied. "Listen, Sully, I'd like to stay and talk, but I'm late for an appointment."

"Sure, sure," Sully said, releasing the lock. "Sorry if I bored you with my troubles."

"Not at all," McGuffin assured him, climbing out of the police car. "Thanks for the loan. I'll leave it with Goody."

"Anytime," Sully called, as McGuffin hurried away, tying his new tie as he ran.

One more close call in a profession where danger lurks at every corner, McGuffin said to himself, as he slipped into the lobby of the Mills Tower in the heart of the financial district. He checked his tie in the glass of the building registry, gave it a last satisfied tug, and hurried for the elevator.

The doors parted on the eleventh floor, and McGuffin stepped out into the carpeted reception area. A pretty young woman looked up from her switchboard and smiled pleasantly as he approached. The large brass letters on the mahogany wall above her head informed any and all that this was the law firm of Knight, Barrett, Worthington, Moss, Ravenscroft, and Goldberg. The last name was new. Somebody has to do the work, McGuffin thought, as he introduced himself to the smiling receptionist.

"If you'd care to have a seat, Miss Potts will be out in a moment," she said, after announcing McGuffin.

"Thanks," McGuffin said. He remembered Miss Potts. A husky, sexy British voice on a fat, fiftyish, balding termagant.

McGuffin picked up the nearest magazine at hand and sat in the chair affording him the best view of the receptionist. The magazine was *Palm Springs Life*, filled, it seemed, with pictures of golf courses and jewelry. Before he had turned many pages, or stolen many glances at the receptionist, Miss Potts came for him.

"If you'll come this way, Mr. McGuffin . . . "

McGuffin got to his feet and followed her, exchanging a quick smile with the receptionist as he passed. They turned at

the end of the corridor, past Mr. Ravenscroft's closed office
and on down to Francis Knight's office at the opposite corner.
Knight rose from his large, clean desk and crossed the thick
carpet as McGuffin entered.

"It's good to see you again—" he looked at his secretary—
"Mr. McGuffin."

"Nice to see you," McGuffin said, shaking the lawyer's
hand.

"Sit down."

McGuffin sat in the chair in front of the desk as Miss Potts
closed the door behind them. Francis Knight remained standing for a moment, the very model of the white-shoe lawyer in
his dark, sharply pressed three-piece suit, Phi Beta Kappa key
dangling at the vest.

"Would you like something? Tea or coffee?" he asked, before getting down to business.

McGuffin shook his head. "No thanks."

"Very well then," he said, circling around to the tall leather
chair behind his desk. He sat stiffly in the chair and laced his
fingers across his flat vest. Perhaps sixty, he had the taut dry
look of a man who exercised regularly, drank little, made love
even less, but derived an almost orgiastic pleasure (although
he would never show it) from a sufficiently large real estate
closing. Other than that, judging from the photographs on the
wall and the trophies on the bookshelves, his greatest pleasure in life was sport, especially golf. "I don't think I've spoken to you since Lydia Curtis's tragic death, have I?" the
lawyer asked.

"No, I don't think so," McGuffin answered, shifting uneasily in his chair. It was a sore point with McGuffin. He had
not only lost his client, George Curtis, in the matter Knight
was referring to, he had also allowed George's wife to be
needlessly killed. The Curtis case had definitely not been one
of McGuffin's shining hours, and even now, years later, he did
not like to be reminded of it.

"A sad affair for everyone concerned," Francis Knight
lamented.

"Yeah," McGuffin agreed, somewhat sullenly.

"I understand you play golf, Mr. McGuffin," Knight said abruptly.

McGuffin nodded. "You've been checking up on me."

"May I ask your handicap?"

"I don't know—I play at the public courses," McGuffin answered, wondering what this had to do with a job.

"What was your best round?"

"I'm not sure," McGuffin answered quickly. "Look, Mr. Knight, I thought I was here to talk about an assignment."

"You are. You are indeed," the lawyer said.

"Then what's golf got to do with it?"

"Rather a great deal, I'm afraid. I need a private investigator who can blend rather unobtrusively into the golf milieu. Or, if you'll allow me to be both blunt and archaic, a detective who can pass for a gentleman."

"I see," McGuffin said, straightening in his chair. "Seventy-eight."

"What?" Knight asked.

"My best score. It was a seventy-eight on the Ocean Course at the Olympic Club when I was about sixteen years old," McGuffin informed him.

Francis Knight stared incredulously at the brash detective. Knight owned the finest custom-made clubs money could buy, had attended all the best golf schools in the country, frequented his club pro, had played golf almost every weekend for most of his adult life, and the best score he had ever posted was an eighty-four, with the help of a red-hot putter. And this man had shot a seventy-eight when he was only sixteen years old? He had chosen Mr. McGuffin for this interview because, despite his well-known shortcomings, he gave the appearance, at least, of something of a gentleman. But— and thank God he had learned before installing him in the company of gentlemen—the man was a craven liar!

"Thank you, Mr. McGuffin," Knight said, getting to his feet.

"Not good enough, huh?" McGuffin said. Golfers understood failure better than most.

"A bit too good, I should say. Especially for a sixteen-year-old," he replied coolly.

"Maybe I was seventeen," McGuffin said quickly, seeing that the job called for a duffer. "Since then I've hardly played. Hell, if I went out this afternoon I probably couldn't shoot better than an eighty-eight."

"Indeed," replied Knight, who hadn't broken ninety for several years. "Thank you for coming," he said, walking across the room to the door.

"Shit," McGuffin muttered, climbing to his feet. He had overplayed his hand. "I've got a bad case of the yips," he added, pausing in the doorway. "Probably have to add two or three a side for that."

Not even the dreaded yips would elicit a response from the stone-faced lawyer. When McGuffin extended his hand, Knight's remained on the doorknob. McGuffin shrugged faintly and stepped into the corridor.

"Oh, Mr. McGuffin—?"

"Yes?" McGuffin answered, turning quickly.

"It may be none of my business, but I'm going to offer you some advice. Never bluff a lawyer, Mr. McGuffin. It's his stock in trade."

McGuffin stood watching as the lawyer closed the door on him. He doesn't believe me, McGuffin realized. "That sonofabitch!" he exclaimed, starting back for the door.

Francis Knight turned, halfway to his desk, when the angry detective lunged into the room.

"You think I'm lying!" McGuffin charged.

"I didn't say that," the lawyer answered, retreating behind his desk.

"If I can prove that seventy-eight, do I get the job?" McGuffin demanded.

"And just how would you—"

"Do I or don't I?" McGuffin interrupted, advancing across the room.

"Well, yes, I suppose so. If the evidence is satisfactory," the lawyer allowed.

"Fine," McGuffin said, sitting on the corner of Knight's desk and reaching for his phone. "Do you mind?"

"Go ahead."

Knight stood with his back against the wall, watching, somewhat apprehensively, as the investigator presented his case. He called information for the number of the Olympic Club, dialed, and asked for the secretary's office.

"This is Smith, *Chronicle* sports desk," McGuffin said. "Approximately twenty years ago, a kid named Amos McGuffin won the Olympic Club Caddies' Tournament. Can you tell me what his score was? . . . Thank you," the detective said, then covered the mouthpiece. "She's looking it up."

Francis Knight nodded numbly. A caddie! He had been tricked. It was one thing for the sixteen-year-old son of a member to shoot seventy-eight, but quite another for a caddie. One might even say it bordered on professionalism.

"Could you repeat that?" McGuffin said, when the secretary returned with the information.

Knight accepted the phone from McGuffin and put it to his ear.

"I said, he shot a seventy-eight. Would you care to know anything else?" the secretary asked.

"No, that's all I wanted to know," Francis Knight replied, as he handed McGuffin the phone.

McGuffin replaced the phone and stood facing the lawyer for a moment before asking: "Do I get the job?"

"First let me tell you what it entails, then you can make your own decision," the lawyer answered.

McGuffin got up from the desk and returned to his chair, then leaned back and tried to look like a detective who could choose between assignments. The lawyer paced slowly behind his desk, as if about to address a jury. He began hesitantly, informing McGuffin that a client and friend named Lyle Boone had suffered a fatal heart attack at some posh Caribbean golf club to which they both belonged. McGuffin listened patiently while the lawyer went on about his feeling of responsibility for the dead golfer, whom he had sponsored for membership in the club, and waited for him to get to the punch. The fact that Mr. Boone had died after winning the club championship and being sworn in as club president made a sad story sadder, but it did nothing to enlighten the de-

tective about his assignment. It was not until the lawyer
mentioned the deep resentment harbored by certain club
members over Mr. Boone's election that McGuffin interrupted with a question.

"Are you suggesting that the president of a country club
was assassinated?" McGuffin asked incredulously.

Knight's smile was reluctant. "Of course not. But don't dis-
miss the power of the presidency of the Palm Isle Golf Club
either," he warned. "The Palm includes some of the richest
and most influential families in America, and the president of
the PIGC has access to most of them. Not that one is expected
to use the office for personal gain, you understand," he
quickly added.

"Of course not."

"No, Lyle was not assassinated," the lawyer said, shaking
his head. "And if it weren't for a few incidents over the past
several weeks, I'd be perfectly willing to accept that Lyle died
of a heart attack, as the coroner said. But when I began thinking about the bonds and the recent explosion aboard the
Francie, it occurred to me that Lyle may have been murdered."

"Wait a minute, wait a minute," McGuffin pleaded, waving
his hands in the air. "What's this about bombs exploding
aboard the *Francie*?"

"Not bombs, bonds," the lawyer said, pronouncing each
word carefully. "Let's begin at the beginning." He rolled the
desk chair back and sat, hands laced across his Phi Beta Kappa
key. "The Palm Isle Golf Club is owned by ten bondholders,
each of whose bond is valued at ten million dollars. I, unfortunately, happen to be one of these bondholders. I say unfortunately because the bond pays no interest or dividends, but
that's neither here nor there. What is important is the fact
that I have suffered something of a cash-flow problem in recent months and I was forced to borrow five million dollars
from a fellow club member, a man named Al Balata."

McGuffin whistled. "That's a good friend."

"Oddly enough, we're not good friends at all. I opposed his
membership—to no avail—because of his connection with

certain organized crime figures. But because nothing was ever proved, and because Balata was willing to pay ten million dollars for a bond when nobody else would, my objections fell on deaf ears—not counting Balata's. He heard about it and has not liked me since. So naturally I was surprised when Al approached me and said he'd heard that I needed some money and he'd be glad to be of help. His terms were generous; he offered me five million dollars, interest-free, for one year, and agreed to hold my bond as security. It was an offer I couldn't refuse—not even when I read the death clause in the promissory note."

"The death clause?" McGuffin asked.

"In the event of my death with the loan outstanding, title to the bond vests automatically in Mr. Balata. My heirs are not entitled to repay the loan and reclaim the bond."

"Resulting in a five-million-dollar windfall to Mr. Balata," McGuffin, no slouch at high finance, quickly deduced.

"Exactly. When I asked about this, Mr. Balata shrugged it off, saying his lawyer had insisted on some sort of quid pro quo in that it was an interest-free loan. Being a lawyer myself, I thought that wasn't unreasonable. And I certainly didn't expect to die within the year, so I signed it."

"So I take it you've had a recent intimation of mortality," McGuffin said. If he was going to the Palm Isle Golf Club, he'd have to start talking like a classy guy. He also vaguely remembered reading of a boat explosion while he was in Los Angeles, and was now sure that it had been Francis Knight's yacht, the *Francie*.

"Yes," the lawyer said, nodding dully, as if he still couldn't believe that the Lord intended that he one day die. "It's my custom every year to take my boat out to watch the St. Francis Regatta. This year, however, I was fortunate enough to come down with the flu, and I wasn't able to take my boat out. As you've probably read in the paper, my boat exploded and burned at the dock, at almost precisely the moment the race was beginning. Had I not been forced to change my plans, Mr. McGuffin, I would surely have been killed." Knight's voice had taken on an indignant tone.

McGuffin made a clucking sound meant to signify sympathy, then asked: "Did the police investigate the explosion?"

"The fire department. There was no suspicion of foul play at the time. It was assumed that the explosion was the result of fumes in the bilge and a short circuit. No one even thought to look for a bomb. And it's too late to look for one now, as the hulk was towed out to sea and allowed to sink."

"Great," McGuffin said softly. "This Al Balata—did he know that you always took your boat out on Regatta Day?"

"I'm sure he could have known—it was common knowledge at the Palm."

"And knowing that, you think he had somebody plant a bomb on your boat, timed to go off at the start of the race?" McGuffin asked.

"I'm not sure what I think," the lawyer answered with a helpless sigh. "One doesn't like to think that a fellow club member would attempt to kill one—not even a member with reputed mobster connections. And yet, while five million dollars may not be a great sum of money to a man like Al Balata, it is at least an inducement to murder."

"At least," McGuffin said, nodding wisely. Hell, he knew guys who could be persuaded to wipe out whole countries for that kind of money. "I can understand why you'd be a little nervous under these circumstances, Mr. Knight, but I don't understand what this has to do with your friend who had the heart attack. Did he borrow money from Balata too?"

"Hardly," Knight replied with a faint smile. "Quite to the contrary, in fact. Balata offered to buy Lyle Boone's bond, but Lyle refused to sell it. He complained to me that Al was being very pesty about the whole thing."

"Pesty enough to kill him?"

"Possibly."

"But why, if that wouldn't get him the bond?"

"Just because Balata wasn't able to buy the bond from Lyle doesn't mean that he won't be able to buy it from his widow."

"Ah, I see," McGuffin said, stroking his chin. "So you'd like me to go down to your golf club with you and have a look around, is that it?"

"Mr. McGuffin, there's nothing I'd rather do right now than go down to the Palm for a little golf—especially with the club championship coming up in a couple of weeks—but I'm unfortunately in the midst of an important trial that threatens to go on for weeks. So if you don't mind, I'd like you to go alone, as my guest. Talk to the coroner, play golf with Al Balata—do whatever you have to do—but find out whether Lyle Boone was murdered or died of a heart attack. If he was murdered I want Balata in jail. But failing that, I want you to come to work for me as my bodyguard until I manage to get this note paid off. I know this won't be an easy assignment."

"Yeah, it sounds tough," McGuffin, who had been thinking of swaying palm trees and lush green fairways, answered dreamily. But somebody's gotta do it, he added to himself.

"I'll phone Horton Ormsby—he's the club president—and tell him I'm sending you down to conduct a confidential investigation into Lyle's death. As far as everyone else is concerned, you'll be my cousin on a golf holiday."

"If you don't mind, I'd prefer that everyone think I'm your cousin, including President Ormsby," McGuffin said.

"Very well," the lawyer said, getting to his feet. "But you needn't worry about Horton. I'd trust him with my life."

"I'm sure," McGuffin said, following the lawyer to his feet. Halfway across the room, the lawyer stopped and turned to McGuffin. "What about golf clubs, Mr. McGuffin?"

"I have an old set," McGuffin answered, which was scarcely an exaggeration.

The lawyer frowned. "Perhaps you'd better use mine. And you'll need some proper golf clothes. I'll arrange for you to charge a few things to my account at Brooks Brothers."

"Great," McGuffin said.

"Just one other thing," Francis Knight said, stopping at the door. "It was your occasional golf partner Judge Brennan who recommended you for this assignment."

"I must thank him," McGuffin answered. Judge Brennan, a habitué of Goody's, played a pretty good stick when he wasn't hung over. But McGuffin had seldom played with him when he wasn't.

"He says you're a good golfer and a good investigator, but you're totally disorganized and you drink too much."

"I'm not *totally* disorganized," McGuffin answered. "And I never drink when I'm on a case."

"Please see that you don't," Knight said. "My reputation at the Palm is most important to me."

"Rest assured, I'll do nothing to tarnish it," McGuffin pledged, raising his right hand.

The lawyer regarded him uncertainly for a moment, then opened the door. "Come, we'll see Miss Potts and work out the matter of finance."

Matter of finance—cash-flow problem, McGuffin repeated to himself as he followed the lawyer down the corridor. He loved the way rich people talked about money.

4

Having deposited Francis Knight's generous advance in his
needy checking account, and added a few golf shirts and slacks
to his equally needy wardrobe, McGuffin was ready to begin
his first paid vacation. Even after phoning Lyle Boone's doctor
from Knight's office and learning that the deceased had been
in excellent health, McGuffin still doubted that the golfer had
been murdered. Francis Knight, apparently overworked and
admittedly in debt, had probably become a bit paranoid, seeing the hand of the Mafia in accidental explosions and natural
deaths. If McGuffin didn't think the lawyer could afford a few
thousand dollars for a frivolous investigation, he might have
felt some guilt at taking the case. But as things were, he felt
only the keenest pleasure in anticipation of a week or two of
golf at, in Knight's words, "undoubtedly the finest golf club in
the world." Even allowing for some chauvinism, McGuffin
was sure it beat waiting two hours to tee off at the local public
course, as was his weekend habit.

This is how I somehow always knew it would be, McGuffin
told himself while hurtling across the country in the first-class
compartment of a 747 the next morning. The dream assignment, the deserved reward for the years of dirty and dangerous assignments willingly borne without a whimper. This
marked the turning point in his career, he was sure. From
now on there would be no more boozy-breath tort lawyers
offering him a grand to come up with a nonexistent witness to
an accident, nor any more interrupted adulterers breaking a

camera over his head. From now on, Amos McGuffin, Private Investigator, would take only those cases suited to his professional stature.

"Pardon me, Mr. McGuffin, would you like a glass of champagne?" the flight attendant asked, as he plucked at the crease of his new buttercup-yellow golf slacks from Brooks Brothers.

McGuffin looked up and smiled sadly. He hadn't had a drink since starting work for Francis Knight, and there would be none until the job was done. "What kind is it?" he nevertheless asked.

"Piper Heidsieck," she answered proudly.

"I think not," McGuffin said with a condescending smile.

She smiled understandingly and continued on down the aisle. That was the nice thing about first class—you met people with such sophisticated taste.

Approximately six hours after departure the flight that had originated in fog ended in bright sunlight at Miami International Airport. McGuffin filed off first with his fellow first-class passengers, mostly businessmen in dark suits, and made his way to the baggage-claim area, a carefree polyester peacock among dull gray sparrows. Beyond the ropes, men in livery prowled about like lost souls, looking for the body whose name they carried on their chest. The one carrying McGuffin's name looked different from the others—creased leather jacket and a face to match. Francis Knight's secretary had described Eddie the Aviator, who would fly him over to Palm Isle in a small plane. It was so far the only part of the assignment McGuffin dreaded.

When McGuffin called, Eddie signaled that he should follow him through the door marked "Authorized Personnel Only." Following the pilot through the door, McGuffin found himself out on the tarmac, where Latins in white jumpsuits were hauling bags out of the plane in which he had just crossed the country. Eddie picked up McGuffin's tattered bag, which had been laid aside, and walked wordlessly to a yellow station wagon with the letters PIGC stenciled across one door. He opened the rear door, and McGuffin slid in, only a moment before it slammed shut. Eddie dropped the bag on the front seat beside him, started the engine, and squealed off in the direction of the plane that would transport them to Palm Isle.

The plane turned out to be even smaller than McGuffin had imagined. "We're going out over the ocean in that?" he asked, as Eddie stowed his bag in the luggage compartment.

"It's a small island—we couldn't land anything much bigger than this," Eddie said.

It was not a reassuring answer, but McGuffin nevertheless crawled in. Eddie started the engine and taxied slowly out onto the airstrip, talking unintelligibly (to McGuffin at least) to the control tower all the while.

"How's the weather?" McGuffin asked, when they came to a halt at the top of the runway. A sudden tropical storm was his last chance for an honorable retreat.

"Not bad," Eddie answered, glancing about for incoming aircraft. "For the Bermuda Triangle," he added, as he suddenly depressed the throttle.

"The Bermuda Triangle—?" McGuffin repeated soundlessly over the roaring engine as the plane began to move.

The little aircraft shuddered noisily, then made a headlong rush against the wind, straining and gathering speed until it broke from the earth and climbed smoothly in the bright sunlight. By the time McGuffin dared to look down, the earth was behind them and they were flying low over the sea. McGuffin clutched the seat and stared straight ahead.

"How long will this take?"

Eddie shrugged. "I'm always so happy just to get there, I never pay much attention to the time."

"Oh shit," McGuffin murmured.

"You didn't happen to notice our compass heading when we took off, did you?" the pilot asked, looking left and right.

"No, I didn't," McGuffin answered.

"Damn," the pilot said, peering intently at the horizon. "Miss It and we better find a gas station right quick. Only thing is, there ain't no gas station till you get to the next set of islands."

"Which islands are those?" McGuffin asked foolishly.

"The Canary Islands," Eddie answered. "And not even Chuck Yeager can do that in one of these itty bitty little planes. But what the hell, you get a couple of hours out over the Atlantic, knowing you should have seen land back when the old fuel gauge started beepin' red at you, and you figure, what the fuck, let's go for it."

McGuffin smiled as if he were about to be airsick, then closed his eyes and tried to imagine he was on a train. He was roused a few minutes later by Eddie's excited exclamation.

"Damn!"

"What? What's the matter?" McGuffin demanded, fumbling in his seat.

"There she is, right where she's supposed to be," Eddie said, pointing.

McGuffin squinted in the bright sunlight, and there, off by itself, was Palm Isle, a dark green hump on an aquamarine sea. As the plane turned, approaching from the south, it resembled a green egg bordered by pink sand. McGuffin could see an enormous yacht approaching a small harbor at the end of the island.

"That boat looks too big for that little harbor," he said, as the plane began to descend. There was a small helicopter on the roof, he observed as they came closer.

"Oh, it'll fit, all right," Eddie assured him. "Though I don't know what it's doing down there now, seeing as how Mr. Boone died a few days ago."

"That's Lyle Boone's yacht?" McGuffin asked.

"Was. Now it belongs to his widow."

"What's she doing here?"

"Got me," Eddie answered, as they swept past the yacht.

They came in low over the boat-dotted harbor and a cluster of buildings at dockside, fairly skimming the tops of tall palm trees, before dropping softly onto a grassy clearing. McGuffin held his breath until the plane slowed to a crawl and began taxiing to a Quonset hut at the end of the runway. When the engine coughed its last, he stumbled out of the plane like a returning hostage.

"Nice flight," McGuffin said, as Eddie hauled his bag out of the luggage compartment and carried it to a waiting golf cart.

"Just follow that path," Eddie instructed, pointing to a trail of crushed clamshell that wound through the tropical forest, "until you see the first green. Mr. Knight's cottage is just to the right, directly above the beach. You'll be able to see the clubhouse."

"Thanks," McGuffin said, sliding under the wheel of his golf cart as Eddie secured his bag to the rear.

When he was finished he slapped the electric cart and McGuffin moved quietly off in the direction of the pink trail. The tall palms and leafy growth formed an eerie arch that scattered shards of sunlight along the path. Here and there a narrower trail forked off to the left or right, affording him an occasional view of a pink cottage through the jungle growth, but he saw no sign of the first green, or even a golf course. He was beginning to think he had made a wrong turn when the jungle gave way to bright sunlight and a paved boulevard, beyond which lay the first green and the ocean. The clubhouse was atop the hill to his left, at the head of the boulevard and the immaculately groomed first fairway, a large and somehow familiar building of a most alarming yellow hue. Because he was eager to see his accommodations, McGuffin drove across the boulevard and down into a copse of trees behind the first green without stopping. Just from the little he had so far seen, McGuffin was satisfied that Francis Knight's claims for the Palm Isle Golf Club were more than idle boasts. He could scarcely wait to play the course.

He found Francis Knight's cottage at the end of the path, a pink stucco building with a clay tile roof, perched on a bluff overlooking the aquamarine waters of the Caribbean. Not bad, McGuffin decided, as he glided to a stop in front of the already open door. A young black woman appeared in the doorway, calling, "Hallo, sah!" as she hurried to his bag.

"Hello," McGuffin said.

He tried to help her with the bag, but she wouldn't have it. She tossed the bag easily atop her head and, hips swaying under her blue maid's uniform, led McGuffin into the cottage. Except for the freshly cut flowers on the coffee table in front of a cracked leather couch, the living room had the Spartan look of a men's club. McGuffin couldn't imagine why, but there

was a fireplace against the far wall. A small kitchen was sepa-
rated from the living room by a bar. A rocking chair with a
coat of arms sat near the fireplace, and a few club chairs were
scattered about the room; an antique writing desk stood beside the front door. A wooden table with six matching chairs
indicated the dining area, and beyond that were three doors,
leading, McGuffin guessed, to the bedrooms. He followed the
maid through the door to the left and found himself in a none
too large bedroom with a window open to the sea. She
dropped the bag on the bed and turned to McGuffin.

"I am Iris and I be de maid, sah," she announced. When
she spoke, it sounded like a calypso song. "Shall I unpack yo'
bag, Mistah McGuffin?"

"No—no thanks," McGuffin said quickly. His gun was on
top of his things, along with the California permit, just in case
of a customs inspection. But as Francis Knight's secretary had
assured him, club members and their guests were seldom
bothered by such formalities.

"Dan I guess dat be all fo' now, sah," she said, taking a last
look around the bedroom. "You'll find something to drink in
de refrigeratah, just as Mr. Knight ordered."

"Thanks, Iris," McGuffin said, reaching into his yellow golf
slacks for a roll of bills.

"Thank you," she said, taking the ten-dollar bill without
expression. Among Palm men, ten dollars was apparently not
a generous tip. "If you need anyting, just pick up de phone
and de receptionist will answer," she informed him, starting
for the door.

McGuffin thanked her again as he followed her into the living room. When she had left, he made directly for the refrigerator, just to see what sort of drinks his client had ordered
for him. There were several kinds of soda, but no wine or
beer. Obviously Francis Knight harbored some misgivings
concerning McGuffin's oath of temperance during periods of
employment. Annoyed, McGuffin slammed the refrigerator
door and walked outside to his golf cart. He would drink at the
bar in the clubhouse, among the gleaming bottles of brown
whiskey. He who watches the stripper is not an adulterer.

He drove past the copse of trees and the first green, then turned up the broad boulevard in the direction of the clubhouse at the top of the hill. Two foursomes of silver-haired gentlemen on the left and right fairways regarded the new man with some curiosity (or suspicion; McGuffin could not be sure) before waving lazily to him. If there were other players on the course, McGuffin could not see them, as the fairway to his left, the ninth, was bordered by a wall of thick tropical forest, and beyond the first fairway lay the Caribbean. It was a spectacular setting for golf.

There were three flags flying from the pole in front of the still strangely familiar clubhouse, the American flag, the Palm Isle Golf Club banner, and the British flag, in descending order, in spite of the fact that the island was a British possession. It wasn't until he pulled into the circular drive and had a good look at the two-story yellow stucco building from the front, with its curious mix of gables and porticos, that McGuffin realized where he had seen the building before. The Spanish stucco had thrown him, but the broad outlines of the massive structure were familiar to anyone who occasionally leafed through the advertising pages of the golf magazines—the PIGC clubhouse was modeled after the Royal and Ancient Clubhouse at St. Andrew's in Scotland.

Seeing no golf carts parked in front of the main entrance, McGuffin followed a narrow path around the corner of the building, past the eighteenth green, where a foursome was just finishing up, and the practice tee, where several players were hitting balls. He parked the cart alongside several others in front of the pro shop at the end of the building. He got off the cart and turned to observe the players on the practice tee, just to see what sort of competition awaited him. Judging from the fact that Lyle Boone had become club champion after taking up the game only several years before, McGuffin assumed that the competition at the PIGC would not be very keen. Watching the dozen or so players on the practice tee for a few minutes did nothing to change his opinion.

The only exception was a dark, muscular man standing alone at the last tee, intently hitting drive after drive far, far down the practice fairway. He was obviously a hitter, on the order of Palmer, not a swinger like Nicklaus or Watson. His stance was wide, his grip strong, and his swing compact. He was forced to block the shot to avoid a disastrous duck hook, and still he was unusually long, rapping the good ones well past the two-hundred-and-fifty-yard stake. He could be even longer if he could learn to swing with his entire body rather than just his hands, but he never would, McGuffin knew. McGuffin understood the muscular golfer's problem because it was his own as well.

McGuffin was a man who liked to control things. He trusted neither sophisticated machinery nor the classic golf swing. He trusted his hands to return the clubface square to the ball at the moment of impact, but he knew better than to trust the other parts of the body to do their part every time. He understood, as well as a neurosurgeon, that every nerve and muscle in the body was a potentially harmful and fearful threat to the golf swing, and like plebeian applicants to an aristocratic club such as the Palm, as many of them as possible should be denied admittance.

The detective had little faith in psychology, yet he believed that a man's golf swing was the key to the mysteries of his psyche. Watching the muscular golfer as he swung powerfully at each shot, McGuffin sensed his personality as well as his game. Not for him the steady, patient round of golf designed to achieve several pars and a few bogeys—and with a little luck a birdie or two. Fairway bunkers and out of bounds be damned, he would go for birdie every time, and doubtless end up with more than a few double bogeys or worse. McGuffin understood this because it was the way he played too.

McGuffin also understood that the swarthy golfer at the end of the line had not learned the classic golf swing as a child at a posh country club, nor had he learned it later at an expensive golf camp for upwardly mobile business executives. His swing, like McGuffin's, was self-taught and pieced together from the largely erroneous advice of fellow players. It was both curious and somehow reassuring to McGuffin that there might be a second impostor at the exclusive Palm Isle Golf Club.

"Mr. McGuffin!" a voice called from the direction of the clubhouse.

Turning, McGuffin was greeted by a display of sartorial splendor unknown since the days of the great Demaret. His pants were baggy plus fours of a silver-gray shade, his shoes were saddle, his knee socks argyle, and his yellow cardigan approximately the shade of his sun-bleached hair. And like the ersatz Scottish architecture, he was vaguely familiar.

"I'm Cuppy Dunch," he said, spikes crunching on the clam-shell gravel as he approached, hand outstretched.

"Cuppy Dunch?" McGuffin repeated. "No wonder you look familiar."

"You remember me?" Cuppy asked, flashing a golf-ball-white smile against a tobacco-tan face.

"Of course I remember you," McGuffin said, pumping the golf pro's hand.

What golfer didn't? The story of Cuppy Dunch was surely one of the saddest in the history of a cruel and heartbreaking game. Several years before, while leading the U.S. Open by a comfortable margin going into the last day, he had been suddenly forced to withdraw from the tournament as the result of a back ailment. Cuppy Dunch had never been heard from again, which had saddened a lot of golf fans, including McGuffin. Unlike most of the wrinkle-free stiffs turned out by the PGA, Cuppy had been a flamboyant figure who occasionally drank too much, always dated gorgeous women (many of them married), and was not intimidated by the waspy officials of the USGA. As far as McGuffin was concerned, the game needed more players like Cuppy, Trevino, and Demaret, and fewer of the sheep in polyester pants who grazed the golden fairways today.

"How's the back?" McGuffin inquired.

"Wha—oh, better," he answered, reaching for it.

"Good enough to go back on the pro tour?"

Cuppy laughed. "No, I think I'll stay right here."

"Imagine that," McGuffin said. He still couldn't get over it. "Cuppy Dunch, club pro at the Palm Isle Golf Club. Francis told me this was a top club."

"It's the finest golf course the world has never seen,"

Cuppy answered. "Your cousin tells me you play a pretty good stick."

"Used to," McGuffin answered. "I haven't played much since I was a ca—since I was a kid."

"It's a little late today," Cuppy said, glancing at his watch. It was the same kind Arnold Palmer wore, and rather gaudy, McGuffin thought. "Plus you're probably a little tired after your flight, but I'd be happy to arrange a foursome for you first thing tomorrow. I think Mr. Knight's clubs should suit you fine, but if they don't I can fix you up with something else."

"I'm sure they'll be fine," McGuffin said. "And by the way, Francis told me to be sure to play at least one round with his friend Al Balata, if he happens to be around."

"His friend—?" Cuppy repeated. "That's Mr. Balata on the practice tee, the dark guy on the end."

"So that's Al Balata," McGuffin mused, watching as he hit another long tee shot.

"I'll see what I can do," Cuppy promised. "But I have to warn you, he's a money player."

"So am I," McGuffin said, wondering how much money they were talking about. Even if it was a one-hundred-dollar Nassau, he couldn't lose more than three or four hundred dollars. And although he had not discussed golf losses with his client, surely they would be considered business expenses, especially if that was the only way to get to Balata. "Maybe I should go over and introduce myself," McGuffin suggested.

"I wouldn't," Cuppy said, laying a hand on McGuffin's arm. "Al takes his golf very seriously now that the club champion is no longer around to defend his title."

"Lyle Boone?"

"You knew him?"

"Sort of," McGuffin answered.

"Now that he's dead, Al's got a pretty good chance of winning the championship, if he can straighten out those tee shots in the next week or so.

"Come on, let me show you around," he offered, turning McGuffin toward the pro shop.

There, amid the gleaming golf clubs and bright golf clothes, four white-haired gentlemen in dark blue blazers were huddled over the putter display. Intent on finding the putter that would cure the yips, they barely acknowledged McGuffin when Cuppy stopped to introduce him.

"You're Frank Knight's cousin, are you?" the eldest of the white-haired gentlemen inquired as he stroked an imaginary ball into an imaginary cup.

"Yes, sir," McGuffin answered.

"How's his slice?" the old man asked.

McGuffin hesitated briefly, then answered, "Terrible."

"Good," the old man said, striking another putt.

As they stepped into the corridor, Cuppy turned to McGuffin and said, "He's one of the richest men in the country, but beat him out of a two-dollar Nassau and he starts chewing the rug. Care for a drink?"

"Maybe a club soda."

Cuppy laughed. "Still not over your flight with Eddie?"

"That's part of it," McGuffin said. "Is there by any chance a boat off this island?"

"There is, but no one takes it. We call it the Ship of Cowards."

McGuffin smiled thinly. He only hoped that when the time came, he would have the courage to make the right decision. In the foyer at the end of the corridor, an attractive black receptionist sat behind a tall counter, routing calls to the outlying cottages. She was obviously having little success, as the rows of boxes on the wall behind her were stuffed with messages. On a day like today at the Palm, no one was in his cottage.

At the top of a broad carpeted stairway, they passed through an arch into a large dining room with a circular bar at the near end. It was here, perhaps on this very spot, that Lyle Boone had suffered his fatal heart attack—or whatever it was that had killed him, McGuffin thought, as he rested his elbows on the polished mahogany.

"Club soda and my usual Haig & Haig!" Cuppy called to the bartender.

"Yas sah," the old man answered, reaching for Cuppy's usual bottle without looking.

"He's getting a little slow," Cuppy observed. "A lot of the members wanted to turn him out to pasture, but after Lyle Boone became president, he wouldn't allow it. He said they'd have to do it over his dead body." The golf pro shrugged. "It'll be interesting to see what happens now."

He stopped talking as the bartender approached with their drinks.

"This is Stymie," Cuppy said, as he reached for his drink. "Stymie, this is Mr. McGuffin from San Francisco. He's Mr. Knight's cousin, so take good care of him, will you?"

"Yas sah, I surely do dat. Specially since you be kin to Mistah Knight, sah," Stymie answered, in the Caribbean rhythm McGuffin was beginning to love to hear.

"Thanks, Stymie," McGuffin said, raising his glass to him.

"To your stay," Cuppy toasted.

"Good golfing," McGuffin replied, lifting the plain club soda to his lips. He sipped it and watched longingly as the golf pro downed his Scotch.

"Come with me—I'd like to show you something," Cuppy said, placing his empty glass on the bar.

Glass in hand, McGuffin followed the golf pro across the dining room and through an archway into a smaller, oak-paneled room with lots of leather chairs and a fireplace as big as some San Francisco apartments. Equally oversized, the club coat of arms hung from the wall above the carved mantel. The wall to the left was lined with bookcases filled with hundreds of old volumes, as well as a display of antique golf clubs.

"Look here," Cuppy said, pointing at the opposite wall, covered with photographs of golf outings past. There were yellowing pictures, beginning at the left, of beaming golfers in knickers and neckties, changing gradually to clearer tones and modern dress.

"Well—?" he said, pointing to the last picture in the bottom row.

McGuffin looked. It showed four men in dark crested blazers standing around a large silver cup. "What about it?" McGuffin asked, after studying the picture.

"Nothing," the golf pro answered, studying McGuffin closely. "I just thought you might want to see a picture of Lyle Boone, seeing as how you knew him."

"Lyle, of course!" McGuffin exclaimed, pressing his nose up close to the photograph. "Without my reading glasses I'm blind as a bat."

"Is that right?" Cuppy remarked flatly. Then, glancing again at his large gold watch, he said, "I've got to get back to the shop. I'll call you later about that game with Al Balata."

"Thanks," McGuffin said, as he watched Cuppy back slowly out of the room, then turn and disappear down the stairs. Was he being paranoid? McGuffin wondered. Or had Cuppy been testing him with Lyle's picture? And if so, why? he asked himself as he turned back to the framed photograph of the golfers crowded around the trophy.

Lyle Boone was no doubt the one with the big grin and the proprietary grip on the silver cup, the PIGC champion. McGuffin had never seen a man who looked more pleased with himself. He had the look of a healthy affable man, a candidate for neither disease nor murder. And yet he had surely been done in by one or the other.

Satisfied that he would recognize the deceased if he ever saw his likeness again, McGuffin strolled across the room to the shelves of old books and ancient golf clubs. All of the books seemed to be devoted to the same subject—golf. Randomly he pulled one of the volumes, whose gold-leaf letters had long since disappeared from its leather spine, down from the shelf and opened it to the title page. It was *The Rules of the Ten Oldest Golf Clubs from 1754 to 1848, by C. B. Clapcott*. Respectfully, McGuffin closed the yellowed pages and returned the book to its place on the shelf, then turned his attention to the ancient hickory-shaft golf clubs that stood in a row behind the glass doors. Each of the strange clubs was identified by a brass plate with an equally strange name. There were baffy spoons and cleeks, bulgers and blasters, water irons and track irons, sammys, jiggers, berwicks, and lofters, and fifty-seven varieties of niblicks and mashies. No wonder the daunting game had once been played by so few—

it required a Philadelphia lawyer to interpret the rules and a lexicographer to identify the equipment.

Intimidated perhaps, McGuffin turned to the purely aesthetic contemplation of the enormous coat of arms over the fireplace. The heraldic shield was of black cast iron, with a golden palm tree in the center, while beneath this a crossed pair of antique golf sticks rested in a knotted scarlet ribbon. The golf clubs, one with a ball attached to its face, seemed from a distance to be authentic classics, drawn possibly from the club collection. Upon closer inspection, however, he saw that they were molded steel or iron, like the rest of the coat of arms, but cleverly painted to resemble the real thing. Even the knotted scarlet scroll proved to be ribbon steel, upon which the words *Golf ad Mortem* had been inscribed in medieval gold leaf.

"Golf till Death," McGuffin, who had studied Latin for four years at St. Ignatius High, translated aloud. How prophetic for Lyle Boone.

Unable to play, McGuffin decided to practice.

"I'll have Mr. Knight's clubs and a bag of balls brought out to the practice tee right away," Tommy, the assistant pro, assured McGuffin, once he had made his wish known.

As promised, the clubs and balls were waiting on the tee when McGuffin emerged from the locker room in his dilapidated spiked shoes. He was pleased to see that Francis Knight's clubs were Pings, one of the most popular makes on the pro tour. McGuffin started with the wedge, punching a few just short of the one-hundred-yard flagstick, before shifting to a longer swing. The wedge felt light, yet he was able to hit the ball much farther than he ever had with his own club. And the same was true of the seven, five, and two irons. He didn't know if it was his swing or just the new clubs, but McGuffin felt that he was hitting the ball as well as he ever had in his life.

The same was true of the woods. He hit drive after drive, with a right-to-left draw, well past the two-hundred-yard flag, until the bag was empty. Too excited to quit, McGuffin hurried to the pro shop for two more bags of balls. Could it be, he asked himself, as he teed up for the next shot, that after all these years, I've finally grooved the perfect swing? The answer came with the next shot, a wild duck hook that went out about a hundred and fifty yards, then turned sharply left and rocketed across the adjoining fairway. He hooked three more and sliced twice that many before managing to get the ball back to a reasonably straight path.

Finally exhausted by the combination of exercise and jet lag, McGuffin repaired to his cottage for a shower and a nap before dinner. Several hours later he was awakened in his darkened room by the phone. It was Cuppy Dunch.

"I've arranged for you to play with Al Balata and a couple of other guys at eleven o'clock in the morning," the golf pro informed him.

"Great," McGuffin mumbled, finding the bedside lamp and switching it on. "What time's dinner?"

"The kitchen closed over an hour ago," Cuppy answered.

McGuffin thanked him and said goodbye, then replaced the receiver and snuggled back up to his pillow. He was hungry, but maybe it was just as well. If they were going to play for big stakes, he would be lean like the hunter.

McGuffin was awakened the next morning by the ringing phone and squawking gulls. Thinking he had slept through tee time, he bolted upright and snatched the phone from its cradle on the second ring.

"McGuffin," he said, looking at his watch, relieved to see that he had more than an hour before teeing off.

"Mistah McGuffin, I have a message from Mistah Dunch, sah," the receptionist informed him.

"Yes?"

"He says he is sorry, but your golf date has to be postponed until tomorrow, sah, because Mistah Balata has another engagement today."

"Well—isn't there someone else I can play with?"

"Don't know, sah."

"Can you put me through to Mr. Dunch?" McGuffin asked.

"Sorry, sah. Mistah Dunch just left with Mistah Balata and some other gentlemen."

"I see," McGuffin said. "Thank you."

"You're welcome, sah," she said, and hung up.

McGuffin replaced the phone and stared out the window at the wheeling gulls. He wondered if, having failed Cuppy's identification test of the day before, the pro had warned Balata that he might be investigating Lyle Boone's death. Or was it just a perfectly innocent postponement? he asked himself, as he threw the sheet back and climbed to his feet. The hell with it. I'll find somebody else to play with.

He was halfway across the room when he realized suddenly that something was wrong. It took him a moment to figure it out—he had no hangover.

McGuffin ate breakfast by himself, downstairs in the men's grill, something called PIGC hash with poached eggs and several kinds of tropical fruit. When he had finished this, he ordered Belgian waffles, more fruit, and a rasher of Canadian bacon.

"I missed dinner," he explained to the amazed waitress.

Feeling satisfied, if slightly uncomfortable after his double breakfast, McGuffin climbed the stairs to the dining room, where he found Stymie dusting bottles with a feather duster. Knowing that a bartender must be alert to the needs of his customers, McGuffin decided that Stymie might be the most reliable witness to Lyle Boone's death. Also, questioning an employee was less likely to cause suspicion than questioning a Palm man.

"Good mahning, Mistah McGuffin," Stymie replied to the detective's greeting. "Played already?"

McGuffin shook his head. "I was replaced at the last minute."

"Sah—?" he said, cocking his head quizzically.

"I'm supposed to be out there now with Mr. Balata's group," McGuffin explained.

"Mistah Balata is not playin' golf, sah," the bartender informed him. "He just got on de jitney to go to de village 'bout an hour ago. I seen him go from de window, sah."

"Was Cuppy with him?" McGuffin asked.

Stymie nodded. "And several othah gentlemen, all goin' to de village."

"Do you know why?"

The bartender shrugged. "Don't know, sah. But it's most unusual. Nuttin' dere fo' de membahs. Can I get you a drink, sah?" he asked.

"No—no thanks," McGuffin replied. He had been staring, fascinated, at the old man's long, bony hands, lightly cradling the worn bamboo handle of the feather duster. With black skin showing dully through a kind of silver talcum, the frail figure seemed almost evanescent. "Tell me, Stymie, were you here on the night Mr. Boone died?"

"Oh yas sah," he replied, nodding his head firmly. "I was standing right heah and Mistah Boone was standing right dere where you ah standing."

"Can you tell me what happened?"

Stymie clutched the duster to his chest and shook his head sadly. "Oh mon, it was sumpin' awful. One minute Mistah Boone be all laughin' an' cuttin' up, dan de nex' he go all stiff an' grin lak de debil an' fall to de floor. Den his body staht to shakin' an' his mouth go to foamin'. Dan jus' lak dot he dead."

"He was foaming at the mouth?" McGuffin asked.

"Lak a mod dog, mon," Stymie answered. "An' dere was nuttin' de doctah could do."

"What doctor?" McGuffin asked.

"Doctah Kilty, sah."

"Byron Kilty?" McGuffin asked. "The heart surgeon?" Kilty had recently been in the news, accused of performing experimental surgery only to enhance his reputation.

"Dot's de mon," Stymie confirmed. "He can take de heart from de dead mon an' put it in de live mon. Liver, lungs, gizzard—everyting! Oh, dot mon really sumpin'."

He was that, McGuffin had to agree. And whatever the ethics of his professional conduct, he should be able to recognize a heart attack when he saw one. Yet there was something about Stymie's description of Lyle Boone's death that troubled the detective.

"You said Mr. Boone was grinning when he died?"

"Lak dot," Stymie said, putting a long finger in each corner of his mouth and stretching his lips grotesquely. "Eben when he was stiff as a board an' Doctah Kilty wipe de foam from his mouth, he still be grinnin'."

"And when he went stiff, did his back arch at all?" McGuffin probed.

Stymie nodded slowly. "Yas, I tink so. Lak de bridge," he said, describing the arc with a graceful hand.

"And Dr. Kilty said then that Mr. Boone had died of a heart attack?" McGuffin questioned.

"Oh yas sah," Stymie answered quickly. "So did de doctah from de village."

"Doctor from the village? Why did he call another doctor when he knew that Mr. Boone was dead?"

"He's de coroner," Styme answered. "Doctah Cavah."

"Dr. Carver?" Stymie nodded. "Did he examine the body too?"

"He took a look," Stymie allowed. "Doctah Cavah don' lak dead folks much, I don' tink."

"Then how did he determine that Mr. Boone had died of a heart attack?"

"Doctah Kilty tol' him," Stymie answered, as if nothing could be simpler.

And of course it must have seemed just that way to the coroner too, McGuffin realized. A village doctor, summoned to the posh Palm Isle Club by a world-famous heart surgeon and told by him that the man on the floor had died of a heart attack—what else would he think?

McGuffin had a few more questions, but when the first contingent of golfers entered the bar, he realized the examination was at an end. "Where can I find Dr. Carver?" McGuffin asked hurriedly.

"If he hab a patient, he'll be in his office on Wharf Street. If he don' he'll mos' likely be downstaihs in de bah."

"Which bar?"

"Only one bah in de village—de Palm Isle Inn."

"How would I get there?"

"De jitney stops in front of de building. But you're not goin' to de village, ah you, Mistah McGuffin?"

"Any reason I shouldn't?"

"I don't tink it's advisable, sah," he warned.

"Thanks, Stymie," McGuffin said, backing away from the bar.

He turned around against the startled golfers, excused himself, and skipped quickly down the stairs and outside to the bus stop. It had been a long time since McGuffin had delved into a toxicology manual, but as best he remembered, Lyle Boone's symptoms were strikingly similar to those of strychnine poisoning.

6

The trip to the village, in a very old bus with no perceptible suspension system, was scarcely less harrowing than the flight over. It was difficult to imagine the distinguished members of the PIGC riding in such a contraption.

"De jitney is mostly fo' de help, sah," the driver explained. "Dere ain't much in de village fo' de membahs."

"But you took some members in this morning?" McGuffin asked.

"Yas, sah. Five of dem."

"Did they say why they were going into the village?"

"No, sah," the driver answered, shifting into low gear as he started up a steep hill. "De village is just ovah de top."

McGuffin gripped the edge of the seat and leaned forward, urging the straining bus up the dirt road. The route had been several miles over a rutted road that snaked through tropical valleys and over eroded hills. When the bus finally nosed over the top of the hill, McGuffin had a brief look at the glimmering, horseshoe-shaped harbor and the clutter of brightly painted buildings. The next moment they were plummeting down the hill along a corkscrew path that had the potential to become a great mudslide. Wishing he were back in Eddie's plane, McGuffin braced himself stiffly and waited for the downward spiral to end. Not until they had clattered safely out onto Wharf Street, which was not so much a street as a broad paved area that meandered around the edge of the harbor, did he relax. The brakes squealed as the bus came to a halt in the center of the village.

"De doctah's office is up dere," the driver said, pointing to a yellow barracklike building with an exterior stairway.

"Where will I find you when I want to go back?" McGuffin asked, crouching low to get through the doorway.

"I'm usually dere at de table wit' my mates," he pointed.

McGuffin looked. There, in front of the Palm Isle Inn, a two-story frame building identified by a crudely painted sign over the open front door, several men were sitting at the few mismatched tables and chairs that had been spread out under a large banyan tree. It was apparently Palm Isle's most fashionable sidewalk café.

When the driver made a U-turn and drove off, McGuffin found himself standing alone on the wharf, the only white in a village of blacks. Native women, selling fruits and vegetables and straw hats and baskets, stared silently from their stalls along the edge of the water, while the men in front of the inn eyed him with an indifference bordering on hostility. He tugged a handkerchief from the back pocket of his yellow golf slacks, mopped his brow, then started across the street in the direction of the doctor's office. The main trunk of the elephant-skin banyan, more than six feet in diameter, all but concealed the men at the tables until he had passed the tree.

"Can I help you, mon?" one of them called.

McGuffin turned and stopped, startled by the sight. The man was well over six feet tall, powerfully built, with long dreadlocks hung with ribbons and tinkling decorations, and in his right hand he held a long staff. He wore sandals and faded khaki shorts, but most startling, a white dashiki-like garment, upon which had been painted several mysterious symbols. Only a coiled snake and a brightly painted cock were readily identifiable to the detective.

"No thanks," McGuffin answered. "I'm on my way to see the doctor."

"You ah from de club," he said.

McGuffin nodded slowly, watching as the large black man circled gracefully in front of him, putting himself between McGuffin and the doctor's office. This holy man, or whatever he was, could be trouble, McGuffin knew. A lot of trouble.

Stymie had warned him that this trip was inadvisable, but he hadn't thought it inadvisable enough to require a gun.

"Den why don' you go to one of de white doctahs from de club?" the black man asked.

"Oh, I'm not sick," McGuffin assured him. "I just want to talk to him about a friend of mine."

His smile was like a shark's. "An' I suppose your *friend* has an unmentionable social disease which he can't discuss with his white doctah, so he is forced to go to de niggah doctah—?"

"Ah, shit," McGuffin mumbled. Even if he was able to take this guy—and the odds were plainly not in his favor—he would probably bust up his hands and wreck a perfectly good golf holiday. McGuffin looked up at the menacing figure, now a few feet from him, smiled disarmingly, and gestured helplessly.

"You're right, I do have an unmentionable social disease," he admitted. "But it's not syphilis or gonorrhea or any of those others. I've got a terminal case of AIDS, and if you don't get the fuck out of my way, I'm gonna kiss you."

The big man danced back and away from McGuffin, more quickly than most humans can run forward.

"I don't think you're contaminated, but just to be on the safe side, you'd better jump in the harbor," McGuffin advised.

He didn't look back to see if the man had taken him up on it, but hurried instead to the yellow building and up the stairs to the doctor's office. A small sign on the door at the top of the stairs read "Gaylord Carver, M.D." Before he could knock, the door was opened by an exotic dark beauty with the kind of body that made even a starched nurse's uniform look like a silk peignoir.

"Can I help you?" she asked, in clipped British. The accents of the island were as varied as the blood.

"I hope so," McGuffin replied, stepping inside.

She closed the door and studied him curiously, as if he might be an appointment the doctor had forgotten to mention. She was the color of copper, with green eyes shaped like slanted almonds, balanced dangerously on high cheekbones.

Who knew what ingredients had gone into this wonderful stew? Spanish, French, Chinese, Indian, half the tribes of western Africa? If the cause of miscegenation, like the March of Dimes, could use a poster girl, she was it.

"Do you have an appointment, Mr.—?"

"McGuffin. But please, call me Amos," he said, coming closer. She smelled of fresh flowers and jungle. "No, I don't have an appointment. I'm not even sick," he boasted.

"Then may I ask why you are here?"

"To meet you," McGuffin blurted. "That's not the reason why I came in the first place, but that's the reason now."

"I see," she said, backing away a step. "And what's the reason you came in the first place?"

"Tell me your name," McGuffin pleaded.

"Liani."

"Liani what?"

"Liani Carver."

McGuffin's pained look brought a faint smile to her face.

"Dr. Carver's—?" McGuffin began. He didn't want to phrase the question, let alone hear the answer.

"Daughter," she replied.

"Thank God," McGuffin breathed.

"Now will you tell me why you've come?"

McGuffin nodded. "I'll tell you everything—my deepest secrets—"

"Mr. McGuffin!" she warned.

"Right," McGuffin said. "I came to see Dr. Carver about a friend of mine—Lyle Boone. He's the man who—"

"I know," she said. "I'm sorry."

"Thank you."

"I'm afraid there's someone with the doctor at the moment." On cue, a child cried, followed by a woman's comforting voice. "But you can wait—over there," she said, pointing to the wooden chair farthest from her desk.

McGuffin walked to the appointed chair and sat stiffly. She remained for a moment in the middle of the waiting room, then turned and walked to her desk, moving like a panther. He hoped she didn't think he was crazy. He was seldom assertive with women, even when drinking, but an occasional woman—they were becoming fewer and fewer—sparked an urge in him that he was scarcely able to control. His ex-wife, when he first laid eyes on her at the No Name Bar in Sausalito, had affected him that way. He hoped this would turn out better than that.

"I saw you talking to Bobaloa downstairs a moment ago," she volunteered.

"Is that his real name?" McGuffin asked. It sounded like an old song.

"I don't know if it is or isn't. But I should stay away from him if I were you."

"That's my intention," McGuffin assured her. "I just hope he'll allow me to abide by it."

He would have inquired further about Bobaloa, but at that moment the door opened and a woman came out with a teary-eyed boy clutching a lollipop. They were followed by a little old man in a white jacket, presumably Dr. Carver. He was of mixed race, but as ugly as his daughter was beautiful, with a lean, knobby face that rested crookedly on a skinny neck. So much for heredity, McGuffin thought. He waited until the woman and her son had left, then got to his feet and waited again while Liani explained the reason for his presence. Dr. Carver looked at the detective the way doctors do, then motioned him into the office.

"Come in, Mr. McGuffin."

"Thank you," McGuffin said, walking across the room. "I'll talk to you later," he whispered, as he brushed past the nurse. She said nothing, but smiled noncommittally, which did nothing to disappoint McGuffin. These things had a way of working out.

"Have a seat."

"Thanks," McGuffin said. There was only one chair in the sparsely furnished room, so he sat on the corner of the examining table.

"First you must please allow me to express my sympathy for the loss of your friend," the doctor said, speaking in a soft Indian accent.

"Thank you."

"Then please allow me to apologize for the rude behavior of Bobaloa. I saw it out the window," he explained, before McGuffin could ask. "I suppose he accused you of stealing the land from his people?"

"Stealing the land? You mean the golf club?"

The doctor smiled and nodded. "Such is the rallying cry of the independence movement. They want the golf club, but they can't decide what they would do with it if they had it. The only thing they agree upon is that it would not be used for golf, as the game is a symbol of capitalist-imperialist oppression." He shook his head and made a clucking noise. "I'm afraid revolutionaries have little feeling for the tourist business."

"If you should see Bobaloa, would you tell him I didn't steal any land, that I'm just a guest at the club?"

"I will tell him that," the doctor promised. "Now, what do you wish to know about your friend Mr. Boone?"

"I'm just curious as to how he could have died of a heart attack when he was in excellent health," McGuffin answered. "I realize that even marathon runners have heart attacks," he went on, waving off the anticipated objection. "But I also understand that it's not always easy to tell if a man died as a direct result of a heart attack, or if something else caused the heart to stop beating."

"That may be true," the doctor allowed. "But in this case, your friend's death was observed by a heart specialist."

"Then you relied rather heavily on Dr. Kilty's diagnosis?"

"I considered it more reliable than any postmortem of mine, yes," he admitted. "After all, Dr. Kilty is a world-renowned heart surgeon."

"I take it you've observed a few heart-attack victims before?" McGuffin asked.

"On these islands, Mr. McGuffin, where malnutrition is common, so too is heart disease. I've observed far too many coronary victims, if the truth be told."

"What about strychnine victims?" McGuffin asked.

The doctor shook his head. "I have not had that pleasure."

"But you are familiar with the symptoms?"

"Strictly speaking, there are no typical postmortem charac-teristics of strychnine poisoning, although the brain, lungs, and spinal cord are usually congested," the coroner informed him.

"Is that right," McGuffin said. The little old man was begin-ning to sound like a doctor after all. Nonetheless McGuffin had his own opinion and would not be dissuaded by contrary medical authority—at least not right away. "Stymie told me that Lyle got a fixed grin on his face, then fell to the floor with convulsions and began foaming at the mouth—and when he died, his back was arched. Does that sound like a heart attack, or strychnine poisoning?" McGuffin asked.

"Who is Dr. Stymie?" the old man asked.

"He's not a doctor," McGuffin answered. "He's the bar-tender at the club."

"Ah, I see," Dr. Carver said. "The bartender is of the opin-ion that Mr. Boone was poisoned. No doubt I should have consulted with this bartender rather than relying so strongly on the opinion of Dr. Kilty."

"Maybe you should have," McGuffin said. "How soon after Dr. Kilty pronounced him dead did you examine the body?"

The doctor thought for a moment. "Within two hours," he answered.

"And when you examined the body, did you find that rigor mortis had already set in?"

"I must admit, I did not examine the body as closely as I might have under different circumstances," the doctor answered.

"Had rigor mortis set in?" McGuffin persisted.

Dr. Carver nodded slowly. "Yes."

"Isn't that unusually soon for a heart-attack victim?"

"It is curious, yes," the coroner admitted.

"But not for a strychnine victim?" McGuffin asked.

Dr. Carver stared off for a moment, as if turning the pages of a vaguely remembered medical text in his mind. "If the victim died of strychnine, rigor mortis may have been almost immediate."

"Then Stymie's observations are consistent with strychnine, are they not?" McGuffin went on. "The death grin, convulsions, the arched back—"

"Yes, but they are not entirely inconsistent with a massive heart attack either," the doctor interrupted. "And when a middle-aged businessman clutches his chest and falls dead, the diagnosis is fairly automatic—especially to a chest man like Dr. Kilty."

"Then you admit that Dr. Kilty might be mistaken?" McGuffin asked.

"Are you a lawyer, Mr. McGuffin?" the old man asked with a thin smile.

McGuffin shook his head. "This isn't a question of malpractice."

"Then it must be a question of murder," the doctor said, still smiling. "Are you a policeman?"

Again McGuffin shook his head. "Just a friend." McGuffin could see that the coroner knew he was lying, but it couldn't be helped. "At first I couldn't believe that a man in Lyle's condition, with no history of heart disease, could suddenly die of a heart attack. But I was willing to accept that—until Stymie told me what he had seen. Now, I don't know enough about medicine to decide one way or the other, but you do. And I think you have to agree that from the symptoms I've described, there's at least a possibility that Lyle was given a massive dose of strychnine."

No longer smiling, Dr. Carver nodded thoughtfully. "I'll admit the possibility that Mr. Boone was poisoned. But that does not mean that it was the result of human agency, does it?"

"Come on," McGuffin scoffed. "It's rather hard in a crowded bar to take a controlled substance like strychnine by accident, don't you think?"

"I wasn't thinking of strychnine, Mr. McGuffin. I was thinking of fish."

"Fish?"

"In tropical waters there are many highly toxic fish. Triggerfish, porcupine fish, parrot fish, filefish, and the most dangerous of all, the puffer fish. A single bite of puffer may be more than enough to kill a man. You say the victim was foaming at the mouth?"

"That's what Stymie said."

"I wonder why Dr. Kilty didn't mention this."

"So do I."

"This is not characteristic of strychnine, but it is characteristic of fish toxins," the old man went on thoughtfully. "And as to the other symptoms described by your Dr. Stymie, the puffer produces a curarelike muscular paralysis whose effects might be quite similar to those he described."

"How long does it take to die after swallowing the fish?" McGuffin asked.

"It would take several hours if he had eaten it," the coroner answered.

"But Lyle Boone died in only a few minutes," McGuffin pointed out. He still favored the strychnine theory.

"I said, if he had *eaten* it," the doctor reminded him.

"How else would he have gotten it?"

The doctor looked questioningly at McGuffin for a moment before inquiring: "Do you believe in zombies, Mr. McGuffin?"

"I prefer straight whiskey," McGuffin answered.

The old man laughed and walked to the single window at the end of the room "I can understand your skepticism," he said, staring at the shacks below. "But I can assure you, the scientific community has begun to take zombies quite seriously. I myself have seen and spoken to one," the old man said, turning to the detective.

Oh, Christ, McGuffin said to himself. I knew that poison-fish business sounded loony. "If you don't mind, Doctor, what does this have to do with Lyle Boone's death?"

"I'm coming to that," the old man promised. "A few months ago, I spoke to a man in Haiti who had died and been buried more than twenty years before. He told me he had been scratched by a voodoo doctor with the poison from a puffer fish, and almost immediately became totally paralyzed. He remembers his funeral and he remembers his casket being nailed shut. He remembers being carried to the cemetery and lowered into the grave. He remembers the sound of the first spadeful of earth being thrown upon his casket, then a few more, then total silence."

"Are you suggesting that Lyle Boone was poisoned by a voodoo doctor while having cocktails at the Palm Isle Golf Club?" McGuffin interrupted.

"That's a question for the, ah, friend," the doctor said, with a knowing nod to McGuffin. "I wish merely to acquaint you with certain scientific evidence that might be of some value to you."

"Okay, go ahead," McGuffin said.

"A short while later, this man was dug up and taken out of the casket by the voodoo doctor and given an unknown antidote. Within a few hours the paralysis disappeared and the dead man, Mr. McGuffin, came back to life. He was brain-damaged and ungainly, but capable of manual labor, and completely under the control of the voodoo doctor—a perfect zombie."

"Amazing," McGuffin said.

"The voodoo doctor took the zombie to a sugar plantation deep in the jungle, where he was put to work with other zombies," the coroner went on. "Twenty years later, after the plantation had become defunct, the zombie wandered back to his village."

"So you think Lyle Boone may be a zombie working on a sugar plantation," McGuffin put in.

"In Japan about sixty people die every year from eating raw puffer fish in sushi restaurants," Dr. Carver continued, ignoring McGuffin's stab at humor. "A few of them, however, have come back to life—so to speak—after having been pronounced dead. And at least one of these victims remembers being fully conscious, but unable to move, until a moment before his autopsy was to begin." The old man looked at McGuffin and smiled.

"Then what happened?" McGuffin finally had to ask.

"The eyelid fluttered, almost imperceptibly, but the doctor noticed. It was only with the aid of an EKG that he determined that the man was alive but paralyzed. The next day, entirely on his own, the man recovered."

"I see," McGuffin said, nodding slowly. "And this is all solid medical fact?"

"It was reported in *Time* magazine."

"Then it must be true," McGuffin replied. "And that means Lyle Boone might have been buried alive."

"Or worse."

"How do you know about this stuff?" McGuffin asked. He didn't believe a word of it, of course, but he was fascinated by it.

"I recently happened to come upon an old book on voodoo, written by a French scientist in the nineteenth century. I've also done a modest bit of research on the possible anesthetic properties of the fish toxin."

"Does anybody else around here know about this stuff— zombies and puffer fish?"

The coroner shook his head thoughtfully, then stopped. "Bobaloa, the fellow you just met, might know something about it—although he didn't hear it from me."

"Then how would he know about it?" McGuffin asked.

"He's a voodoo doctor."

McGuffin waited for the old man to laugh. When he didn't, McGuffin asked: "You wouldn't be having me on, would you, Doc?"

"I assure you, Mr. McGuffin, everything I've told you is true beyond the shadow of a doubt."

McGuffin clasped the back of his neck and stared thoughtfully at the doctor. This was a place where street smarts didn't count for much. "If the body was freshly scratched, that should have shown up at the autopsy, shouldn't it?"

"It should have, had there been an autopsy," the doctor answered.

"There was no autopsy?" McGuffin asked, incredulous.

The doctor shook his head. "I don't believe Mrs. Boone wanted it."

"But isn't it mandatory?" he asked.

Again the coroner shook his head. "Not if two physicians sign the death certificate."

"You and Dr. Kilty—" McGuffin said, moving his finger metronomically. "That's why you were called. The widow—or somebody—didn't want an autopsy. Look, Doctor, I don't want you to think I'm entirely sold on this zombie business, but let me ask you a hypothetical question. If the body was exhumed, would the scratch marks still be visible? If they were there in the first place," he added.

"Assuming decomposition has not progressed too far—and after only a few days, I'm sure it has not—the marks would still be visible. And unless the wound was thoroughly cleaned, evidence of the toxin might be found in the damaged tissue."

"Great," McGuffin said. He was becoming enthusiastic in spite of himself. "If I can get the widow to agree to an autopsy report, will you sign an exhumation petition—or whatever is required?"

"If there's a chance the man was murdered, I could do nothing less," the coroner answered. "Besides, Mr. Mc-Guffin, by now I'm every bit as curious as you are," he said.

"Thank you, Doctor, this has been very illuminating," McGuffin said, walking across the room to shake the old man's hand.

"You're entirely welcome, Mr. McGuffin. But I'm afraid you might have some difficulty in convincing Mrs. Boone that her husband may have been the victim of foul play."

"Yeah, I know," McGuffin said. Especially if she already knows, he added to himself, as he opened the door and stepped out into the waiting room. An elderly couple sat on either side of the window, framing the beautiful harbor and the widow Boone's yacht in the distance. Liani, however, was nowhere to be seen.

Not to worry, McGuffin told himself, as he hurried down the exterior stairs. When the time came, he would know where to find her.

7

The men at the tables stared as McGuffin hurried past. Bobaloa, the voodoo doctor, had apparently left. He had probably gone home to take a bath, McGuffin guessed. The Boone yacht lay at anchor in the middle of the harbor, beyond the small moored fishing boats that lay scattered across the bay. Not knowing how he would get out to the yacht, McGuffin made for the women at their stalls along the edge of the wharf. No doubt one of them had a fisherman husband anxious to make five dollars by ferrying him out to the yacht.

"I want to get out to that yacht," McGuffin said to a fat woman sitting amid a pile of straw hats and baskets, as he pulled a role of bills from his pocket.

"Dahlin', fo' five dollahs I'd swim out dere wit' you on my back," she said. "But none of us got no boat."

"What about those men at the inn?" McGuffin asked, pointing toward the banyan tree across the street.

"Dose men ah retired," she said, raising a cackle from her colleagues.

"Damn," McGuffin muttered. He walked to the edge of the wharf and stared out at the yacht. It was, he estimated, a driver and a wedge away. Not a long swim, were he dressed for it. There were several brightly painted wooden boats tied side by side at the foot of the wharf. He was debating borrowing one when he heard the sound of a motor turning over out on the bay. He looked up to see a motor launch from the yacht making for the dock. The pilot, a tanned young man in a white shirt, maneuvered the launch between the moored fishing boats, then eased her bow gently against the wharf at McGuffin's feet.

"Hurry, sir, they're waiting!" the young man called over the idling engine.

McGuffin hesitated for only one brief, confused moment before jumping aboard the launch. He walked along the side deck, then ducked under the canopy and took a seat on the slat bench in the first row. The pilot backed the launch out, then turned it around and headed back to the mother ship. Who are the *they* who are waiting for me? McGuffin wondered. And who the hell am I supposed to be?

The pilot brought the launch around to the far side of the yacht and edged up next to the landing platform hanging near the stern. While the pilot held the launch firmly against the platform, McGuffin jumped aboard the yacht. He turned, expecting the pilot to throw him a line, but the launch was already moving off, around the bow and back in the direction of the wharf. For more passengers? McGuffin wondered. He shrugged and started up the jack ladder to the promenade deck, expecting someone to appear at any moment and unmask him for the pretender that he was. Exclusive golf clubs and luxurious motor yachts were not this detective's usual beat. The promenade deck of the *Cricket*—the name on the life preservers along the bulkhead—was unoccupied.

"Hello?" McGuffin called.

Getting no answer, he opened the nearest hatch and walked into a sumptuous wood-paneled stateroom, with brass lamps and antique furnishings carefully scattered over a blue carpet dotted with gold anchors.

"Nobody here?" McGuffin called out in the plainly empty room.

The next room was the dining salon, larger than many restaurants, and no less empty than the last.

"Mrs. Boone?" he called.

Again getting no answer, he plunged on into the next room. This one had a fireplace and a grand piano, but still no sign of life. What the hell is this, a ghost ship? McGuffin wondered.

A door on the right was open to a large bedroom with a canopied bed. Peeking in and finding no one there, McGuffin crossed the room to a second door, which he opened to a sybaritic bath and sauna. A floating massage parlor, McGuffin marveled, walking to the edge of the sunken tub. Standing on the marble, he suddenly felt the vibration of the accelerating engines and nearly lost his balance as the ship surged forward.

"Christ, I'm being shanghaied!" he exclaimed, rushing back into the adjoining stateroom. He threw open a door and stumbled out onto the promenade deck. "Where the hell is everybody?" McGuffin shouted, starting forward.

The passenger quarters may be empty, but dammit, there has to be somebody on the bridge, he reasoned. When he climbed the ladder and stepped out onto the next deck, he saw that he was still not as high as the bridge. At the forward end of this deck there was still one more flight of stairs to be climbed. McGuffin started up the stairs, then, seeing the woman in the bow below, he froze.

Standing down there, with her long blond hair and white gown trailing in the wind, she was a beautiful, luminous figurehead. When she removed her shoes, McGuffin didn't know what she had in mind. But when she started up the bow ladder, clutching a small package in her arms, he knew that she was about to jump. He opened his mouth to shout, then thought better of it. It would only startle her and perhaps push her over the edge.

Instead he backed down the ladder, then ran to the next one and down onto the promenade deck. Agile as a fireman, he spun himself around the rail and along the deck. He ran recklessly across the forward deck, stumbling once over the anchor chain, and fairly threw himself into the bow. The woman screamed and struggled violently as he wrapped his arms around her legs. Something hard bounced off his head, and a moment later they were thrashing about on the filthy deck while she continued to scream. A second blow to the head was far more telling than the first. There was little pain, just a dull, numbing sensation followed by nothingness, deep and dark as the sea.

When McGuffin regained consciousness a few moments later, he found himself lying on the deck, his bright polyester golf costume coated with black grime. The woman in the white dress, now besmirched with the same grime, stood several feet away, tears coursing down her dirty cheeks. When McGuffin tried to get to his feet, he was quickly hauled back down.

"Keep him away!" the woman cried.

"Not tryin' to hurt her," McGuffin mumbled, probing the back of his head with his fingertips. He came away with blood. "Jus' tryin' to save her."

"Save her from what?" a disembodied voice demanded.

"Suicide—jumpin'—" McGuffin mumbled, pressing a hand to his head wound.

"He thought she was going to jump?" It was another disembodied voice, incredulous.

"Good God, man, don't you know what you've done?" a new voice demanded.

"What?"

"You've interrupted a memorial service!"

McGuffin blinked and managed to get, unmolested, to a sitting position. A hand clutching a pewter urn dangled in front of his face. "You mean this—these are—?"

"The ashes of Lyle Boone, you imbecile!" the same voice informed him, followed by a wail from the widow.

"No!" McGuffin wailed, almost as loud. "Why'd you do that? Why'd you have him cremated?"

"What business is that of yours?"

"The gall of the man."

"Who is he?"

"His name is Amos McGuffin," a familiar voice informed his inquisitors. It was Cuppy Dunch. "He's Francis Knight's cousin."

"Frank Knight's cousin?" a skeptical voice repeated.

"That's right," McGuffin said. He was able to make out Cuppy, among a group of blue blazers, each with the PIGC crest over the left breast.

"He still has no business here. This is a private service," a man with a white pompadour said.

"I'm sorry," McGuffin said, climbing to his feet. He was covered with Lyle Boone's ashes.

"Moron," the pompadour muttered.

"Don't," the widow said. "It was just a mistake. And I do think *some* of Lyle's ashes blew into the sea."

"Oh, I'm sure some of him made it," McGuffin said with a weak smile. When he shifted uneasily, Lyle's ashes made a grating sound under his feet. "If you'll tell me where the broom and dustpan are, I'll be happy to sweep this up."

"The crew will take care of it," Mrs. Boone assured him, turning from McGuffin to the men in blue blazers. "If you don't mind, we'll dispense with the rest of the service and go straight to the dining room. I'll join you just as soon as I've cleaned up."

"Terribly sorry," McGuffin said, as the widow in the soiled dress walked stiffly past him.

"Are you okay?" Cuppy asked.

"I think so. Who hit me?"

"I did," a blue-blazered man announced, proudly, it seemed.

McGuffin was able to place the aquiline nose and cap of tight curls in only a moment. He was Dr. Byron Kilty. "I thought doctors were supposed to save people," McGuffin said, gently probing his wound. The blood had not yet stopped.

"I thought I was," the doctor remarked coolly. "Come inside, and I'll have a look at your head."

McGuffin followed him aft, along the promenade deck and into the dining room, where stewards in white jackets were putting the last touches to the memorial buffet. The man with the white pompadour fairly glowered at McGuffin as he followed the doctor across the room. He was flanked by Al Balata and a skinny younger man with dull blond hair. Other than Cuppy Dunch, there were no other mourners in evidence.

"Rather a small group for Lyle's memorial," McGuffin opined, as he followed Dr. Kilty into the head.

"It was to have been limited to those of his golfing buddies who happened to be around. Not strangers," the doctor said, with a disapproving backward glance.

"Sorry," McGuffin apologized.

"Sit on the head," the doctor ordered.

McGuffin did as instructed. Dr. Kilty opened the medicine cabinet and surveyed its contents with a critical eye. "You know, it's really not entirely my fault that I'm here," McGuffin said. "I was just standing on the dock, minding my own business, when this guy came by in a boat and said to hop in. Not that you should blame him either," McGuffin quickly added.

"I don't," Dr. Kilty answered, rummaging through the medicine cabinet. "How is it that you happened to be standing on the dock in the first place—minding your own business?"

McGuffin shrugged. "I just came into town to do a little sightseeing."

"Was there anything in particular you wanted to see?"

"No."

"Or anyone in particular?" he asked, gazing pointedly at McGuffin.

"Doctor, I'm a stranger here. Who would I be going to see?"

"I can't imagine." Kilty continued to stare at McGuffin, a bottle in one hand, a bandage roll in the other, then he ordered, "Turn around."

"Please, no head transplant," McGuffin said, as he twisted around on the toilet seat. A moment later he felt a wet compress applied to his wound, followed by a searing pain. "Jesus!" he wailed.

"Does that burn?" Kilty asked, pressing the compress firmly against the open wound.

"Like a branding iron," McGuffin answered, beginning to squirm.

"Hold still," the doctor ordered. "There may be some of Lyle in that wound."

"I get the feeling you're enjoying this," McGuffin said through clenched teeth.

"Hmm," Kilty answered, as he went on poking at the wound. "I wonder if there's a needle and thread aboard this boat."

"Never mind the needle and thread, what about the anesthetic?" McGuffin asked.

"Oh, I'm sure there's none of that," Kilty answered, continuing to probe painfully at the patient's head.

"How about a little fish toxin?" McGuffin asked.

Dr. Kilty's probing suddenly stopped. "Fish toxin?" he repeated, removing his hands from McGuffin's head.

"Yeah, I understand it has anesthetic properties," McGuffin answered. "Unless, of course, you use too much."

"Are you in the sciences, Mr. McGuffin?" Kilty asked.

"In a remote sort of way," McGuffin answered.

"And in what way is that?"

"I'm in the investment business." It was the cover his client had suggested.

"I see," Kilty said, replacing his hands on McGuffin's head. This time the probing seemed cautious and less painful. "I'm afraid if I don't put a couple of stitches in this it might leave a scar," the doctor warned.

"I can bear the emotional pain—spare me the physical," McGuffin instructed.

"Very well, I'll put a pressure bandage on it." He opened the roll of gauze and unwound a few feet. "Hold this."

McGuffin held the gauze loosely while the surgeon wrapped his head several times. When he was finished, he tied a large bow over McGuffin's eye.

"Not bad for a field hospital," Kilty said, stepping back to admire his work. "Take a look."

McGuffin got to his feet and looked at himself in the mirror. It looked as if he were wearing a cast. "The bow is in my eye," he complained.

"I think it's cute," Kilty answered. "Come along, I'd like the others to see it. I'm sure they have no idea that I'm capable of such mundane medical work," he said, opening the door for McGuffin.

Knowing that Kilty was enjoying making him look foolish, McGuffin nevertheless followed him into the dining room. Al Balata and the white pompadour, standing together in the middle of the room, stared at him as he was led across the floor.

"My God, he looks like a mummy," the pompadour observed.

"It'll only be for a week or two," Kilty said. "This is Horton Ormsby, club president since Lyle's death."

"How do you do?" McGuffin said, shaking hands. Horton Ormsby had the look of a stern jurist, with a large head, well suited to an eventual stone bust. "I'm sorry about the ashes," McGuffin apologized.

"I don't suppose it matters to Lyle," Ormsby replied, somewhat grudgingly perhaps. "Have you met Al—Al Balata?"

Balata acknowledged McGuffin's greeting by dropping his eyelids once. He had thick black eyebrows and a face seamed and browned by many hours of golf.

"I'm sorry we had to cancel our golf game," McGuffin said.

"Yeah, me too," Balata said, as if hearing about it for the first time. "We only found out about the service this morning."

"Maybe we can play tomorrow," McGuffin suggested.

"I'm afraid we already have four," Balata replied, nodding in the direction of the blond youth across the room who was engaged in an animated discussion concerning the golf swing with Cuppy Dunch.

"Another time then," McGuffin said, smiling but disappointed.

"Sure," Al replied, with little enthusiasm.

"We may be able to use an alternate," Ormsby said. "Lyle's death has left me with a lot of administrative work," he explained, in response to Balata's steady gaze. "I won't be able to play tomorrow."

Al Balata turned to McGuffin with little visible enthusiasm. "How do you play?"

"I used to break eighty once in a while." Balata's eyelids again lowered and lifted. "But I haven't played for a while."

"We play for money," Balata warned.

"So do I."

"We'll play tomorrow," Al promised.

"I'm looking forward to it," McGuffin said, as Mrs. Boone, now changed to pleated slacks and a pale silk blouse, entered the dining room. She saw McGuffin's bandage and brought her hand to her mouth as Dr. Kilty hurried across the room to her. She took his arm and whispered something to him as he led her across the room to McGuffin.

"That's a very pretty bow, Amos McGuffin," she said, failing to suppress a grin.

"And that's a very pretty blouse, Mrs. Boone," he observed. She had sharply pointed breasts, from which the silk material hung like a tent. She still had the long, lean lines of a model, and the hard, wise eyes of a woman who knows the next step—marriage to a rich, older man, followed by a quick divorce. Or murder. The only difference between Marian Boone and a vulture, McGuffin suspected, was nail polish.

"Thank you, Mr. McGuffin," she said, releasing Dr. Kilty's arm and stepping back so that both men could better admire her.

Charming woman, McGuffin said to himself, with a smile that resembled a prosthetic device. Judging from the admiring look of the surgeon, he was too concerned with flesh and bone to bother with the psyche.

"Why, Mr. McGuffin, you don't have a drink!" she exclaimed, suddenly grasping his hand.

"I'm not drinking," McGuffin said. "It only makes me clumsier."

"Then by all means have nothing to drink. Darling, find something harmless for Mr. McGuffin to drink, would you, like a dear?" she asked, turning to the doctor.

"I have no idea what that would be," the doctor remarked flatly.

"Club soda will be fine," McGuffin answered.

"Yes, bring Mr. McGuffin a club soda. While I ask him a few questions. If you gentlemen don't mind," she added to Ormsby and Balata, as she tugged McGuffin away. It wasn't until she released his hand, after they had crossed the stateroom, that McGuffin realized his hand was still smudged with the ashes of her husband. He covered it and was trying to rub the mark away when the widow turned to him with her professional smile.

"Did you know my husband, Mr. McGuffin?" she asked.

"Casually," he lied, continuing to rub the dead man's ashes. "Somehow I feel I've grown closer to him since his death."

"I know what you mean," she said. "What brings you to Palm Isle, Mr. McGuffin?"

"Golf."

"What else," she said, with a weary shrug. "That's all that goes on here."

"Are you sure?"

"Why, Mr. McGuffin," she said, grinning wickedly. "Don't tell me you know something I don't know."

"Not yet," he said.

She stepped closer and peered intently at him, as if her eyesight were bad. "I wonder why Lyle never introduced us. You seem like a lot more fun than the rest of his golf buddies," she said, indicating the others with a toss of her head. When she moved, the tip of one breast pressed against the back of his hand.

"You've got a nice boat," he said.

"It's a yacht," she said, stepping back.

"Why is it called the *Cricket?*"

"That was my professional name, Marian Cricket. I thought it was kind of catchy."

"It was," McGuffin agreed. "Why did you have your husband cremated?"

"Because he was dead," she answered. "If it's any of your business."

"Let me phrase it another way," he tried. "Did Lyle direct in his will that he be cremated?"

"Not specifically. I mean, there are only two choices, aren't there? And cremation is so much more civilized, don't you think?"

"Unless it contravenes the will of the deceased," McGuffin qualified.

"Oh, I wouldn't contravene anyone's will," she said, looking up at McGuffin with an innocent smile. "Lyle told me he wanted to be cremated. Not that he expected to die soon, you understand. We were just talking one night, while we were standing on the deck in the moonlight, and Lyle turned to me and said: 'When I die, I'd like to be cremated and my ashes scattered at sea off Palm Isle.'"

"With a few of his golfing buddies in attendance," McGuffin added.

"That was my idea," she said.

At that moment, one of Lyle's golfing buddies called her away. Byron Kilty crossed the room with McGuffin's drink, handed it to him, and turned to Marian Boone. "Horton would like to speak to you."

"And I bet I know why," she said.

She excused herself and walked across the room to where Horton Ormsby stood alone in the corner. He reminded McGuffin of a lion in a small cage. Byron Kilty stared intently at her as she went. Both of them were thinking the same thing, McGuffin knew. She had a great ass.

"A man could kill for a woman like that," McGuffin said.

"Some men," Kilty agreed, without looking away.

"But not you?"

Kilty turned to McGuffin. "I don't have to kill for women like that."

"Must be nice." McGuffin said, glancing at Marian and Ormsby, huddled together in the corner. He was too far away to hear their conversation, but it had obviously quickly become an agitated one. Ormsby prowled around her, hands waving, while she answered with a jabbing finger and thrust chin.

"Lyle wouldn't have approved!" Ormsby suddenly shouted, his voice filling and silencing the room.

"Who are you to tell me what my husband would approve or disapprove?" the widow demanded.

"You at least owed us the opportunity to bid! Lyle loved the Palm—he wouldn't want his bond owned by an outsider!"

"Hypocrite!" she replied, her volume matching his own. All

attention was now on the combatants. "You got Lyle to buy those shares simply because you ran out of bluebloods willing to tie up ten million dollars. You let Lyle buy himself into the company of gentlemen like yourself, but you never stopped reminding him that he had no business here!"

"We elected him president, for God's sake!"

"You *sold* him the office! A million here, a million there! You may have taken him, but you won't take his widow! I sold those shares in the good old capitalist tradition you're all so fond of. So thanks very much for attending Lyle's memorial service, but you can't get blood from ashes. So if you don't mind," she said, turning to the stunned mourners, "I wish you would all leave now."

Glasses were replaced and partings murmured as the blue-blazered Palm men shuffled to the door. It wasn't often that men such as these were spoken to in such a way by anyone—least of all a beautiful blond ex-model from California. McGuffin had rather enjoyed it.

"Good show," McGuffin said, as he filed past.

There was a hint of a conspiratorial smile in her glance, McGuffin thought, as he stepped out onto the promenade deck. Did she know that he was an impostor? Had all that money for preppy golf clothes gone for nothing?

McGuffin sat in the back of the launch, while Horton Ormsby snorted and huffed like a tethered bull. The blond kid too seemed worried, pointing out that this was the first time a bond had ever been owned by a nonmember—whoever he was. Al Balata nodded sympathetically from time to time, but his voice was absent from the indignant chorus.

McGuffin was both amused and concerned at the revelation that Marian Boone had sold Lyle's bond to a mysterious purchaser. It occurred to him that because the sale had to have taken place almost immediately after Lyle's death—he had been dead only for four days—it might have been agreed to by Marian and the purchaser prior to Lyle's death. In fact, Lyle's death could have been arranged by the purchaser in return for Marian's agreement to sell. McGuffin studied Al Balata, who was staring calmly shoreward while Ormsby raged helplessly beside him. Did he look like a man who now owned twenty percent of the PIGC—Lyle's bond as well as his own? Or more to the point, did he look like a man who would kill for ten million dollars? Was there a man who wouldn't?

Or a woman? No, Marian Boone was not likely to kill for money, he decided. She already had more than she could ever spend. When a woman like Marian kills her rich old husband, it's usually for the love of a younger man. Suddenly McGuffin snapped up in his seat and peered all around the boat. Byron Kilty, he realized, had remained aboard the yacht with the angry widow.

8

McGuffin stood on the practice green, knocking ten-foot putts at the hole, while his opponents watched from the first tee. He missed some and made some, but the stroke felt good, and all in all, he felt ready to play. Cuppy Dunch had worked with him on the practice tee for nearly an hour, and after a few adjustments, the golf pro had pronounced him fit for competition.

"Just keep it slow," Cuppy had cautioned.

It was the simplest instruction in golf, yet the most difficult to obey.

When McGuffin made three in a row from ten feet, he retrieved the balls from the cup and walked to the first tee. Besides Al Balata, he was playing with Byron Kilty and Churston Brown, the skinny blond kid he had seen aboard the *Cricket*.

"Good of you to join us," Churston said, bounding across the tee to shake McGuffin's hand.

"Good of you to have me," McGuffin replied, shaking the eager hand.

"We haven't had you yet," Al Balata said, the voice of reserve.

"What happened to my bow?" Dr. Kilty asked, pointing to McGuffin's bandage. The bow had been snipped off, leaving a tight knot over one eye.

"It was interfering with my golf swing," McGuffin said.

"That was the idea," the surgeon said. "Cuppy tells me you hit the ball pretty well."

"I just hope I can hold up my end," McGuffin replied modestly.

"You don't have to worry about that," Al Balata said. "In Skins it's every man for himself."

"Is that the same as Skats?" McGuffin asked.

"The same thing," Churston replied. "It's a four-way match, low ball wins the hole, but it has to be par or better. One tie all tie, with carryovers until there's a winner."

"Plus double for birdies, triple for eagles, and an extra Skin for sandies," Al added.

"Right," McGuffin said, trying to take it all in. A greenie, he knew, was a ball hit on the green with one stroke to a par three hole. So a sandie, he guessed, must be a par from a greenside bunker, a sand-blast shot and a single putt. Even at five dollars a hole he couldn't lose much more than a hundred dollars, including sandies, he calculated. Surely his client wouldn't complain about the expense, especially if it was the only way to get next to Al Balata. And now Byron Kilty, his newest suspect. "How much are we playing for?" he asked.

"Just enough to keep it interesting," Churston Brown said, beaming amiably from behind his round wire-framed spectacles. "A hundred dollars a hole."

"One hundred," McGuffin repeated, just to be sure he had heard it correctly. Nobody corrected him. He quickly calculated: lose all eighteen holes to a few birdies and sandies and he'd be out close to three thousand dollars. Still, he couldn't lose them all. And each hole he won was worth four hundred dollars at least, including his own hundred. Hell, I might even make a couple thousand dollars, he decided. In which case he saw no reason to mention it to his client.

They tossed coins, and McGuffin elected to hit last, an advantage in match play, he felt. Each hole, he noticed as he studied the scorecard, was given a name. The first, because of its resemblance to the famous eighteenth at Pebble Beach, was appropriately called Pebble. It was a five-hundred-and-three-yard par five, curling gently from right to left along the edge of the ocean. The tee shot, if the golfer elected to carry the water, had to fly almost two hundred yards to a lush green

fairway that resembled a bobsled run, with a large fairway
bunker on the high right shoulder. Hit it short, McGuffin calculated, as Byron teed up for the first shot, and he'd be in the
water. Hit it long and he'd be in the bunker. But hit it extraor-
dinarily long and he'd fly the bunker, catch the side of the hill,
and scoot down to the center of the fairway, leaving himself in
position to reach the green in two—if he didn't catch the
creek in front of the green. It was a godlike hole, generous to
the humble in spirit but terrible in its wrath to the golfer of
false pride. It was scarcely the percentage shot, but McGuffin
knew that if he got it all, he could clear the bunker and reach
the green in two. He would wait to see what his opponents
did before deciding.

Kilty chose a three wood, punching it just short of the
bunker, a good shot but a long way from the green. Balata,
who had stood watching with a wood in each hand, dropped
his three wood on the ground and unsheathed a metal driver.
A man after my own heart, McGuffin said to himself, as he
watched Balata bring the club back. He hit it well, but not
well enough. It missed clearing the bunker by only a few
yards.

"Damn!" Balata exclaimed, slamming his club to the
ground.

"Too bad it's not horseshoes," Churston Brown said, as he
walked to the front of the tee.

Balata glared at Brown as the young man went obliviously
about his business. He took two practice swings before hitting
a long high drive that started out to sea, then drifted right and
fell softly on the lush fairway, some thirty yards past Kilty's
ball. Balata was possibly out of it, while Kilty and Brown were
both planning to lay up for easy fives, McGuffin decided. So
what the hell, why not go for it.

Remembering Cuppy's advice on the practice tee, "The farther you want to hit it, the slower you take it back," McGuffin
cranked it back slowly, held it for an instant at the top, then
brought the clubhead down with a mighty rush. He heard the
heavenly click and felt the solid impact that told him he had

gotten it all, then looked up to see his ball climbing and turning left over the bunker like an aerobatic jet.

"Jesus!" Kilty breathed.

"He's got it!" Churston announced.

"Hell of a drive!" Al Balata said.

"Ah, I didn't get it all," McGuffin complained, as he bent
over to pick up his tee. It was probably the best tee shot he
had ever hit in his life.

Kilty stared stonily at him as he climbed aboard the cart.
They curled along the edge of the water, then made a straight
line to Kilty's ball. McGuffin remained on the cart while Kilty
hit his shot. He laid up in front of the creek, and Churston did
the same, both of them serviceable shots. Balata was forced to
hit a sand wedge out of the bunker in order to clear the front
lip, leaving his second shot just a short distance beyond
McGuffin's first.

McGuffin's ball was sitting up nicely on the lush carpet—
there didn't seem to be a bad lie on the entire golf course—
just begging to be spanked up on the green, about two
hundred and twenty yards away, with a smooth easy three
wood. But it was not to be. He snapped the club back with a
quick jerk and hit a shot that slithered through the grass like
a snake.

"You looked up," Byron offered, as McGuffin slumped onto
the cart.

McGuffin glanced at him out of the corner of his eye. He
was smiling that same smile he had smiled while probing at
McGuffin's head wound.

McGuffin and Balata both missed the green with their third
shots and took bogeys, but Churston and Byron tied with
pars.

"No blood," the doctor said, as they walked off the green.

They drove past the cottage where McGuffin had spent the
night, then across the drive to the second hole, the Bottle, so
called because of its shape. A long narrow neck led through
the tropical forest before opening to a broad saucer-shaped
fairway with the green nestling in the bottom of the Bottle.
Kilty and Brown both threaded three woods safely down the

bottle's neck, but well short of the opening, while Balata knocked a long one through the opening and down into the saucer. A birdie here would be worth twelve hundred dollars. McGuffin decided to go for it.

"Just get the key in the keyhole and the door will open," Churston advised, as McGuffin addressed the ball.

Thinking fondly of his first tee shot, McGuffin reared back and let it fly. He not only failed to get the key in the keyhole, he missed the door. The ball went out about one hundred and fifty yards, then ducked into the jungle on the left like a hound after rabbits.

"Too quick," Byron said with that same smile.

"Will I be able to find that?" McGuffin asked, reaching for the ball in his back pocket.

"Yeah, but I wouldn't go look for it if I were you," Churston said.

"Why not?" McGuffin asked.

"Coral snakes," Byron answered.

"Oh," McGuffin said, pulling the ball from his pocket. If there was one thing he disliked more than small airplanes, it was small poisonous snakes. He hit the next one through the clearing about twenty yards past Al Balata's ball. But with the stroke and distance penalty for the lost ball, he was out of the hole.

"I woke up with a headache last night and phoned you a couple of times," McGuffin informed the doctor as they rode down the fairway. "Apparently you were out."

"That's to be expected," Kilty said. McGuffin looked at him. "The headache, I mean." He stopped the cart in front of a gnarled banyan tree, with the dense jungle foliage beyond. "Do you want to look for your ball?" he asked, pointing into the dark tropical forest.

McGuffin shook his head. "I'll play the second one."

"You're hitting three," he said, smiling again.

"Thank you," McGuffin said, smiling back.

McGuffin hit a beautiful shot dead on the stick for a gimme bogey, while the others all made par.

The next hole is worth twelve hundred dollars, McGuffin

reminded himself, as Byron steered the cart through a jungle path to the next tee. Cuppy had been right—a player could scarcely see from one fairway to the next on this magnificent golf course. And so far each surprising hole was entirely dissimilar to the last. The first resembled an oceanside links in California, while the second resembled Augusta, and this, the third, looked as if it belonged in a Japanese garden. It was a par three from an elevated tee to an undulating island green in the middle of a clear pond, connected to the mainland by an arched oriental bridge, perhaps the one Stymie had likened to Lyle Boone's back. Two white swans floated aimlessly on the pond, and when McGuffin walked to the edge for a closer look, a school of goldfish flashed in the water like scattered doubloons.

"A beautiful hole," McGuffin said, as he stood appraising the green. It seemed as large as Australia, with a few innocuous bunkers scattered about, like so many piles of sugar.

"Don't be deceived by her beauty," Churston warned. "She's called Devil's Island."

A piece of cake, McGuffin told himself.

Yet Byron and Churston both missed Devil's Island, slicing five irons into the pond. Al hit a six iron onto the green but left himself a long twisting putt. Trying to think of his swing and not the money at stake, McGuffin was a bit quick, pulling his six iron to the left of the stick. At first he worried that it would find the water, but it was hit badly enough that it began slicing and ended up about ten feet from the hole.

"Not very pretty," McGuffin allowed, as he bent to retrieve his tee.

"Unlike bullfighting, style isn't everything in this game," Churston remarked charitably.

Neither Byron nor Al Balata said anything. With them you always knew where you stood.

With McGuffin in position for a sure par and three Skins worth twelve hundred dollars—unless somebody tied him— Al Balata suddenly had two partners. Churston lined Al's putt up from behind the hole, Byron from behind the ball.

"It breaks about four feet from right to left," Churston said.

"Maybe more," Byron added. "Just don't leave it short."

McGuffin stood calmly to the side while all three players combined their advice and skill in an effort to deprive McGuffin of victory. Balata struck the ball to the right of the hole, but not nearly hard enough. The putt drew up six feet short of the cup, as his advisers groaned audibly.

Without any help from his friends, McGuffin lined up his putt. He could safely two-putt for a par and if Balata missed his six-footer, pocket twelve hundred dollars, or make it for a birdie and earn sixteen hundred dollars. He decided to go for it.

Don't leave it short, he told himself, before taking the putter back. He didn't. His ball rolled more than three feet past the cup. Not to worry, he told himself, as he marked his ball. Tom Watson knocks these in all the time.

"We don't want to put any unnecessary pressure on you, Al," Churston said, as Balata lined up his six-footer. "But right now this putt is the single most important event in all of our lives."

Nervously, Al Balata knocked the putt into the hole.

"Nice putt," McGuffin said flatly, when his friends had finished congratulating him.

Now McGuffin was the most popular man in the foursome. Byron and Churston rushed to help him with his three-and-a-half-footer, while Balata waited, outwardly calm, at the edge of the green.

"Hit it on the left side of the hole," Byron advised.

"In the middle," Churston corrected.

McGuffin chose the former. All putts broke, however slightly, one way or the other. To aim for the middle of the hole was unwarranted optimism. McGuffin struck his putt and looked to see if it had gone into the hole, though not in that order, and missed on the left.

"Dad luck," Al called happily as he turned and walked briskly to the bridge, twelve hundred dollars richer.

Byron and Churston filed slowly over the bridge while McGuffin stayed behind to hit his putt twice more. He made it both times.

McGuffin parred the next three holes, very nearly making birdie on two of them, but so did Byron and Al. Churston's long smooth swing was beginning to give him trouble, and the adjustments he had made were not working. With sixteen hundred dollars now riding on the seventh hole, a long par five, it was beginning to look like a three-way match.

Churston's drive off the seventh tee caught the left rough, while the other three found the middle of the fairway. Byron's drive was the big surprise, sailing some thirty yards past McGuffin and Balata.

"A lot of pros don't hit it that far," McGuffin said, as he chauffeured Kilty to his ball.

"That felt good," Byron allowed.

The second shot was a blind shot over the top of the hill. Churston was forced to hit an iron out of the rough, lobbing the ball gently over the top of the hill and out of sight. Al hit a soft five iron not much farther.

"The pin is in line with that tallest tree," Byron advised as McGuffin halted the cart beside his ball. "You can reach the green if you get it all."

Remembering how he had muffed his second shot on the par five first hole, McGuffin decided this time to play it safe. Better a sure par than a possible bogey, he told himself as he took a stance over the ball. He swung slowly and smoothly, caught the ball squarely on the screws, and watched it rocket over the crest of the hill directly at the tallest tree.

"If it's long enough you're on the green," Byron said. "Great shot."

"Thanks," McGuffin said. He replaced his three wood in the bag and slid under the wheel. It had to be long enough; he couldn't hit it any farther.

Much to McGuffin's surprise, Byron too hit an easy five iron over the hill that landed approximately where Al's ball had landed. When he reached the top of the hill and saw what lay below, McGuffin saw the reason for their caution, and understood immediately why the seventh hole was named Normandy. From the bottom of the hill to the green, a distance of more than one hundred yards, lay the most awesome stretch of bunkers he had ever seen. Great walls of sand, like storm-tossed waves, reached high into the air to snatch and bury well-hit balls otherwise destined for the green. There were greenside bunkers and fairway bunkers, church pews and pot bunkers, and a random scattering of inkblot bunkers that defied definition. There were three balls lying short of the sand, and McGuffin knew his was not one of them.

Byron made a clucking sound with his tongue that was supposed to signify sympathy. "I'm afraid you're in the Devil's Asshole."

"The Devil's Asshole?" McGuffin repeated.

"You see that deep hole in front of the green with the ladder sticking out of it?" McGuffin nodded. It appeared that the maintenance crew was doing some work on the watering system. "Well, that pot bunker is called the Devil's Asshole," the doctor informed him.

McGuffin stared incredulously at the steep-sided hole and shook his head slowly. "And the ladder is so I can get down into the hole?" Kilty shook his head. "It's so you can get out."

And Byron was not exaggerating, McGuffin saw, when he stepped off the last rung of the ladder and into the sand. He was standing in a hole about the size of a large bedroom, with ten-foot clay walls, smooth and straight as tile. It took three blasts of the sand wedge to get the ball up and out of the pot bunker, which knocked him out of the running for the sixteen hundred dollars. All he could do now was pray that Al and Byron tied with fives, which appeared likely, as both of them were lying three, but safely out of birdie range.

McGuffin retrieved his ball from still another trap in front of the green and walked off in the direction of the next tee to await the outcome. Churston had mishit still another shot that ended up in a deep greenside bunker near where McGuffin stood.

"I shoulda stood in bed," Churston muttered, as he disappeared into the bunker with a rake and a wedge.

As McGuffin continued on in the direction of the next tee, Churston's ball flew out of the bunker on a tail of sand, bounced twice, and rolled into the hole for a birdie four. Al

and Byron, who had been intently lining up their own birdie
putts, stared wordlessly at the occupied hole.

"How'd I do?" Churston called from the bunker.

"Not bad," Al answered.

McGuffin stood tensely on the tee and watched as Byron
and Al both missed their birdie putts to tie. Not bad at all,
McGuffin said to himself. That blind birdie out of the bunker
had been worth two thousand dollars to the kid. Not to worry,
McGuffin told himself. There's still forty-four hundred dollars
riding on the last eleven holes.

One of the most puzzling mysteries of golf is how news of an
unusual event travels from the remotest corner of the golf
course to the clubhouse in less time than it would take to get
through by phone. Cuppy Dunch claimed to know of a particularly tight-fisted golfer who shot a hole-in-one, then raced
immediately back to the clubhouse bar to close his account—
only to find the entire membership already drunk at his
expense.

In the case of Churston's miraculous two-thousand-dollar
sand shot, it perhaps took a little longer for the word to drift
back to the clubhouse. Thereafter, however, the reports arrived, by various labyrinthine means, with a regularity and
efficiency the major television networks might envy. It was
reported that the next three holes were tied with bogeys, but
that the guest, McGuffin, had birdied the eleventh hole.
Then a minute later it was reported that Byron had also had a
birdie on eleven. The same thing happened on fifteen, after
they had tied the previous three holes, only this time the
birdies were by Al and Churston. After tying sixteen and seventeen with pars, there was forty-four hundred dollars available to the winner of the final hole. Although this was a
modest sum for the wealthy members of the PIGC, it was
sufficient to whet their appetite for competition and draw a
modest gallery around the eighteenth green, including even
Cuppy Dunch. He stood behind the green in white plus
fours, waiting for the golfers to emerge from behind the tree
line, more than two hundred yards down the fairway.

The eighteenth was the number-one handicap hole at Palm Isle, a four-hundred-and-sixty-seven-yard dogleg par four, requiring a long tee shot to clear the trees, followed by a wood or long iron to an elevated green. There were three balls lying in the fairway beyond the trees, but Cuppy didn't know yet to whom they belonged. While the spectators waited, somebody's second shot appeared from behind the trees and settled gently on the left side of the fairway, about a hundred yards from the green, the best a player could do if he failed to get his tee shot past the trees.

When the carts came around the trees and each player proceeded to his ball, Cuppy saw that it was Byron Kilty who was lying two, while all the others were lying one. Churston, who had about two hundred and thirty-five yards to the green, hit a wood short and a little left, not a bad shot. Al Balata hit an iron that ended up short in the right rough, while McGuffin hit an iron that landed in front and managed to trickle onto the edge of the green. He had a very long putt, but right now Cuppy would have had to rate McGuffin the favorite to win the forty-four hundred dollars.

As Cuppy watched the players approach, Tommy, the assistant professional, swept down to the green on a cart and braked beside his boss.

"Mr. Ormsby wants to see you," Tommy said.

"Tell him I'll be there in a little while," Cuppy answered, watching as Byron Kilty walked to his third shot.

"He said right away," Tommy warned.

"Shit!" Cuppy muttered, turning and walking to the cart. On or off the golf course, Horton Ormsby's problem was timing.

9

Following the round, McGuffin went directly to his cottage to phone his client with the news. It turned out, however, that Horton Ormsby had gotten to Francis Knight before him.

"Horton has already told me about the incident aboard Marian's yacht, and I must say, McGuffin, it has left me more than a little disturbed."

"Yeah, well, I can explain that," McGuffin said. "If you had been there, I'm sure you would have agreed—that woman looked like she was going to jump."

"Jump? What woman? Have you been drinking, McGuffin?" the lawyer inquired frostily.

"No, of course not," McGuffin answered quickly, realizing that Ormsby had somehow neglected to mention his failed rescue attempt. "Why don't you tell me what you heard, then I'll tell you what I heard."

"Very well," the lawyer answered hesitantly. "I received a call from Horton Ormsby this morning, while you were out playing golf, which only confirms my worst suspicions. Marian Boone sold her husband's bond, or at least contracted to sell it, to something called the Devon Corporation, about which Horton knows nothing. He's assigned me the job of finding out who the principals of this corporation are, but I'm afraid I already know the answer."

"Al Balata?" McGuffin asked.

"Undoubtedly. But I'll let you know just as soon as I've confirmed it."

"Yeah, please do," McGuffin said, writing "Devon Corporation" in his notebook, in large bold strokes.

"Now tell me what you've heard."

McGuffin dropped the pencil beside the pad and rose from the bed. He talked better on his feet. "Well, just for openers, I discovered that Lyle may not have died of a heart attack, as Dr. Kilty claims. He was with Lyle when he died, yet he called in the local coroner, a Dr. Carver, to corroborate the cause of death."

"Isn't that rather excessive?"

"Not if you wish to avoid an autopsy," the detective replied. "Apparently in British jurisdictions no autopsy is required as long as two physicians sign the death certificate and agree as to the cause of death. The coroner agreed with Byron's diagnosis, but almost entirely on Byron's say-so, even by his own admission. Dr. Carver hardly even looked at the body."

"You think Byron may have been mistaken," Knight summed up.

"To put it politely," McGuffin replied.

"And do you have any forensic evidence to confirm this?"

"Only Stymie's description of Lyle's death. Judging from what he observed, there's a good chance Lyle was given a massive dose of strychnine shortly before he died. Dr. Carver agrees now that Lyle may have been poisoned, but he's not sure it was strychnine." McGuffin had decided to hold the puffer-fish theory until later. It seemed much too exotic for so early in the investigation.

"I'm not sure I understand exactly what you're saying," Francis Knight put in. "If Lyle was poisoned—and it was apparent even to a bartender—how would Byron mistake his death for a heart attack? Or are you suggesting that it was not a mistake?"

"That's at least a possibility," McGuffin answered. "Especially after what I observed last night."

"And what did you observe last night?"

"Byron Kilty spent the night with Marian Boone, aboard her yacht." The faint gasp from the other end of the line told McGuffin he had made his point. "I think Byron Kilty and

Marian Boone have been carrying on an affair for some time, but so far it's only a guess. Let me prove it and we've got a strong motive for Lyle's murder."

"Not Al Balata?" the lawyer asked, incredulous.

"I haven't ruled him out yet," McGuffin answered. "But if it turns out that Balata has no connection to this Devon Corporation, we're going to have to take a hard look at Dr. Kilty and the widow."

"Yes, of course," Knight agreed, but not without some reserve. "This is rather a lot to assimilate all at once. Balata, yes. But Byron Kilty? Why, the man is every inch a gentleman. No one has ever accused him of miscounting so much as a stroke."

"Yeah, he plays an honest game of golf," McGuffin had to agree.

"And Marian?" he said, less incredulous, it seemed. "I didn't believe that she married for love, but still, that's a long way from murder. I have a thought!" he said brightly.

"What's that?" McGuffin asked.

"We'll have the body disinterred. Marian wouldn't dare oppose it if there was any suspicion that Lyle had been poisoned. Or if she did, we'd know that there *is* something to your theory after all."

"That's why I'm *sure* there's something to my theory," the detective answered confidently. "Marian shipped Lyle's body to Florida and had him cremated the next day."

"No."

"Yes."

"Lyle told me that when he died he wanted to be buried on a hill overlooking a golf course."

"According to his widow, he had a change of heart at the last minute. His ashes were scattered at sea last night. Or at least most of them were," McGuffin added. "I'm surprised Horton Ormsby didn't mention it this morning."

"Yes, so am I," the lawyer admitted. "I suppose he was preoccupied with the bond and this Devon Corporation. I was sure it had to be Al Balata," he said thoughtfully. "But Byron Kilty—the man's a very good golfer, you know."

"I know," McGuffin answered. "Which brings me to my

next item of business. I had to write a draft on your account for two thousand dollars."

"Two thousand—what the hell for?" the lawyer spluttered.

"That's how much I lost at Skins this afternoon," the detective explained. "I know we didn't discuss golf losses as a business expense, but believe me, it was the only way I could get next to Al and Byron."

"You played Skins with Al and Byron?" Knight asked, incredulous.

"And Churston Brown," McGuffin added.

"And Churston? Don't you know those are three of the best players in the club?" he wailed.

"I know it now," McGuffin answered. "But I could have beaten them out of forty-four hundred bucks this afternoon, except that Byron hit a seven iron dead on the stick for his third shot, and I got nervous and three-putted. But it won't happen the next time. I can beat those guys—I'll get your money back for you," McGuffin swore desperately.

"I'll pay your losses this time, Mr. McGuffin, but I don't want you to go near that Skins game ever again."

"But if I don't play in the Skins game I won't be able to talk to them," McGuffin pleaded. That was partly true, but more important, he wanted to get in the game and recoup his losses. And with a little luck he might even pick up an extra several thousand dollars before this case was finished.

"Do you seriously think you can beat them?" Knight asked.

"I'm sure of it," McGuffin insisted. "They aren't that good. I almost beat them today, and this was the first time I played the course."

"All right, Mr. McGuffin, I'll allow you to play one more time, if that's the only way I'm going to get my two thousand dollars back."

"Not to worry," McGuffin assured him. "By this time to-morow you'll have your two thousand back."

And I might have a couple thousand of my own to go with it, McGuffin thought, as he replaced the phone after bidding goodbye to his client. McGuffin was no math wizard, but he understood that on this case his fee was bus money compared to the seventy-two hundred dollars riding on each Skins game.

10

McGuffin stood in front of the bathroom mirror and carefully unwound the bandage from his head. Some blood oozed from the wound when a bit of scab came away with the bandage, but it quickly coagulated after a couple of blottings with the towel. As he dropped the stained towel in the sink and returned to the bedroom, McGuffin wondered if the excessive bandage had been Dr. Kilty's idea of a joke. He would ask at dinner.

He was almost out the door when the phone rang. That would be one of the Skins players, McGuffin knew, when he glanced at his watch. He was fifteen minutes late for dinner.

"I'm on my way," he called into the phone.

"On your way to where?" a lovely, British-accented woman's voice inquired. It was Liani Carver. "You left without saying goodbye," she said in a teasing voice.

"I couldn't find you," McGuffin said.

"And after all that sweet talk. I'm terribly disillusioned, Amos."

"I don't blame you," McGuffin said. "What can I do to make it up to you?"

"You could take me to dinner."

"My very thought."

"Do you have a car?"

"No."

"Then I'll pick you up in front of the clubhouse at eight o'clock."

"Wouldn't you like to come in for a drink?" McGuffin proposed.

"No," she replied tersely.

"I'll be on the front steps," McGuffin promised.

McGuffin said goodbye and slowly replaced the receiver, as the opening lines of a piece of pulp fiction he had read more than twenty-five years before leaped suddenly and unaccountably to mind.

> *It was late and I was fagged, so I decided to stack a few ZZs on the old office Chesterfield. The last sheep had just cleared the fence when she busted in—and I mean busted!—a platinum blonde, built like a Maginot bunker, and naked under a long chinchilla coat.*

This dusky island beauty was certainly no blonde, and almost as certainly she didn't own a fur coat. And no doubt the tough private eye of that long-forgotten novel would never cancel an appointment with a prime suspect just to have dinner with an irrelevant figure, no matter how lush and exotic that figure might be. But to McGuffin, who had been drawn to this romantic vocation as an impressionable youth, only to suffer a career of steadily grinding disillusionment over the ensuing years, the lovely Liani, blonde or no, was finally, he was sure, his promised professional destiny. Al Balata and Byron Kilty would have to wait their turn.

They had dinner at Jezebel's Creole Restaurant, in a small but once grand house on the side of a hill overlooking the village and bay of Palm Isle. A Victorian gingerbread behind a picket fence and trellised entry, it was all but hidden by leafy palms and, judging from the dark faces of the diners that surrounded them, known only to a few islanders of relative wealth and keen eyesight. When he entered with the cinnamon-skinned Liani, McGuffin's white, sunburned face had stirred some curiosity, but no overt hostility. He behaved as if color-blind, ate everything she ordered for him, including conch chowder, squid, and eels, and a local lobster that tasted

nothing like the Maine variety. Mindful of his pledge, Mc-
Guffin pretended to drink the rum-and-coconut-milk con-
coction that Liani had ordered for them, but she was not
deceived.

"You don't like your drink?" she asked, toward the end of
dinner.

"I've never tasted a drink I didn't like," McGuffin corrected. "But I never drink before an important golf match." It
was the excuse he had prepared earlier.

"I can't imagine taking a game so seriously," she said, with a
disapproving shake of her head.

"I might as well take it seriously," McGuffin said with an
easy shrug. "I came all the way from San Francisco just to
play."

"Is that the only reason you came?" she asked, studying
him closely through green, almond-shaped eyes.

"What do you mean?" the detective asked.

"In my father's office, you said you came here only to meet
me," she reminded him.

"That has lately taken priority," McGuffin admitted, returning her stare. Her eyes glittered like jade in the flickering
light from the hurricane lamp in the center of the table. These
and the wax-encrusted sconces on the walls provided the only
illumination in the room, scattering shadowed curtains with
each puff of tropical breeze that blew through the open
windows.

"What do you do in San Francisco?" she asked.

"Nothing very exciting—I'm in the investment business."

"With which firm?"

"Firm?" McGuffin repeated. What could this sultry woman
of the islands know or care about Montgomery Street? "I'm
private."

"Amos McGuffin, Private Investments?" she asked.

McGuffin coughed and covered his mouth with his napkin.
"Close enough," he answered. "Now let's talk about you."

"I'm afraid you won't find me at all interesting," she
warned. When she leaned forward, her breasts swelled and
threatened to spill over the top of her low-cut dress.

McGuffin's stolen glance bordered on grand larceny. "I already have," he answered. "In fact, I find it curious that a woman as interesting as you would be on an island such as this."

"I stayed in London for a few years after graduating from college, but I finally had to come back. I suppose it's guilt," she said, with a shrug of her bare shoulders.

"Where did you graduate from?" McGuffin asked.

"The London School of Economics."

"Wow," McGuffin said softly. "You didn't study nursing there."

She shook her head. "I learned that from my father. But my training in economics hasn't been wasted," she added. "Most of my time is spent trying to get development funds for Palm Isle from government and private sources."

"What are you developing?" McGuffin asked.

"At the moment a medical center," Liani answered. "After that I intend to develop certain local industries—baskets, straw hats, that sort of thing."

"Tourism?" McGuffin asked.

"I'm afraid there isn't much chance of that as long as the golf club remains here. There are only a few good beaches on Palm Isle, and they're all owned by your club," she informed him.

"Wait a minute, it's not my club. I'm just a guest here," McGuffin protested. He'd be damned if his romance would be destroyed by politics. "I've already had trouble with one of the natives over that mistake."

"If you're speaking of Bobaloa, he does not wish to be referred to as a native. And neither do I," she added coolly. When she stiffened, her breasts bulged defiantly against the frail dress.

Shit, I'm blowing it, McGuffin thought. "I'm sorry. Your father mentioned revolutionaries who want control of the golf club, but he didn't seem to take it seriously, and so neither did I. But please don't think I have no concern for social injustice." Hell, they could have the golf club and all the beaches, if he could just have one night with the lovely Liani.

"You needn't worry—the Mau Maus won't slaughter you in your bed," she said with a forgiving smile that quickened McGuffin's pulse.

McGuffin slid his hand across the table and placed it on top of hers. "Nevertheless, I'd feel better if I had a hostage."

Liani stared at him for a long time without moving. Candlelight and shadow played across her face at the whim of the wind, changing her color from bronze to brown. "Would you like dessert?" she asked.

"What do you suggest?"

"The melons are especially good."

"I'll have the melons."

She slid her hand gently from under McGuffin's and raised a lissome, golden arm in the undulating light. "Waiter!" she called.

Barefoot, unmindful of the long expanse of thigh flashing from beneath her skirt as she clutched and braked, Liani pushed the tiny English Ford mercilessly over the twisting road that led to the golf club, while McGuffin, folded up to resemble an *in utero* giraffe, clutched the passenger seat with both hands. When at last the lighted clubhouse appeared through the trees, a golden glow at the top of the hill, McGuffin relaxed his grip and brought his knees down as far as the cramped compartment would allow. He glanced down at her well-shaped leg, glowing warmly in the instrument light, and sighed.

"Exhilarating."

"Where is your cottage?" she asked.

"Through the gate and turn right," McGuffin answered cheerfully. "If you hadn't already turned me down, I'd invite you up to the clubhouse for a drink."

"I'm not in the mood for a drink," she answered, flashing between the gateposts that marked the entrance to the PIGC.

Good, McGuffin thought, suddenly remembering that there was nothing to drink in his cottage except the several kinds of soda his client had thoughtfully provided. "What are you in the mood for?" he asked.

"I feel like a walk on the beach," she answered.

"That sounds interesting," McGuffin said, with little enthusiasm. Just be patient, he reminded himself, as he raised his hand and pointed at the road ahead. "Turn here."

She turned right, past the white flag fluttering limply in the faint moonlight, then coasted to a stop at the end of the crushed-clamshell drive. She switched the engine off, but left the headlights on, illuminating the sandy trail that sloped upward to the top of the cliff.

"The beach is at the bottom of the hill," McGuffin informed her.

"I know," she said, switching the headlights off.

"You've been here before?" McGuffin asked, opening the door and squeezing out.

"Many times," she answered, stepping out and closing the door. "This is the best beach on the island and the only safe access. You'd better take off your shoes," she warned.

"I will when I get down to the beach," McGuffin said, falling in step beside her.

They could hear the surf rising and falling lazily as they climbed to the top of the cliff. McGuffin could see the ribbon of surf in the dim moonlight from the top of the cliff, but the trail down was a black hole. When Liani suggested going first, McGuffin stepped back quite willingly. She appeared and reappeared below him as she zigzagged nimbly from station to station. Clutching at sea grass and sand, McGuffin followed in her footsteps as best he could. Partway down, his leather-soled cordovans, always equal to the challenge of Telegraph Hill, slid out from under him, and he did the last twenty yards on the seat of his golf slacks. Liani stood over him, grinning with amusement.

"Now will you take off your shoes?"

Mumbling, McGuffin untied his laces and removed his shoes and socks. He carefully placed them at the foot of the path and climbed to his feet. "I'll leave them here to mark the trail."

"Are you going somewhere?" she asked.

"You said you wanted to go for a walk on the beach."

"I've changed my mind," she said, turning her back to him. "I'm going for a swim." She placed her hand behind her neck and lifted her long mane of black hair. "Would you unzip me?"

"It would be a pleasure," McGuffin said, oozing calm and confidence.

Be calm, fingers. When he pulled the zipper it made a tearing noise that went from his head to his loins. She hunched her shoulders and extended her arms, then gave a little wriggle, and the dress fell to the sand in a heap. She stood with her smooth brown back to him, bisected by only a white band of panties, which she quickly slid over her hips and dropped atop the dress. McGuffin watched breathlessly as she strode, with a grace beyond nature, across the beach to the water's edge. She walked out until the water was at mid-thigh, then dived into the white wall of incoming breakers. She surfaced in front of a bigger wave, then swam for shore and rode it in. She rose up from the sea and stood in front of the awed detective, glossy as a wet panther.

"Aren't you coming?" she called.

The idea had crossed his mind. He slipped quickly out of his pants and shorts and ran for the water, pulling his alligator shirt over his head and flinging it away a second too late. The alligator floated briefly on the tide, then sank to the bottom as its owner followed his Caribbean Nereid to deeper water. Although his ungainly crawl was no match for her graceful stroke, his enthusiasm was such that he quickly overtook her. When his fingers trailed over her back and buttocks, she stopped and treaded water. They circled each other in a feverish silence, more like wrestlers than lovers. When he touched her lightly on the hip, she came to him. She placed her hands on his shoulders and kissed him lightly as his hand trailed over her body, along the sharply angled hip to the tight waist, stopping at the full breast and hard, erect nipple. When he felt her legs lock around his back and felt her tongue deep in his throat, he grasped her buttocks and returned her fierce kiss— until he felt seawater running down his throat and realized they were sinking. He let go of her ass and reached for the surface, pulling Liani, still locked around his waist, along with him. He broke the surface, coughing and gasping for breath.

"What do you say," he began, the sentence punctuated by briny coughs, "that we continue this in my cottage?"

"How very boring," Liani said with a frown. "I want this to be special, or not at all."

"Not at all?"

"Not at all," she repeated.

"The beach!" McGuffin said.

Liani shook her head. "Too sandy."

"How about the first green?"

She gestured wearily. "You call that unusual?"

"The backseat of the car?"

"Oh, please."

"Then where?" McGuffin pleaded, in a desperate, water-logged voice. "I'll go anywhere you say. Just tell me where you want to do it."

"Right here," she said.

"Here? In the ocean?" She nodded. "That's impossible. Humans can't make love in the ocean."

"How do you know if you don't try?" she asked.

"Believe me, I know. I sometimes have trouble under the best of circumstances, let alone the ocean," he said, as a wave broke over his head. "I'll meet you halfway. We'll do it standing in shallow water," he proposed.

Liani shook her head. "Here or not at all," she said, raising her toes and lying flat on the water. She was smooth and glossy as rounded stones at the edge of the sea. She placed her feet lightly against McGuffin's chest and, as he reached for her ankles, pushed off, driving him underwater. When he surfaced she was several yards away and stroking hard out to sea. Feeling foolish but helpless, McGuffin stroked after her.

When he finally caught her, she came to him, unresisting. They kissed while treading water, sank briefly, then quickly resurfaced, laughing and spluttering. When McGuffin tried again to kiss her, she twisted away, slippery as a seal. The water lapped over her chin as she circled McGuffin, eyeing him warily. In the changing moonlight she looked sometimes seductive, sometimes dangerous. When McGuffin came close enough to lay a hand against her breast, she allowed it to remain for a moment before backing away.

"Was Lyle Boone really your friend?" she asked.

"What? Is that why we came out here—to discuss Lyle Boone?" McGuffin asked.

"Can't we talk while making love?" she asked.

"I can talk while making love," McGuffin said, dog-paddling in front of her. "And I might even be able to swim while making love. But I doubt if I can talk, swim, and make love all at the same time."

"Then perhaps we should eliminate love," she said.

"Okay, I'll talk," McGuffin answered. "Yes, Lyle was my friend."

"And you think he was murdered?"

"Is that what your father thinks?"

"Uh uh," she warned, sticking a finger out of the water and waving it like a dorsal fin. "If you're to get your reward, *you* must answer the question, not I."

"All right, it's possible he was murdered. Now let's get on with this aquatic erotic experiment before I become exhausted."

"Be patient," she chided. "Do you know who killed him?"

"No."

"Any suspects?"

"None."

"Well, you certainly aren't a very good policeman, are you?"

"I'm not a policeman, I'm in the investment business," McGuffin reminded her.

"Oh, come on, Amos. Even without your clothes you look like a policeman. Tell me, are you an FBI agent?"

"No."

"CIA?"

"Why would the CIA be interested in Lyle Boone?"

"Maybe they aren't," she answered. "Maybe Mr. Boone is just a pretext. Or a cover. Isn't that the word?" McGuffin said nothing. "Maybe your mission is political."

"Political?" McGuffin asked.

"Why did you stop and talk to Bobaloa?"

"I didn't," McGuffin protested. He was about to explain the circumstances of their meeting when he heard a marine engine, not very far away. "Listen," McGuffin said. "There's a boat coming toward us, but I don't see any lights."

Liani listened for a moment, then replied, "It's all right. It's way offshore."

"I think we'd better get in," McGuffin said, not at all assured.

Liani did not protest. When McGuffin turned to shore, he saw a quick flash of light from the beach at a place somewhere near the trail they had come down. He felt Liani's hand on his shoulder when he stopped swimming, and realized that she had seen it too.

"Who could it be?" McGuffin asked.

Liani treaded water silently for a moment, then replied, "It must be someone from the club."

The light flashed again, for scarcely a second. The boat was somewhere to the right and sounded as if it would pass close by.

"Why would anybody from the Palm Isle Golf Club be signaling to a boat without running lights in the middle of the night?" McGuffin asked, as at last the small boat began to take shape. It was scarcely visible when it went past, several hundred feet away, making directly for the onshore beacon. The light flashed again, and a minute later the motor stopped. "They're either loading or unloading something," McGuffin said.

"What do you suppose it is?" Liani asked.

"I don't know. And I'm sure they'd rather have it remain that way. Let's go in," he suggested. "And don't make any noise."

While they were swimming silently toward shore, the marine engine kicked over and the boat headed back in their direction. The loading or unloading of the assumedly illicit cargo had taken only a few minutes. When McGuffin's feet touched the sand, Liani wrapped her arms and legs around him, and they stood with only their heads sticking out of the water while the unseen boat approached.

"It sounds as if it's headed straight for us," Liani said.

"He wouldn't come in this close," McGuffin said uncertainly.

But when the boat flashed past a few moments later, it was very close indeed. Close enough in fact for McGuffin to get a good look at the driver.

"It was Bobaloa," McGuffin said.

"You're mistaken," Liani said.

"I'm not mistaken. I saw him clearly."

"I'm afraid all blacks look alike to you," she said, starting for the beach.

"Don't give me that," McGuffin said, following her out of the water. "You know as well as I that that was Bobaloa."

"I know nothing of the sort," she replied, hurrying across the sand to their clothes. "And I resent the implication that I'm lying."

"Why are you protecting him?" McGuffin asked.

"I'm not protecting anyone," she answered, picking up her dress and giving it a shake. Then, still dripping wet, she stepped quickly into it. "Except perhaps you," she added, turning her back to McGuffin.

"Me?" McGuffin said, reaching for the zipper. But that wasn't why she turned. "Hey, where are you going?" McGuffin called, as she walked away.

"Home," she answered.

"Wait a minute!" McGuffin shouted. Her white panties were lying on the sand. "You forgot your panties!"

"Keep them," she replied. "Because that's all you'll get from me."

McGuffin stared sadly at the empty panties, while trying to figure out what had happened. *A few minutes ago I was about to make love like a whale and now I'm beached.* As he gathered his clothes and started for the path, leaving Liani's panties on the beach, he heard her drive away. *She recognized Bobaloa, there's no doubt about that,* McGuffin told himself. *And he was up to no good, there's little doubt about that. But* what was he doing? Running guns? That is the sort of thing revolutionaries do, isn't it? Or is he smuggling dope? I wouldn't think there'd be much call for that at the PIGC.

Carrying his clothes, McGuffin climbed naked to the top of the path and walked slowly back to his empty cottage. Bobaloa had ruined what could have been a wonderful evening, and McGuffin was annoyed, as well as puzzled. Why is she protecting him? McGuffin wondered. Racial loyalty? Or is there something more between them? And what about all those questions she asked me? Does she really think the CIA sent me down here to thwart a revolution? It's a heady and humorous notion, McGuffin said to himself as he opened the front door to his cottage.

He walked into the bedroom and switched the overhead light on, then looked at the empty bed and sighed. There were a great many questions about Liani and Bobaloa, but McGuffin was in no mood to entertain them. After all, McGuffin asked himself, as he turned down the sheet, what could they have to do with Lyle Boone's death?

11

Churston Brown and Al Balata were already on the practice tee when McGuffin arrived at the clubhouse, but Byron Kilty was not yet among the dozen or so swingers who lined the tee. Balata, at his usual place at the end of the line, waggled his driver in a lazy salute as the detective drove past him on the cart, looking for an empty place on the tee. He found it next to Churston.

"I'm sorry I had to miss dinner last night," McGuffin apologized, as he stepped off the cart.

"Oh, hi, Amos," the blond young man said, looking up from his teed ball. He was hitting driver and his blond hair was damp with sweat. "I hear you had dinner with Liani Carver," he said with a smirk.

McGuffin, sorting through his clubs for a wedge, looked up with a surprised expression. "Who told you that?"

Churston laughed. "This is a small island, Amos."

"Apparently," McGuffin said, pulling his wedge from the bag. With a bag of balls in one hand and a club in the other, he walked up onto the tee to an unoccupied place beside Churston. "The practice range is rather popular today," he observed.

"It's almost time for the club championship," Churston replied, still smirking. "Let somebody else win the titles, I'm after the Skins."

"So am I," McGuffin said, dumping the bag of new white Titleists—no striped range balls for the privileged members

104

of the PIGC—on the manicured tee. "Have you seen our fourth player yet?"

"Not yet. But don't worry about Byron. He wouldn't miss a Skins game unless he was dead," Churston assured him.

"Or unless he found something better to do," McGuffin added, as he went into his warm-up routine. He held the club across his back in the crook of his arms and rotated his upper body from side to side.

"What can be better than a Skins game?" Churston asked.

"The love of a beautiful woman."

"The only beautiful woman on this island, I mean truly beautiful, is the one you were out with last night."

"Aren't you forgetting Mrs. Boone?" McGuffin grunted as he twisted and stretched from side to side.

Churston's eyes opened wide behind his wire frames. "Byron and Marian Boone—?"

"Why not? Lyle suspected she was having an affair with someone," he lied. "Not that it matters now. Lyle was only concerned that the other members shouldn't find out about it." McGuffin removed the club from behind his back and began swinging it easily, watching Churston as he did. Churston addressed his ball after a moment's hesitation, then stepped away and turned to McGuffin.

"Lyle needn't have worried," he said.

"No one knew?" McGuffin asked, continuing to swing the wedge back and forth in a lazy pendulum arc.

"No one but me," Churston replied.

"You knew?" McGuffin asked. Churston nodded slowly. "How?"

"I saw them together."

"How do you mean, saw them together?"

"The same way you do—*in flagrante delicto*. It happened the night I dreamed the secret of golf. I remember, I ran all the way to Cuppy's cottage, shouting: 'I've found the secret of golf!' Only that wasn't all I found," he added softly. "I found the two of them in bed together."

"You found Marian and Byron in Cuppy's bed?" McGuffin questioned.

"Not Byron," Churston said, shaking his head. "Lyle's wife was having an affair with the golf pro."

"No," McGuffin replied, disappointment and annoyance showing on his face. If Marian was having a serious affair with Byron, he had a motive. But if she was fucking everybody, McGuffin too was fucked. "You're sure it was Cuppy?" he asked helplessly.

"Absolutely. Why did you think it was Byron?"

"Because it's been Byron who has been staying overnight on Marian's yacht, not Cuppy," McGuffin answered.

"I'll be damned," Churston said, owlish eyes widening. "I wondered why he was never in when I phoned. The sly fox."

"Just don't say you heard it from me," McGuffin warned.

"Oh, I won't," Churston promised. "Unless it becomes absolutely necessary," he added, with a mischievous grin.

"What do you mean by that?"

"Nothing," Churston answered, turning his back to the detective. He hit a drive with a right-to-left draw, unusual for him, that rolled well past the two-hundred-and-fifty-yard marker.

McGuffin pulled a new white ball from the pile with his wedge, hit it fat, and watched it drop well short of the first practice green. He muttered irritably and slammed the wedge to the ground. "By the way, Churston, what was the secret of golf that came to you in your dream?" he asked, as he pulled another ball from the pile.

"I don't know," Churston answered sadly. "I was so shocked at seeing them in bed together, it went completely out of my mind."

"That figures," McGuffin mumbled, as he set up over his second shot. Like all golfers, he had many times discovered the secret of golf, usually on the last hole on the last day of the season, only to forget it over the winter. The only secret of golf, McGuffin reminded himself as he took the club back, is a good swing. He hit the ball squarely with a solid, descending blow, then looked up to watch it rise and fall softly on the back of the green. Hit them all like that and you'll be a rich man before this day is out, McGuffin told himself.

True to Churston's prediction, Byron showed up for the Skins game just as McGuffin was hitting the last of his practice balls.

"Just let me hit a few and I'll join you on the first tee in a minute," Byron called as he jumped off his cart.

"Okay, but hurry up," Churston said, as he strapped his bag to McGuffin's cart.

"I'll try not to keep you from your work," the doctor replied, facetiously it seemed to McGuffin.

"What did he mean by that?" McGuffin asked, as they drove to the first tee.

"He's just trying to get on my case," Churston answered. "I'm writing a book on the history of these islands, which Byron doesn't consider real work."

"What's your real work?" McGuffin asked.

"The family owns a few banks. I worked in the Paris branch for a while, thinking an exotic setting might make a dull life tolerable, but it didn't. I'm afraid I'm a hopeless anthropologist to the chagrin of my father."

"I don't see why," McGuffin said. "Anthropology is a noble calling."

"I knew you were a cultured man," Churston said, smiling eagerly. "Are you interested in the history of Palm Isle?"

"As a matter of fact, I am," McGuffin answered.

"It's quite a bloody history," he warned. "The land this golf course sits on was virtually ripped away from the islanders by the founders of the PIGC just after the First World War. The blacks who lived here were forcibly relocated to an out island and forbidden ever to return. But one of them, a voodoo doctor according to the legend, defied the order and returned. He got as far as the beach, then he was shot and left for the turkey buzzards, as a warning to the others."

"What happened to the guy who shot him?" McGuffin asked, as they glided to a stop beside the first tee.

"He wasn't prosecuted, if that's what you mean. But the voodoo doctor may have had his revenge after all. If you subscribe to the legend," he added, as he stepped off the cart.

"Which is what?" McGuffin asked, without getting off the cart.

Churston walked to the front of the cart and stood facing McGuffin. "The village elders insist there were no coral snakes on this island prior to the time the voodoo doctor was killed. Then, while his body lay rotting on the beach in the moonlight, just below your cottage, as a matter of fact, coral snakes began crawling out of his carcass. And when the sun came up the next morning, the beach was teeming with small, brightly banded, lethal snakes. Then the turkey buzzards, which had refused to eat the voodoo priest, fell on the snakes and carried them off to the hills," Churston said, with a fluttering motion of one hand. "Of course, this is only a legend, but it has nevertheless had a strong influence on the lives of these people."

"You mean they practice voodoo?" McGuffin asked.

"Oh, they practiced voodoo long before 1920," Churston assured him. "Since then they've added serpent worship to their religion."

"Fascinating," McGuffin said. "It's sort of like the legend of St. Patrick, only they got it backwards."

"Perhaps you'd like to attend a voodoo ceremony with me sometime," Churston suggested.

"Perhaps," McGuffin said, with a short laugh. "But what's all this got to do with the revenge of the voodoo doctor?"

"I was coming to that," Churston answered. "A short while after the voodoo doctor was killed, old Kilty himself died, after being bitten by a coral snake."

"Old Kilty?" McGuffin repeated.

Churston nodded. "It was Byron's grandfather who shot and killed the voodoo doctor."

"I'll be damned," McGuffin said softly. "No wonder Byron's annoyed about your book. Bitten by a coral snake," he mused, shaking his head slowly. "What a terrible way to die."

"Not all the members feel that way," Churston said, as he went to his bag.

"What do you mean?"

"He was bitten on the finger while bending over in a

bunker. Obviously he was bitten while improving his lie in a sand trap," he said, sliding the driver from his bag.

"The villain!" McGuffin exclaimed, jumping off the cart as Kilty and Balata appeared from behind the clubhouse, making for the first tee. "In that case it was no more than he deserved."

Byron headed down the clamshell path at top speed, then skidded to a stop just inches from Churston's shins, very nearly crushing him between the carts.

"What do you think you're doing?" Churston demanded.

"Sorry," Byron said, alighting from the cart.

"He's pissed because you wouldn't give him time to hit any balls," Al explained.

"If he hadn't stayed out all night, he'd have had plenty of time to hit balls," Churston said.

"Who says I stayed out all night?" Byron demanded.

"Oh, shit," McGuffin breathed.

"Well, didn't you?" Churston asked.

"That's none of your business!" Kilty replied, snatching a driver from his bag. He stalked angrily onto the tee, then turned to Churston for a last volley. "I suppose you want me to hit first."

"It's still your honor," Churston replied evenly.

Muttering, Byron teed his ball up, took a single practice swing, and addressed his shot. He swung quickly and hit a vicious duck hook into the ocean.

"Bad luck," Churston said, grinning, as he stepped onto the teeing ground.

Churston hit a high, fading shot that landed safely on the right side of the fairway, well short of the bunker. Balata swung easily and rifled his tee shot straight down the fairway to the left of the bunker. McGuffin selected a three wood and placed it in the middle of the fairway only a few yards short of Al's ball.

"It looks like the big knocker is playing it safe today," Churston remarked, as they drove to his ball.

"Right," McGuffin said. He had learned on the first day that the PIGC was a course to be managed, not overpowered.

And like it or not, that's the way he would play today. With this strategy in mind, McGuffin managed to par the first three holes, as did Al and Churston.

McGuffin lost his touch on the fourth hole, hitting his second shot into a greenside bunker for a bogey, but Byron at last found his swing and managed to equal Churston's par. On the fifth the good doctor saved them again, this time tying Al's par, while on the sixth they all made par.

"There's twenty-eight hundred riding on this one," Churston reminded them, needlessly, as they stood on the seventh tee surveying the hole called Normandy.

"I don't know what we'd do without you," Byron remarked, as he watched Al tee his ball up.

All four of them hit safely to the middle of the fairway, then drove grimly to their second shot. As the money increased, the banter grew less frequent. With the wisdom of experience and the caution of a banker, McGuffin punched a six iron over the top of the hill and well short of the dreaded Devil's Asshole. He struck his third shot to within ten feet of the pin, while Churston and Al both left themselves with long, snaking putts that might well require three strokes. Trying to keep his mind on his putt and not the money, McGuffin watched as Byron hit his third shot.

"Nice shot," he said flatly, as Byron's ball rolled inside his own.

"Spoken like a true gentleman," Byron called, as he climbed back onto his cart. It was the first time he had smiled in seven holes.

"You're going to have to make that putt for birdie just to tie the hole," Churston said miserably as they drove past the Devil's Asshole.

"Thanks for the information," McGuffin said, peering into the deep, steep-sided bunker. There were plenty of golfers, McGuffin thought, who could never get their ball out of such a bunker. Hell, without the ladder they couldn't even get themselves out of that hole.

Byron marked his ball and walked off the green while Al, who was away, squatted down to align his putt. Byron's putt was little more than six feet, while McGuffin's was close to twelve. Everyone would be putting to make it.

Al made a good try, narrowly missing the hole but knocking the ball more than ten feet past. He took two more putts for a bogey six, then retired to the sidelines to watch the putting duel.

Churston was next. He took a long time to line up his long putt, visibly annoying Byron, which was plainly his intention. When at last he seemed ready to stroke the putt, but then stepped away, Byron groaned audibly and Churston smiled faintly. In spite of all his preparation, when it came it was a terrible putt, traveling scarcely halfway to the hole.

"Goddammit!" Churston cried, as he knocked his ball off the green.

"That's what you get for taking so much time," Byron said.

Churston glared angrily at the doctor for a moment before replying: "I'd rather be a bad putter than a cuckold."

"Churston—" McGuffin warned in a soft voice, knowing already that it was useless.

"What did you say?" Byron demanded.

"You heard me," Churston answered, thrusting his chin at the doctor. "The golf pro is getting it on with your mistress. Cuppy Dunch is fucking Marian Boone."

Byron swung, but Churston was ready. Agile as a bantam-weight, Churston easily ducked a clumsy right hand and danced away as Byron came for him. McGuffin and Balata rushed across the green at the same time, Balata pouncing on Kilty while McGuffin grabbed Churston from behind. Kilty wrestled with the stronger man, trying to get at Churston, who offered McGuffin no resistance at all. He had obviously only meant to rattle Byron's nerves prior to his all-important birdie putt, and at this he had succeeded admirably.

"Now let's see him make birdie," Churston whispered.

McGuffin released his charge while Byron continued to struggle. If there had been any question before as to whether or not Byron Kilty and Marian Boone were having an affair, there was none now, McGuffin knew.

"Cut it out, you're wrecking the green!" Al shouted, as he gave the smaller man a last violent shake.

Sobered by the sight of the torn-up green, Byron stopped struggling. The line between his ball and the hole was unscathed, but McGuffin's line had great chunks of sod ripped from it. As Byron surveyed the damage, his anger gave way to a pleased smile.

"It's your putt, Amos," the doctor said.

McGuffin stared incredulously at the gouged green. "What do I do about this?" he asked, pointing to the damage.

"You putt over it," Kilty answered, with the same pleased smile.

"He's kidding. You can move the ball," Balata said.

"By what authority?" Byron asked.

"Come on, you don't expect him to putt over that, do you?" Al asked.

"I most certainly do," Byron answered. "I not only expect him to putt over it, I refuse to allow him to repair the damage. Those are cleat marks, not ball marks. And Rule Sixteen plainly states that cleat marks may not be repaired."

"But you're the one who made that damage!" Churston wailed.

"That makes no difference. Either putt the ball or concede the hole," he instructed.

McGuffin looked uncertainly from Kilty to Balata. "Is he serious?"

"I'm afraid he is," Al, who knew him best, answered.

"Jesus," McGuffin breathed, as he stooped over to place his ball on the mark. "You're out for blood."

"Just your Skin," the doctor corrected.

McGuffin looked at the clumps of sod and black holes lying in his path and shook his head helplessly. Just to get the ball over these holes and clods would require an extremely hard knock, and even if the ball made it over this obstacle course on a straight line to the hole, it would almost certainly be going too fast to drop.

"What the hell," McGuffin said, stepping up to the ball. He brought the putter back and hit the ball hard. It immediately hit a clump of sod and leaped into the air, then landed and skittered like a pinball from post to post, leaped once again, and fell into the hole like a shot bird. It rattled from wall to wall for a moment, as if trying to escape, then lay quietly in the bottom of the hole. All four golfers stared at the hole, expecting perhaps that the ball might still climb out.

"It's your putt, Byron," McGuffin said, stooping to retrieve his ball.

Following the expressions of disbelief, there was a sudden shift of alliances. Even though Byron had tried to knock his head off only a few minutes before, Churston was now right there with Al, counseling and urging the good doctor to make this putt and save them all. It was a six-footer, straight as a die, they all agreed.

"Just don't be short," Churston urged.

"Never up, never in," Al added.

McGuffin stopped breathing as Byron, after due deliberation, took a stance over the ball. He struck the ball firmly and it rolled straight for the hole. McGuffin looked away. The ball was going in the hole, and he couldn't bear to watch. He waited for the hollow sound of the ball dropping, but was treated instead to an anguished wail. The ball had rolled five feet eleven and three-quarter inches, to the very edge of the hole, but would go no farther, not even with three men jumping up and down on the green.

Thirty-two hundred dollars richer (including double for the birdie), McGuffin sauntered off the seventh green while Al and Churston turned their collective wrath on the wretched cuckold. Churston was red-faced, and his eyes bulged alarmingly, McGuffin saw, when he slumped beside him on the cart.

"When I was a kid I decided to give up this game because I knew there had to be something more to life than golf," McGuffin mused, just to lighten things up. "But now I'm beginning to think I may have been wrong."

"You're still wrong," Churston replied, jamming the accelerator violently. "There's nothing more to life than winning."

McGuffin laughed politely, then suddenly stopped.

Churston's boyish face was contorted by a wrathful glare that McGuffin would not have thought possible. Churston looked away, perhaps because of McGuffin's quizzical glance. By the time he looked back, at the next tee, the demonic expression had been replaced by his usual affable one. But McGuffin was not reassured. He had the uneasy feeling that during his brief ride from green to tee, he had been in the company of two different men.

12

When McGuffin and Churston came around the clubhouse on their cart, Eddie the Aviator and a young man with a blond ponytail, who presided over the club storage room, were engaged in an intense conversation. Seeing them, Eddie drifted back into the club room while the bag boy came forward to collect their bags from the back of the cart. Churston thanked him, but he said nothing as he snatched the bags from the cart and carried them into the club room, where he would clean the clubs for the next day's round. He had a distinctive ape-like gait that caused McGuffin to wonder if he had seen him someplace before. McGuffin glanced back at the young man for a moment before he and Churston walked around the corner of the clubhouse. Eddie had reappeared and the conversation had resumed.

"I can't help thinking I've seen that bag boy someplace before," McGuffin said, as they walked around the building to the front entrance.

"You probably have," Churston said. "But you'd better not call him the bag boy to his face or he'll tear your head off. Cuppy says he's the caddiemaster and that's what he wants to be known as. I know," he said, anticipating McGuffin's question, "we have no caddies at the PIGC. That's just another of the many mysteries of golf. His name is Angelo Caudie, and he used to be Cuppy's caddie, while Cup was playing the tour."

"Of course!" McGuffin remembered. He had seen him

many times on television, looking more like a hippie than a caddie and consequently nearly as well known as his "bag," as the caddies called the players. It seemed to McGuffin that the caddie had been banned from a few tournaments, because of either his dress or his conduct, McGuffin couldn't remember which. "Didn't he get in some kind of trouble?" McGuffin asked.

Churston nodded. "He was accused of running drugs into Florida, but he beat it, thanks to Cuppy."

"What did Cuppy have to do with it?"

"Cuppy was Angelo's surprise witness. He claimed Angelo thought he was only going night fishing when he jumped aboard a boat owned by a Bolivian narcotics dealer—until they rendezvoused with a freighter and started taking on drugs. Unfortunately, by the time Angelo figured out what was happening, the Coast Guard had also figured it out. They arrested the whole bunch of them."

"And the jury believed that?" McGuffin asked, incredulous.

Churston shrugged. "There must have been a few golfers on the jury. And it probably didn't hurt that Cuppy had just won the Miami Open."

"Apparently," McGuffin said, as they skipped up the front steps, spikes scratching on the concrete. "It sounds as if Cuppy was willing to risk a perjury charge for his caddie."

"Good caddies are hard to come by," Churston replied, in the somber tone of a man who had suffered greatly at their hands.

"That's true," McGuffin, the former professional, agreed as he opened the door for Churston.

They walked across the carpeted corridor to the desk, where the receptionist was busily taking phone messages and stuffing them into the appropriate boxes. The boxes again were filled to overflowing.

"Nuttin' fo' you, Mistah Brown, but two fo' Mistah Mc-Guffin."

"Thanks," McGuffin said, taking the messages. The one from Francis Knight required an answer, the one from Liani Carver didn't. She and her father had been called away on a medical emergency for a few days, but she would call when she returned. "Where can I make a phone call, Churston?" he asked.

"Privately?"

"Yes."

"The first door on the right," Churston replied, pointing down the carpeted corridor. "I'll see you in the locker room or the bar."

"Yeah, thanks," McGuffin said, starting down the corridor.

It was a small room with three writing tables, each with an ample supply of PIGC stationery and a telephone. McGuffin picked up the first phone and spoke to the receptionist just outside the door. "I'd like to speak to Mr. Knight in San Francisco," he said, and gave her the number. While he waited he doodled on a piece of stationery. Under the crossed golf clubs and the motto *Golf ad Mortem* he sketched a horizontal figure with an arched back.

"Yes, Mr. McGuffin?" Francis Knight said.

"I won!" McGuffin blurted into the phone. "I won all your money back and a few hundred dollars besides!" McGuffin had decided not to mention that after paying his client the two thousand dollars he had lost, his "few hundred dollars" actually amounted to twenty-eight hundred dollars.

"Why is it, Mr. McGuffin, that when you lose it's 'we,' but when you win it's 'I'?" Francis Knight asked.

"Sorry," McGuffin apologized.

"I trust your investigation is coming along as well as your golf game?"

"The investigation is proceeding smoothly," McGuffin answered, shifting to his best professional tone. "I've learned that Byron is definitely having an affair with Marian Boone." He didn't mention that this information had contributed in a large measure to his winnings that afternoon. "And I also learned that she's been having an affair with Cuppy Dunch."

"The little tart!" Francis Knight exclaimed.

"My thought exactly," McGuffin said. "Obviously the affair doesn't mean as much to Marian as it does to Byron, who is right now ready to kill Cuppy. Maybe Marian too."

"You're speaking figuratively, of course," the lawyer put in.

"Unfortunately," McGuffin agreed. "But if Cuppy should happen to turn up dead, it would sure as hell make my job a lot easier."

"It doesn't sound as if your job has been all that difficult to date," the lawyer observed. "Have you managed yet to question Al Balata?"

"I'm meeting him and Churston in the bar just as soon as I've had my shower."

"What happened to Byron?"

"Byron disappeared right after the round—he was a little unhappy with his game." Byron had been the big loser, shooting nothing but bogeys and double bogeys after missing his birdie putt on seven. Churston had won four Skins and Al three, while McGuffin, with four more Skins on the back nine, had been the big winner. "I think he went to the yacht to be comforted by Marian." And to inquire about her affair with the golf pro, McGuffin thought, but didn't say. Instead he asked: "Have you found out anything about the Devon Corporation yet?"

"As luck would have it, I have," the lawyer answered. "It's a Florida corporation, recently formed for the express purpose of acquiring and developing real estate. The president of the corporation is a Miami woman named Gina McKay, with whom I briefly spoke by phone this morning."

"Did you get anything out of her?"

"Scarcely anything."

"What about the Balata connection?"

"She denied it and claims she doesn't know him, but I think she's lying. It's just my lawyerly instinct."

"I'll find out," McGuffin promised, reaching for a clean sheet of stationery. "How do you spell McKay?" Knight spelled the name for him. "Who are the other officers?"

"Gino and Richard McKay."

"Probably sons," McGuffin deduced, adding their names to their mother's. "Balata already owns a bond of his own, doesn't he?"

"Yes," Knight answered. "He was required to purchase one

as a condition of membership, as was Lyle and as was I. There are only ten bonds in existence, so it's quite possible that Balata now owns twenty percent of the PIGC. And if anything happens to me before I pay off my loan to him, he'll own thirty percent." The lawyer's voice carried a faint tone of panic.

"Take it easy," McGuffin said, jotting a column of ten numbers on the stationery. Beside the first three he wrote the names of Al Balata, the Devon Corporation with a question mark after it, and Francis Knight. "Who are the other seven bondholders?"

"Byron Kilty owns one. His grandfather, poor fellow, was a founding member."

"Yeah, I heard about his accident with the snake," McGuffin said, adding his grandson to the list. "What about Churston Brown?"

"His father owns a bond. As does Horton Ormsby."

"That makes six," McGuffin noted, as he added the last name to the list. "Enough for a controlling interest."

"If you ask Horton, he'll tell you who the other four are," Knight informed him.

"Thanks," McGuffin said. "I'll call you just as soon as I've had a chance to question Balata about this Devon Corporation."

"There's one more thing before you go," the lawyer said, as McGuffin got up from the desk.

"What's that?"

"It has to do with my backing you in the Skins game."

"Don't worry, I can beat these guys," McGuffin assured him.

"That's all well and good for you, Mr. McGuffin, I'm sure. But, to put it baldly, what's in it for me?"

McGuffin was taken aback. "You mean you want a piece of the action?"

"Well, it hardly seems unreasonable—seeing as how I'm putting up all the money."

"How much do you want?" McGuffin asked.

"Seventy-five percent," he answered. "After all, the risk is entirely mine."

"That's true," McGuffin had to agree. "But I'm afraid that if I had to play for only twenty-five cents on the dollar, I might find it hard to really put my heart into it."

"I'll make it sixty-forty," the lawyer replied.

"Fifty-fifty," McGuffin countered.

"Done."

McGuffin said goodbye and hung up, then walked to the door. He would have a shower and a steam bath, and possibly even a massage. Then he would go upstairs to the bar and join his golf buddies for a drink, albeit nonalcoholic. When the PI business was bad, McGuffin thought as he walked down the corridor, past the smiling faces of the old boys in their plus fours, it was very bad. But when it was good it was outrageous.

McGuffin lay on the table—a pile of pinkish flesh except for his newly tanned face and arms—while the strong black hands of the thickly muscled masseur kneaded and pummeled each golf-weary muscle. How am I ever going to go back to publinx golf? McGuffin wondered as, still tingling with pleasant sensations, he climbed heavily to his feet. He wrapped the towel around his middle and gave his abdomen a proud pat. Already exercise and abstinence had noticeably flattened the beginning bulge that had hung threateningly over his belt for the past few years. Twenty minutes in the steam bath and the loss of a few more pounds and he would look like a movie detective, he decided, as he padded across the tile to the steam room.

The thick, moist air hit him in the face like a hot towel when he opened the door. He let the door fall shut behind him, then stood in the swirling steam, thicker than even a San Francisco fog, and tried to see to the back of the room.

"Over here, lucky," a deep voice growled from behind the wall of steam. It was Al Balata.

"A guy knocks in an easy little putt over twelve feet of plowed field and you call it luck?" McGuffin grumbled, as he inched through the steam. A red glow pierced the steam briefly, then faded. McGuffin moved after it, until finally the figure of Al Balata, sitting naked and cross-legged on the high-est ledge, appeared at the back of the steam room. The red glow had come from a thick cigar clenched between his teeth. "What are you doing way up there?" McGuffin called from the floor. Al's head was only a few feet from the ceiling.

"It's hotter up here," Al answered. "And easier to keep my cigar lit. Come on up."

Although it was more than hot enough for McGuffin on the floor, he quickly scrambled up the four concrete ledges. This was his first opportunity to speak to Balata without interrup-tion, and he would do nothing to destroy it. "It's very nice up here," McGuffin gasped. It was impossible to tell where the cigar smoke stopped and the steam began. "I just hope my heart can take it."

"A little heat is good for the heart," Al said. He dragged on his cigar and watched a thick cloud of smoke bounce off the ceiling like a sloppy balloon.

"It seems to me I heard Lyle say that," McGuffin said, hop-ing to get quickly to the important questions. No one could safely remain in the steam room for more than thirty minutes and he didn't know how long Balata had already been in. Or-dinarily the detective preferred to work slowly, feeling his opponent out with a few innocuous questions designed to es-tablish an easy rapport, then gliding seamlessly to the more telling interrogatories. But a steam room was unfortunately no place for the practice of so fine an art.

"You knew Lyle?" Al asked, cocking his head toward the detective.

"Casually," McGuffin said. He could now at least recognize his photograph.

"Lyle never took the steam," Balata said, shaking his head.

McGuffin shrugged. "It must have been somebody else who said it."

"It was me," Al said. "I just told you that, I was always telling Lyle to take the steam, but he never would." He took two short puffs on his cigar and blew smoke into the wet air. "So now he's dead."

"Of a heart attack."

"Yeah, a heart attack," he said, turning his head again to McGuffin. "What else?"

"I don't know," McGuffin answered. "I just find it hard to believe that a man in Lyle's condition could have died of a heart attack."

"Believe it," he said with a short nod. "I was there."

"You saw Lyle die?" McGuffin asked, with quickening interest.

"No, but I was there. I was too far back to see anything. Not that I wanted to anyway. Byron was there—Lyle didn't need anybody else," he said, sticking his cigar in his mouth.

Except possibly a bodyguard, McGuffin thought to himself. "It must have been a terrible loss to you."

"Yeah, it was," Al said, talking around the cigar. "Lyle was a hell of a player—never out of the hole."

"You can't say much more than that for a man."

"No, you can't. I miss the guy. Even if he did take me for a lot of money."

"Speaking of money, I just got off the phone with my cousin, Frank Knight. He told me to tell you that Gina McKay said hello."

Al removed the cigar from his mouth and turned his head slowly to McGuffin. Smoke seeped from the corner of his mouth as if a fire were burning in his belly. "Gina McKay?" he asked.

"You know her, don't you, Al? The president of the Devon Corporation?" McGuffin asked, an innocent inquiry.

"She's my sister," Balata answered evenly. "But I don't know why your cousin should take an interest in my family."

"You know Frank, always looking after people," McGuffin replied with a shrug.

"Yeah, Frank's like that," Al said. "But tell him I said I wish he'd look after himself."

"I will," McGuffin promised.

Al brought the cigar almost to his mouth, then stopped and turned to the detective. "By the way, how's Frank's health?"

"He's still a little shaken up after the boat accident," McGuffin answered.

"Boat accident?"

"I though you'd heard. His boat blew up at the dock on Regatta Day."

"That's a shame," Al said flatly.

"Yeah," McGuffin agreed. "Fortunately he wasn't on the boat when it blew up."

Balata grunted. "I hope he had insurance."

"It's hard to insure against that kind of accident," McGuffin said.

"Is that right?" Al asked. "I don't know much about the insurance business."

"Exactly what is your business?" McGuffin asked.

Al brought the cigar up to his face and studied it for a moment before replying. "Same as yours—investments."

"Investments," McGuffin repeated. "That seems like an unlikely occupation for a man who would make a five-million-dollar loan without charging any interest."

"You and Frank don't seem to have any secrets from one another," Al said, continuing to study his cigar.

"We're very close," McGuffin replied.

"Apparently."

"He also told me that if he should die before paying off his loan to you, you'd inherit his club bond."

"That's true."

"Which would put you in a rather difficult position."

"How so?" Al asked. He seemed more interested in his cigar, in which he had apparently discovered a flaw, than in the answer to his question.

"Just imagine how you'd feel if Frank had been on that boat when it blew up. You'd hardly know whether to grieve the loss of a friend or celebrate the inheritance of a bond."

Deciding perhaps that the cigar was all right, Balata inhaled deeply of it. Then he looked at McGuffin and smiled, yellow smoke seeping from between his teeth. "To me, friends are more important than bonds, Amos."

"That's exactly what I told my cousin," McGuffin said. "But then he told me that you had tried to buy Lyle's bond while he was still alive, but Lyle wouldn't sell. So you formed this

Devon Corporation, naming your sister president, and you bought Lyle's bond from his widow. So you see, Al, you mustn't blame my cousin if he thinks bonds are very important to you—maybe even more important than friends."

Al Balata stared evenly at the detective for a long time, then asked: "What's your real business here, McGuffin?"

"Golf."

"Horseshit."

"Why have you formed a corporation to buy PIGC bonds?" McGuffin demanded.

Al's cigar sizzled when he stabbed the wet cement between McGuffin's legs. McGuffin didn't flinch. He looked down at the smudge, inches from his exposed genitals, then looked up at Al Balata's dark eyes. Threats weren't unusual in the detective's line of work. By taking them all seriously, he had so far managed to avoid lasting injury or death, even while recognizing that some threats were more serious than others. As much as the gun or the knife, it was the eyes that were the measure of the danger. Some glowed with a jittery fear (usually dangerous) while others burned with the religious fervor of the kamikaze (usually fatal). Then there were those eyes that were no more than cold, empty corridors, carrying their unvarnished, primordial message to a state-of-the-art killer computer. These were the most frightening and dangerous eyes of all. And Al Balata had them. In spades.

"You know, Amos, too much steam can be bad for you," he warned.

He was probably right, McGuffin knew, but he plunged ahead anyway. "You intend to take over this club and convert it to a public resort," McGuffin charged.

"No!" Balata replied forcefully. "That's not what I intend to do! But that's what'll happen if *somebody* doesn't do something to stop these phony sonofabitches!" he added, angrily throwing his cigar butt across the room.

"What phony sonofabitches? Who are you talking about?" McGuffin demanded.

"You know who! Your cousin, for one!" he said, jabbing a thick finger at the detective. "He came to me for money because he was broke and now he's crying about the terms? So tell him for me he can go fuck himself. All you fucking WASPs are alike. You think people like me owe you something for letting me join your fucking club, but I know better. I know the old family fortunes are drying up and you fucking WASPs are in trouble. The only way you're able to live in the style to which you think you're entitled is by selling off all the assets your ancestors busted their ass to get. The only reason I'm buying bonds is to make sure you fucking WASPs don't sell them off to some hotel chain after you've gone through your inheritance."

"I'm not a fucking WASP," McGuffin announced indignantly, when it appeared that Balata was winding down. "And I'm not stupid. I know nobody would pay sixty million dollars to get control of the PIGC unless he could make a profit on it."

"It wouldn't cost near that much," Balata replied, shaking his head impatiently. "This fucking club hasn't redeemed a bond for full value in years. When a member dies the board of directors goes to the widow and pleads poormouth. They tell her there's only a few million in the treasury, but she should take it and give the bond to the club, because that's what her husband would have wanted. Then do you know what they do when they have the bond?" McGuffin shook his head. "They sell it to somebody like me or Lyle, who would give anything to belong to the PIGC, for the full ten million dollars. That's the kind of people you're working for, McGuffin," he said, jabbing a finger against the detective's bare chest.

"That may be," McGuffin said, pulling away from the jabbing finger. "But what they're doing is perfectly legal."

"So is what I'm doing," Al said. "All I'm doing is bidding against the club and making sure the widows get a fair price for their bonds. What's wrong with that?"

"Nothing," McGuffin had to admit. As long as you're not making them widows, he added to himself.

"Believe me, Amos, all I want is for the PIGC to go on just like it always has. And if I have to buy a few bonds to keep it that way, I don't mind."

"To control this club, you'll have to own six bonds," McGuffin pointed out. "Now maybe I'm just a country boy, but it seems to me that even if they only cost you thirty or forty million dollars, that's still a hell of a lot to pay just to be sure you have a reserved tee time on Sunday morning."

"Not to me it isn't. To me the PIGC is a lot more than just a place to play golf," Al replied, staring dreamily into the steam.

"What else is it, Al?" McGuffin asked.

He turned to McGuffin, as if suddenly aware he was not alone. "You'd think it was stupid," he said, shaking his head.

"Try me," McGuffin urged.

"You got to understand, I was born poor, really poor," Al Balata said, chopping the steam with his hand. "I mean I grew up on the Lower East Side in tenements rats wouldn't live in. In fact, I think I would have been dead or in jail by now if it wasn't for the subway."

"The subway?" McGuffin asked.

"Yeah, the subway. I hated my life so much when I was a kid, I even thought of killing myself. Then one day I got on the subway—I didn't know where it went and I didn't care—and I rode it all the way to the end of the line. Then when I came up out of the subway, I was in a place like I'd never seen before—except in pictures in the *Saturday Evening Post*—clean streets and kids and dogs and that kind of shit. So I walked through this town, it was way out in Queens, then up a long hill, with no idea where I was going. And when I got to the top of the hill, I looked down into this valley and I saw something more beautiful than anything I'd ever seen before."

"What was it?" McGuffin asked.

Al turned to him. "A country club."

"A country club?"

He moved his hand through the steam, as if he were un-covering a picture. "A big white clubhouse with a striped tent on the lawn and lots of kids in the swimming pool with their good-looking mothers and big shiny cars in the parking lot and all these old guys knocking a little white ball around with a stick. It was all a mystery," Al said, turning back to McGuffin.

"I'd never seen anything like it before. But suddenly I understood something. I understood that there was them and there was me. And I decided then and there that one day I was going to get into that club, or I'd die trying."

"And did you?" McGuffin asked.

"In a way," Al answered. "I got a job as a caddie for a few years. You may not believe it, but that's how I learned how to play golf."

"No!" McGuffin said.

"Yeah." He nodded. "I applied for membership after I made my first million, which wasn't much later, but they turned me down. They said I was a hoodlum element. *Hoodlum element*," he repeated, shaking his head sadly. "I'll never forget that. Of course, they never said it to my face," he added quickly.

McGuffin didn't doubt it. "That's a sad story," he said, truthfully.

"Yeah, but it had a happy ending," Al said with a quick smile. "A few years later I bought the fucking place and paved it over."

"Good for you," McGuffin said, not insincerely. "But as I'm sure you can understand, that's hardly the kind of behavior that will put the members of this club at ease."

An injured look came over Al's face. "Are you kidding? You think I could do something like that to the PIGC?"

"You did it before," McGuffin reminded him.

"That wasn't the same thing, Amos. That wasn't the same thing at all," he protested in an injured tone. "That was just some shitty little country club with a bunch of snobs who thought they were better than everybody else. But this is the PIGC. These people really are better than everybody else. These are some of the oldest and best families in America. They may think I'm a hoodlum element, but they don't care. They're still willing to have me as a member. That tells you something about these people, Amos. Don't you see that?"

"Yes, I do," McGuffin answered uncertainly.

"Surely you don't think I could betray that kind of trust, do you?" he asked, wide-eyed and eager.

"No, of course not," McGuffin said, shaking his head.

"So you can tell Frank and anybody else who asks that the PIGC has got nothing to fear from Al Balata," he said, getting to his feet. He stood on the next ledge down and got into his white robe, pulling the hood over his head. He turned to McGuffin with a peaceful smile and a faraway look on his face. "When I look at this place," he said, opening his arms, "I'm not looking at it through the eyes of a hoodlum element. I'm seeing it through the eyes of an innocent child. I see the big striped tent and the beautiful young mothers, and the old boys knocking it around, and I know—I know, Amos, that this is what America is all about."

McGuffin stared as Al Balata turned and descended into the swirling steam and quickly disappeared.

"God how I love this place," Al Balata's disembodied voice proclaimed from the steam.

A moment later the door closed and McGuffin was left alone in the steam room. There goes a real Palm man, McGuffin said to himself as he slid down to the next ledge. Or a real actor, he added.

It was three o'clock in the morning when McGuffin's body awakened him for a drink. No booze, we're on a case, he reminded his body. After a moment, however, he realized that it had not been the sound of Bacchus murmuring in his ear that had awakened him, but rather the more prosaic sound of a motorboat at sea. It was Bobaloa on another mission, McGuffin was sure. What was he delivering and who was he delivering it to?

He had earlier dismissed the possibility of drugs, but realized now that this had perhaps been a hasty decision. With all the money and diversity among the membership of the PIGC, there had to be some demand for cocaine. Or girls. McGuffin had observed a few ass-patters moving among the waitresses in the dining room.

"Damn!" McGuffin muttered, whomping the pillow. It would be a long time before he would get back to sleep with these questions and a motorboat buzzing in his head.

Then, suddenly, the engine stopped. McGuffin threw the sheet back and walked naked to the open window overlooking the sea. The sliver of moon shining fuzzily behind scudding clouds was sufficient to shed some light on the offshore breakers, but beyond that all was inky black and ominously quiet. He waited for a few minutes and was about to return to bed when he saw three quick flashes of light from far out at sea. A few seconds later there was a longer answering flash from the beach, at a spot on or very near the dock below the clubhouse. McGuffin dressed quickly and hurried outside to his golf cart.

He drove down the path to the main boulevard, then turned up toward the darkened clubhouse. Once past the first green and across the creek, he turned off the noisy clamshell and onto the lush, quiet fairway. Sensing as much as seeing the first tee, he angled off toward the sea, then up the trail along the edge of the sea cliff.

Several hundred feet from the clubhouse grounds, he stopped the cart beneath a sand hummock, then proceeded the rest of the way on foot, crouching low behind the sand knolls and sea grass between him and the sea. When the wooden railing and steps leading down to the dock came into view, some thirty or forty yards ahead, he crawled up over the sand dune to the edge of the cliff for a view of the beach and dock below. While he was climbing, he heard the motor again, revving powerfully this time and, it seemed, coming in his direction.

When he poked his head through the sea grass, a sudden stream of light appeared on the water below. And at the source of the stream, unmistakable in the ambient flashlight, Angelo and Eddie stood at the end of the dock, awaiting the arrival of the incoming boat. A few moments later the boat appeared at the side of the dock, driven by Bobaloa. Eddie held the boat to the dock while Bobaloa passed several packages to Angelo. Then, after scarcely a minute, Bobaloa backed the boat away from the dock and sped off along the shore in the same direction he had taken the other night.

McGuffin pressed down against the sand as he heard their feet on the wooden stairs. Both men were breathless when they reached the top. Angelo dumped his parcels carelessly at the top of the stairs—it seemed to McGuffin there were four of them, each about half the size of a shoe box.

"I'll get a cart," Angelo said softly.

Eddie said nothing as Angelo disappeared in the direction of the clubhouse. Wishing he had concealed his cart more carefully, McGuffin hugged the sand and waited. The packages obviously contained drugs, cocaine most probably, obtained from a freighter offshore. Apparently the caddie's previous brush with the law had done nothing to dissuade him from a life of crime. And no wonder. There was perhaps a million dollars' worth of cocaine lying in a neat pile at the top of the steps.

Presently Angelo returned on a golf cart with, to McGuffin's surprised amusement, two sets of golf clubs still strapped to the back of the cart. But when they began stuffing the packages of dope into the bottom of the golf bags, McGuffin's amusement gave way to amazed admiration. Their smuggling operation was immediately clear—and brilliant. Bobaloa picked the stuff up and delivered it to Eddie and Angelo, who then stuffed it into a couple of innocent-looking golf bags and flew it to Miami the next day. Eddie was a familiar figure with American customs, hauling golf clubs for former Presidents and other members of the New York–Washington power structure, hardly the sort of servant to be interrupted by a federal employee looking forward only to an uneventful retirement. All Eddie had to do was carry the bags through the airport, deliver them to a waiting accomplice, and be back on Palm Isle within the hour. It was the sweetest drug-smuggling operation McGuffin had ever seen. And to think I gave up caddying because I thought there was no money in it, McGuffin said to himself as he watched Eddie and Angelo drive off with a fortune.

Okay, so you've got no head for business, you're still one hell of a private eye, he told himself as he walked back to his cart. You're not even fully awake yet, and already you've uncovered a major drug-smuggling operation.

And it occurs to me, McGuffin thought, as he climbed onto his golf cart, that if Lyle Boone discovered the same thing and threatened to end it, that might explain why he was murdered. Suddenly the case was pregnant with motives. Now all he had to do was select one from column A and apply to the murderer in column B. Detective work was a piece of cake.

14

Byron Kilty missed the Skins game the next day. He had left a message for Horton Ormsby with the receptionist, asking Horton to take his place in the foursome, but giving no reason for his absence. Still preoccupied with his presidential duties, Horton lost heavily, as did Churston, while Balata managed to come out a few hundred dollars ahead after making a long snaking putt on the last hole that broke McGuffin's greedy heart. After the obligatory drinks in the bar (McGuffin kept to club soda) and the settlement of accounts, McGuffin went looking for Cuppy Dunch. The news that his trusted employee had, even after Cuppy's court appearance on his behalf, returned to a life of crime should affect the golf pro in one of two ways, McGuffin had decided. He would either be greatly disappointed by Angelo's recidivism, or extremely annoyed at McGuffin for having discovered it.

"Mr. Dunch is busy in his office," Tommy, the assistant pro, dutifully informed McGuffin.

"Where's his office?" McGuffin asked, looking around the pro shop for a door.

"Off the corridor," Tommy said, pointing to the bowels of the clubhouse. "I'll tell him you'd like to see him."

"Don't bother, I'll tell him myself," McGuffin said, racing Tommy to the door.

Tommy watched with a worried look as the winner of the race pushed through the door and into the corridor.

"Yeah?" a voice growled from behind the door when McGuffin knocked.

"It's me," McGuffin said, opening the door and stepping into the dimly lit office. The draperies had been drawn over the mullioned glass, and the golf pro lay sprawled over the leather couch like a Dali watch. There was a half-filled bottle of Haig & Haig on the floor and a neat bandage on the point of Cuppy's chin. "What the hell happened to you?" McGuffin asked, closing the door and switching on the light.

"Ahyeh!" Cuppy exclaimed, bringing his hands to his eyes. "I cut myself shaving," he said, after a moment.

McGuffin looked at the bandage. It was no piece of toilet paper. "You didn't happen to run into Dr. Kilty, did you?"

Cuppy continued to rub his eyes. "Nope. Come to think of it, I haven't seen him around lately at all."

McGuffin waited until the golf pro had pulled himself up to a sitting position. He stopped rubbing his eyes, then yawned and rested his elbows on his knees. McGuffin walked across the room, picked up the bottle of Scotch, and placed it on the desk. "Take it from somebody who's been there," McGuffin said, turning to the golf pro. "If you like your job, keep the drinking separate."

Cuppy laughed softly. "And if they fired me, who do you think they'd get to stay on this godforsaken island twelve months of the year? Arnold Palmer?"

"I didn't know you were unhappy here," McGuffin said.

"Even paradise gets boring," the golfer answered.

"Then why don't you go somewhere else? A pro with a record like yours—you could go to work at almost any club in the United States. And probably earn a hell of a lot more money than you're making here, couldn't you?"

"Probably," Cuppy agreed, running his hand through his blond hair.

"Or maybe you have some sort of personal reason for staying here," McGuffin went on.

"Personal?"

"Yeah, you know—like a friend you can't leave? Something like that?"

"It's a job, that's all, just a job," the pro answered, followed by a weary sigh.

"Right," McGuffin said, nodding. "Strictly business. You

don't by any chance have another business on the side, do you?"

"Another business?" Cuppy said, taking his hand from his head. "What kind of business?"

"I don't know," McGuffin answered, sitting on the corner of the golf pro's desk. "You sell golf equipment to the members, don't you?"

"Yeah. So what?"

"So do you sell anything else?"

Cuppy stared at the detective for a moment, then replied slowly, "I don't know what you're driving at. I sell golf clubs and I give golf lessons and that's it, period."

"What about your caddiemaster?"

"Angelo?"

"Yeah, Angelo. He must have a lot of free time on his hands, seeing as how he has no caddies to supervise."

"He keeps busy."

"He was certainly busy last night," McGuffin agreed. "He and Eddie were down at the beach unloading a boat driven by one of the locals, a guy named Bobaloa. Do you have any idea what might have been on that boat?"

"How should I know?"

"You're right, you shouldn't," McGuffin agreed. "But do you know what I think was on that boat?"

"What?"

"Drugs," McGuffin answered, watching the golf pro's eyes. They didn't blink. He should have known. Any man who could calmly knock in six-foot putts for fifty thousand dollars was not a man to be rattled by a gumshoe. "I'm afraid Angelo has let you down."

Cuppy stared thoughtfully at the detective for a moment, then picked up his glass and got to his feet. He walked across the room to the desk, opened the bottle, and poured himself a drink. "Do you want one?"

"No thanks."

Cuppy placed the bottle next to McGuffin's leg. He sipped his drink and stared thoughtfully at the wall for a moment before inquiring, "Are you a narcotics officer?"

"No," McGuffin answered.

"Then what are you doing down here?"

"Just keeping my eyes open."

"Yeah," Cuppy answered, dubious but helpless. "Have you told anybody about this?"

"Just you."

"Do you plan to tell anybody else?"

"I don't know," McGuffin answered. "What do you think I should do?"

Cuppy shook his head slowly. "I don't know. I thought he was finished with that shit."

"Why did you testify for him when he was arrested the first time?" McGuffin asked.

"I felt sorry for him."

"Is that all?"

The golf pro turned his narrowed, bloodshot eyes on the detective. "What else?"

"Even the narcotics business requires start-up costs, and Angelo and Eddie don't have that kind of money. I think they may have a financial partner right here on Palm Isle," the detective informed him.

"And you think it's me?"

"Why else are you staying here if you're not happy?"

"Not for that reason," Cuppy replied, shaking his head emphatically.

"Then why?" McGuffin persisted.

Cuppy took a quick drink and looked away from the detective. "I'm here because I can't leave."

"What do you mean?" McGuffin asked, sliding off the desk. "Why can't you leave?"

"I can't tell you that."

"You mean you won't."

"I mean I can't!" he said, turning on McGuffin. "If you want to turn Angelo over to the cops, that's your business, go ahead! But I've told you as much as I can."

"Okay," McGuffin said, stepping away from Cuppy. "If you've told me all you can, I'll just have to ask somebody else." McGuffin walked to the door, opened it, and turned back to the golf pro. "But if you should remember anything, give me a call."

McGuffin slammed the door, then walked down the corridor, through the pro shop, and outdoors. Even if Cuppy wouldn't answer his questions, there was still somebody who would.

He found Angelo in the workshop at the rear of the club storage room, bent over a wood club clenched tightly in a vise at the end of a long, scarred bench. He didn't look up from his work when McGuffin walked into the room and peered over his shoulder. With the care of a portrait painter, Angelo was staining the newly sanded clubhead with a clear varnish that left each whorled grain of wood fairly shimmering with light.

"It looks as good as new," McGuffin observed. The small talk would be first, the hard questions later.

"It's better than new," the caddiemaster corrected, as he added another stripe of varnish. "That's a thirty-year-old block cut from the heart of the persimmon tree and oil-hardened for almost a year. That ain't just wood no more, that's stone and steel," he said, straightening up for an admiring look.

McGuffin was surprised. Until now he hadn't heard more than a few words from the taciturn caddiemaster. Apparently his enthusiasm was greater for things than for people. Still he didn't look at McGuffin. Both men just stood there admiring the driver.

"Is it yours?" McGuffin asked.

"Don't I wish. Naw, it's Cuppy's," he said, going back to his painting.

"It's a good-looking club," McGuffin said. Although the markings were long gone, he guessed that it was a MacGregor Tourney and now worth its weight in gold.

"Yeah, we won a few tournaments with this stick, me and the Cup. But now we don't use it much no more."

"That was too bad," McGuffin sympathized. "A lot of great players have been hurt by back problems."

"Yeah, back problems," Angelo mumbled, putting a final brush stroke to the wood.

There was a note of resentment in the caddie's voice that McGuffin couldn't miss. "You sound either bitter or dubious," McGuffin observed. "Which is it?"

Angelo threw the brush into a varnish-crusted coffee can, as if he were throwing a dart. "There are some things you can't do nothin' about, so why talk about 'em," he said, snatching a stiff, darkly stained rag from the bench.

"You mean there's nothing you can do about Cuppy's back?" McGuffin asked.

"Yeah, that's what I mean. I ain't no doctor," he said, dipping the rag into a turpentine-filled coffee can. His hands became nearly as dark as the stained rag as he rubbed them with the solvent. Then he tossed the rag onto the bench and walked across the room to the sink.

"It must be rather boring for you and Cuppy on this island after all the excitement of the pro tour," McGuffin called from the bench.

"Sometimes," Angelo said, rubbing his hands briskly under the water.

"What keeps you here?"

Angelo walked back to the bench, drying his hands on a clean white towel bearing the PIGC crest and the *Golf ad Mortem* motto. "I need the job," he said simply, tossing the towel onto the bench. His hands were clean except for the fingernails and the deep lines in the palms.

"But Cuppy could get a job anyplace," McGuffin pointed out. "Why does he stay here?"

Angelo regarded the detective for a moment, suspiciously, it seemed, before replying. "You'll have to ask him that."

"I already did."

"What did he say?"

"He said he can't leave Palm Isle."

Angelo shrugged. "Then there's your answer."

"Why can't he leave?" McGuffin asked.

"I don't know," Angelo answered.

"I think you do," McGuffin countered. "I think you know very well why Cuppy can't leave, but you don't want to tell me."

"Everybody's entitled to their opinion," the caddie answered, faintly annoyed. "I don't owe you any answers."

"Why can't you tell me, Angelo? Are you and Cuppy running a little business on the side—something you don't want the members to know about? Because I'm not a member, Angelo."

"You got a lot of questions, Mr. McGuffin. Any particular reason?"

"Island fever," McGuffin answered. "When I get bored I like to talk. And take long walks," he added. "Especially in the middle of the night. Like last night, for instance. I'll bet you'd never guess where I went walking last night."

"Where?" Angelo asked. The word had the hollow sound of a golf ball dropping into the cup for a double bogey.

"On the beach. And you know what I saw, Angelo? I saw a guy in a boat delivering some packages to a couple of guys on the beach. A tall guy with dreadlocks and a dashiki. At first I thought he must be the United Parcel man, until I realized— and this will come as a shock to you, Angelo—that this was a drug boat! Does that surprise you, Angelo?"

"Yeah, that surprises me," Angelo said, eyeing the hunter like a fox in a trap.

"I don't understand how anybody could fail to recognize a drug boat when he sees one. You must have been a very innocent young man when you jumped on that drug boat in Florida."

"The jury thought so," he answered.

"Thanks to Cuppy's testimony," McGuffin added. "Why would Cuppy want to do something like that for you?"

"I was a good caddie. Good caddies are hard to get."

"They aren't as unusual as caddiemasters without caddies," McGuffin pointed out. "Why did Cuppy bring you here with him after he quit the tour?"

"I don't know. Maybe for old times' sake. What are you, some kind of a cop?"

"Yeah, some kind of a cop," McGuffin said, reaching for his back pocket. He had intended to whip his PI badge quickly past Angelo's nose, but the pocket was buttoned. The move was sloppy but eventually successful. "You're in deep shit, Angelo. But if you help me, I might let you haul yourself out."

"What do you want?" Angelo asked.

"Answers," McGuffin said, backing Angelo up against the bench. "Was Cuppy involved in your drug-running business in Florida?"

"I wasn't in no drug business!" Angelo blurted. "I was tried and—"

"I know, I know," McGuffin interrupted, raising his hands to block the words. "You were found not guilty by a jury of hackers. But I'm no hacker, Angelo. I've got enough to put you and Bobaloa and Eddie away for most of the rest of your lives, and I will if you don't start giving me some answers. I'm not interested in narcotics. If I was, I would have busted all three of you last night. So give me what I want and I might just give you a break."

Angelo was bent backward over the bench, but there was no getting away from the detective. "Okay, back off," he pleaded. McGuffin leaned back an inch. "Just for the record, I don't know nothin' about no drugs, okay?"

"Just for the record," McGuffin agreed. "Now what about Cuppy? Was he involved in drugs, either in Florida or here?"

Angelo shook his head. "Cuppy don't know nothin' about no drugs neither, honest. But you're right, I got somethin' on him."

"What?"

"It's hard to talk with you leanin' in my face," he complained. Satisfied that he was hooked, McGuffin gave him more line. "Cuppy ain't got a bad back. That was just some bullshit the PGA put out after Cuppy agreed to quit the tour rather than face a hearing."

"A hearing for what?"

"Cheating," Angelo answered.

"Cheating!" McGuffin exclaimed. He was prepared for drugs, perjury, possibly even homicide. But cheating at golf? Golf was a royal and ancient game, played by gentlemen to whom honor was sacred. "How?" McGuffin asked.

"Lotta ways," Cuppy's former caddie answered. "I had a

hole in my pocket, and I always carried an extra ball. If Cuppy hit it in the woods, I always found it on the edge of the fairway. If he hit it in the rough, I always made sure it was sittin' up nice on the grass. It was pretty easy when he was an unknown and he had no gallery. But after he started winnin' it got a little tougher and some of the pros began to notice things. So that day at the Open when Cuppy hit one in the woods and I found it in the rough, the pros he was playin' with lodged a complaint after the round and we didn't know nothin' about it. That night the rules committee went out with flashlights and looked for Cuppy's ball."

"And found it?"

"Yeah. They called me and him in the next morning and told him he could quit the PGA tour and nothin' would ever be said about it, or he could have a hearing. Cuppy knew they had him, so he pulled out of the tournament—because of a bad back. Then a couple of weeks later he announced his retirement because of a chronic back problem."

"And that's when he came here as club pro?"

"Yeah."

"And you're the only one here who knows Cuppy was thrown off the tour?"

"The only one besides Dr. Kilty," Angelo answered.

"Byron? How does he know?" McGuffin asked. And if he did, why would he have a golf cheat as club pro? Dr. Kilty was as respectful of the game as anyone McGuffin had ever played with.

"He was chairman of the rules committee at the club where it happened," Angelo answered. "It was him who got me and Cuppy this job."

"That seems rather generous under the circumstances," McGuffin remarked, puzzled.

"Yeah, that's what me and Cuppy thought at first. But generosity ain't got nothin' to do with it. Kilty wants to be president of the club, and bringin' Cuppy here to work for practically nothin' is a good way of gettin' the job. Kilty's blackmailin' Cuppy. If he tries to quit and go to another club, Kilty'll blow the whistle on him. This may be Palm Isle to you, Mr. McGuffin. But to Cuppy and me it's Devil's Island."

So it was true—Cuppy couldn't leave Palm Isle. At least not so long as Dr. Kilty remained here. It was harsh punishment, McGuffin thought. But not too harsh for a man who cheated at golf.

"Okay, Angelo, you did pretty well," McGuffin informed him.

"You ain't gonna bust me?"

"Why should I want to bust you? As of now you're out of the drug business. Right, Angelo?"

"Yeah, yeah, right," Angelo said. "No more drugs for me."

"And when you announce your resignation to Eddie and Bobaloa, don't mention my part in your decision. Nobody on this island but you knows I'm a cop. And if anybody finds out, I'm gonna come back here and clean my spikes on your face," McGuffin said as he turned and started for the door.

"Don't worry, you can trust me!" Angelo called after him.

Sure I can, McGuffin thought, as he crunched across the clamshell to his golf cart. Anybody who would cheat at golf, even a caddie, was scarcely a man to be trusted. Promise or no promise, just as soon as he got to Florida, he would inform narcotics of Angelo's golf-bag operation. Some people might consider this a breach of trust, McGuffin knew. But they didn't understand the criminal mind as well as he did. Angelo was about as likely to give up the drug business as was the Eli Lilly Company.

Francis Knight listened quietly while McGuffin described his meeting with Al Balata in the steam room. The attorney wasn't surprised to learn that Balata and the Devon Corporation were one, nor that Balata intended to buy as many PIGC bonds as he could for as little as possible. But about Balata's professed motive, the preservation of the PIGC, Francis Knight was more than a little dubious.

"That hypocrite!" he blurted. "Al Balata has no feeling for anything or anybody. He wants control of the club so he can exploit it for profit."

McGuffin agreed. "But there's nothing illegal about it that I can see," he pointed out.

"It may not be illegal, but it is reprehensible," the lawyer fumed. "A man's own club, for God's sake. And murdering people to get their bond is certainly illegal!" he said, suddenly remembering a forgotten point of law.

"And almost impossible to prove without a body," the detective remarked gloomily. "Unless he should strike again," he added.

"I'm afraid that's exactly what he will do," Knight replied soberly. "Therefore I've decided to bring you back to San Francisco."

"San Francisco?" McGuffin repeated. He was looking out the window of his cottage at an almost full moon with a palm tree growing in the middle like a gunsight, shooting a glittery trail from the ocean's horizon to the shore. He was winning big at Skins, the beautiful Liani would soon be back, and winter, despite Mark Twain's comment about summer, was not the best time to be in San Francisco. "Why would you want to do a thing like that?"

"Because having you on Palm Isle if Al Balata tries to kill me in San Francisco is not going to do me much good, that's why," the client answered.

"But you hired me to find out who killed Lyle Boone," McGuffin pointed out.

"And you said you can't because you have no body."

"I still might be able to prove it," McGuffin argued, rising from the bed. He threw the telephone cord over the bed and walked to the window. "I'm onto something else."

"What?"

"Drugs."

"What does that have to do with Lyle's death?"

"Plenty," McGuffin said, wondering what indeed the connection might be. Nonetheless he told the lawyer what he had observed on the beach a few nights before.

"So Angelo and Eddie are involved in drugs," Knight said, obviously unimpressed by this information. "I still don't see what that has to do with Lyle's death."

"Well—obviously there's got to be a money man somewhere in the background," McGuffin said. "Maybe even a Palm member."

"What?" Francis Knight gasped.

"Or maybe not," McGuffin quickly amended. "It could be your golf pro."

"I very much doubt that," the lawyer said.

"Did you know that he was thrown off the pro tour for cheating?" McGuffin asked.

"No!" Francis Knight exclaimed. Drugs were one thing, but cheating at golf was quite another.

"It's true," McGuffin said. His continued presence on Palm Isle, he recognized, depended upon his making a case against the golf pro. "Angelo told me all about it. He was once arrested on a drug charge in Florida, but Cuppy testified for him and he managed to beat it."

"I know all about that," the lawyer said impatiently. "I want to know about this golf thing."

Patiently, McGuffin explained just how Cuppy and his caddie had been able to cheat at golf, just as Angelo had explained it to him. It was apparent by the time he finished that Francis Knight was totally nonplused by the whole thing.

"Cheating at golf—our club pro—" he repeated. "I can't believe it."

"I know, I wouldn't have believed it myself," McGuffin said, clucking sympathetically. "Except that Dr. Kilty was privy to the whole thing."

"Byron knew? And he did nothing?" the Palm man asked, the incredulity rising in his voice.

"That's another story—which I haven't yet been able to follow up on," McGuffin answered. "Byron's been spending a lot of time with Mrs. Boone lately. But that's not important. The big question is, why would Cuppy risk perjury for his caddie, unless they were partners in the drug trade and Angelo was threatening to implicate him?"

"I still find it hard to believe such a thing of Cuppy," the lawyer said softly.

"A lot of solid citizens are involved with drugs," McGuffin said.

"I'm not talking about drugs, I'm talking about golf," Knight muttered impatiently.

"Right," McGuffin said. "As you can see, there's a lot going on down here, and I'm sure I can prove that it's all somehow connected to Lyle's death if you'll just give me a little more time," he pleaded, pacing back and forth in front of the open window.

"I don't know, McGuffin," the client replied slowly. "It seems to me that the connection between drugs and Lyle's death is tenuous at best. Not that I doubt for a minute that anyone who could cheat at golf might also become involved with drugs," he quickly added. "And he might even be capable of murdering Lyle for having discovered it. But that wouldn't explain the attempt on my life, nor does it explain why Al Balata is secretly buying up club bonds."

"That's true," McGuffin replied thoughtfully. He had been so intent on making a case against Cuppy that he had almost forgotten Francis Knight's real bogeyman. "I've thought about that and I've decided that it's also possible that Al Balata is the financial partner in Angelo's drug operation, either alone or with Cuppy. And if he is, that would explain why Al is trying to get control of the PIGC."

"It would?" Knight asked.

"Sure. Lyle was a loyal Palm man, was he not?"

"The best."

"So if he became aware that Balata was using his club to run drugs, he would undoubtedly demand his resignation—or worse. He might even threaten to go to the police. And if that happened, Balata would obviously have to kill him. Would he not?"

"Yes," Knight agreed. "But why would he want to gain control of the club?"

"To make sure nothing like this ever happened again," McGuffin answered. "Once he has more than fifty percent of the voting stock, he'll be free to run the PIGC like his own little fiefdom. If anybody gets curious, as Lyle may have done, Al can simply throw him out of the club."

"I don't know that the bylaws would allow that, but I do see your point," the lawyer answered. "And I'm sure Al has just the sort of mob connections that would lend themselves to a drug operation."

"Exactly," McGuffin said with a sigh of relief.

"If I allow you to stay a while longer, Mr. McGuffin, could you give me some idea of just what your investigation will entail?"

"Of course," McGuffin answered. "I want to lean on Eddie a little—see if he'll crack. He's been flying a lot, because of the championship coming up, and I haven't been able to pin him down yet. I'd also like to talk to one of the locals, a guy named Bobaloa who drives the boat for them. If I keep the pressure on, something will break—it always does," McGuffin promised. It was not a lie, just an optimum prediction.

"Very well, you can stay on a bit longer," the lawyer assented. "But if this doesn't pan out very soon, I'm going to have to bring you back."

"I understand," McGuffin said.

He said goodbye and hung up the phone, then stood staring out to sea. The only way he could stay on for any length of time, he realized, was if someone else was murdered. He felt strangely ambivalent.

16

McGuffin was sitting alone on his golf cart at the head of the airstrip, waiting for Eddie the Aviator to return from Florida with one last group of golfers. When the sun had all but disappeared behind the wall of jungle that lined the west side of the clearing, he sighed wearily and turned the cart for the clubhouse. Eddie had either decided to spend Saturday night in Miami, as he had the last two nights, or was avoiding the detective. Painful though it was, McGuffin finally had to admit that Angelo Caudie was not a man of his word. The moment he left the bag room, Angelo had no doubt run to Eddie with the news that the detective was onto their drug scam, just as McGuffin had known he would. Oh well—now it'll be that much easier to turn you over to the narcs, McGuffin said to himself as he turned onto the boulevard and headed up the hill to the lighted clubhouse.

The cocktail crowd was the largest McGuffin had seen, but few of the faces were familiar. As the day of the club championship matches drew nearer the crowds increased, but few of them, according to Churston, were serious contenders. Although Churston and the others in McGuffin's Skins group all professed indifference to the club championship, McGuffin knew better. Each of them was a keen competitor, especially Al Balata, and unable to play except to win, even though the stakes be only honorific. Even Horton Ormsby, McGuffin noticed when the club president raised his glass to him, had lately switched from whiskey to plain club soda.

McGuffin found an empty place at the bar and sadly ordered a club soda for himself, but not because he was in training for the club championship.

"Can I get you anyting else, Mistah McGuffin?" Stymie asked, as he placed the glass of bubbling water on the bar.

"Alas, no," McGuffin said. The old bartender was a keen judge of clientele, the detective knew. "It's rather busy tonight," McGuffin observed.

Stymie looked down the bar and nodded. "Yas sah, it is."

"As busy as the night Mr. Boone died?"

"Oh no sah, not dat busy. Dat was de President's Day, sah. Ain't no day busier dan de President's Day."

"A big day, huh?"

"Yas sah, very big day."

"You remember it well?"

"Very well," the bartender said, nodding softly.

"Do you remember who was standing beside Mr. Boone when he died? Besides Dr. Kilty?"

"Well, let me just tink on dat fo' a minute, sah," the old man said, cupping his chin in a long, bony band. "Dere was Mrs. Boone, of course—she was standin' on de left side. And Mistah Ormsby was right behind him when he fall. And Mistah Brown and Mistah Revell," he went on, counting to himself. "Oh, and Mistah Balata," he remembered.

"Al Balata was there?" McGuffin exclaimed.

"Oh yas sah, I remember. He was standin' at de bah right in front of Mistah Boone all de time until he fall."

"Then what happened? Where'd he go after that?"

Stymie thought for a moment, then looked at McGuffin and shook his head. "Funny, I can't remembah seein' him after dat."

"But you're quite sure he was there when Mr. Boone died?"

"Yas sah, quite sure," Stymie replied.

"Do you remember if Mr. Boone had a drink in his hand when he died?"

"I don't remembah dat, sah," the bartender answered, shaking his head slowly.

"Did somebody mop the floor or sweep up any broken glass?"

"No sah," Stymie answered after a moment.

"Then Mr. Boone had a glass sitting on the bar?"

The bartender smiled. "Yas sah, dere was plenty of glasses on de bah dat night."

"I'll bet there were," McGuffin said.

"Excuse me, sah," Stymie said, turning away from Mc-Guffin.

McGuffin waited until Stymie finished with the customers at the end of the bar, then waved his empty glass. The bartender filled a new glass and carried it to McGuffin.

"Tell me, Stymie, do you know a tall guy from the village, wears dreadlocks and a dashiki with funny pictures?" McGuffin asked quickly.

"Bobaloa?" Stymie answered uncertainly.

"That's the guy. Do you know where I might find him?"

"Saturday night, sah, everybody be at de church."

"The church?" McGuffin repeated. Somehow the dope dealer hadn't seemed the church type. "Where's the church?"

"Outside de village on de end of King's Road."

"Thanks, Stymie," the detective said, sliding off the bar stool.

"But I wouldn't go dere, sah. It ain't de kind of church you tink," the bartender called after McGuffin.

McGuffin didn't doubt it. But he could be very ecumenical.

McGuffin waited in front of the clubhouse for almost half an hour before the bus lights appeared at the bottom of the hill. But it wasn't the jitney, he quickly realized, as he watched the vehicle racing toward him in the bright moonlight. It was a jeep, and it was being driven by Churston Brown.

"What are you doing out here by yourself?" Churston called, as he glided to a stop in front of the building.

"Waiting for the jitney," McGuffin said, approaching the idling jeep.

"I'm afraid you'll have a long wait. I just saw the driver at the Palm Isle Inn, and he didn't look like he was in any hurry to leave."

"Shit," McGuffin muttered.

"Big date?" Churston grinned.

McGuffin shook his head. "As a matter of fact, I was going to church."

"Church?"

"The church at the end of King's Road. Do you know where it is?"

Churston's wide-eyed look gave way slowly to a pumpkin grin. "Yeah, I know where the church is. Hop in, I'll give you a lift."

"You're sure I'm not keeping you from anything?" Mc-Guffin protested politely as he pulled himself into the jeep.

"It's my Christian duty," Churston answered, still grinning.

McGuffin braced himself between the windshield frame and the seat edge as Churston spun the jeep in a tight circle and headed for the village. "I didn't know you had a car," he said, speaking loudly over the wind.

"An anthropologist has to have wheels," Churston answered. "I didn't know you were a religious man."

"I'm not. I have to see a man about some drugs," McGuffin answered.

"Drugs?" Churston repeated. When he looked at McGuffin the pumpkin grin had disappeared.

"Yeah," McGuffin answered. "You wouldn't know anything about drugs on this island, would you?"

"A bit," Churston replied. "The voodoo people sometimes use marijuana in their rites. They call it ganja."

McGuffin shook his head. "I mean big-time cocaine smuggling, the kind of thing Angelo was into once before."

"Angelo is smuggling cocaine?" Churston asked, wide-eyed.

"Along with a guy from the village, a big guy with dread-locks, wears a dashiki with weird symbols painted on it."

"Bobaloa?"

"You know him?"

"Very well. It's his church we're going to," Churston answered.

"You're kidding."

"You'll see."

Past the Palm Isle Inn, where the jitney driver and several of his friends were gathered about the tables, Churston turned off the wharf and up a muddy street, past rows of shanties, some of them painted red, yellow, white, or pink, and all of them glowing brightly in the moonlight. Each postage-stamp lot was defined by a ramshackle fence of scavenged materials that left a crazy-quilt border along both sides of the muddy street, where barefoot children ran squealing through puddles beside the jeep, before tiring and peeling off. All of the shacks rested on pilings or concrete blocks, suggesting dressed-up ladies delicately lifting their bright skirts before stepping off into the muddy street. There were crudely painted signs on some of the buildings. One was a tailor shop, another a grocery, then a barber shop, and finally the tavern on the corner, a concrete-block house boasting "Life Rake & Scrape."

"It's music played on saws and files," Churston volunteered in reply to McGuffin's unasked question. McGuffin winced, remembering a nun with long fingernails and short chalk, as Churston went on, unbidden. "The materials have changed, but the technique was observed by anthropologists in Africa in the nineteenth century."

"Fascinating," McGuffin said, as Churston turned the jeep onto a wider but equally muddy road. This was King's Road, McGuffin knew, when he saw the white, spired building at the end of the road.

"The voodoo temple," Churston said, lifting one finger from the steering wheel.

"Looks just like a Christian church," McGuffin remarked.

"There's a bit of that in it too. The cross on the spire is painted black, just as it was long before Christ was crucified. Both Judaism and Christianity have borrowed heavily from the voodoo faith," Churston informed him.

"Faith?" McGuffin questioned. "I thought it was supposed to be black magic."

"That's the sensationalistic underbelly," Churston replied.

"It's true, voodoo has its devil worshipers, just as Christianity does, but that doesn't make it any less a religion."

McGuffin wouldn't argue. As they approached the voodoo temple he heard singing from inside that sounded much like the Latin of his Catholic youth. Churston stopped the jeep in front of the picket fence that staggered across the front of the temple, and they both got out. "What are they chanting?" McGuffin asked. It sounded like "Dumb Wally" over and over again.

"They're praising Damballa, the symbol of God," Churston answered. He was standing beside the jeep, hands on hips, staring up at the black cross atop the spire. "Did you know that Africans worshiped bulls and serpents even before it was recorded in *The Bacchae* of Euripides?"

"No, I didn't know that," McGuffin answered absently. He too was looking at the temple, wondering how he was going to have a word with the voodoo priest. Would Bobaloa stand on the steps and greet his parishioners after the service, like any country cleric? Or would they stay inside for the rest of the night, smoking ganja and biting heads off chickens or whatever the faithful did at a voodoo service? "What did you say about a snake?" McGuffin asked.

Churston grinned. "You aren't afraid of a little snake, are you?"

"No more than a little airplane," McGuffin answered. "Tell me, Churston, is it safe for me to go in there?"

"It's perfectly safe. As long as you're with me," he added.

"You're coming in with me?" McGuffin asked, not at all displeased with the idea.

"I wouldn't miss it for the world," Churston answered, walking around the jeep. He grabbed McGuffin by the elbow and led him through the gate.

"How am I going to talk to him when he's conducting a service?" McGuffin asked over the chanting, *Damballa Damballa*, as they approached the closed door. Like a timid salesman making his first call, McGuffin would, if given the slightest excuse, have been happy to come again another day. But Churston was not accommodating.

"We'll watch the service, and when it's over I'll introduce you to him," he said, as he pulled the door back.

Feeling Churston's hand on his back, McGuffin stepped into the dimly lighted temple. It looked like a candlelit Baptist church in the woods of Georgia, except that there were no pews. Women in white dresses, their heads wrapped in scarves, stood in the middle of the room, chanting and weaving to the monotonous beat of a single drum, while the men in their Sunday suits stood in a circle around them, clapping hands to the beat. The chanting sounded like "Red Rover Red Rover let Johnny come over" until McGuffin was able to make out the words.

> *Damballa, Damballa,*
> *Praise be Damballa.*

They chanted it over and over, without changing the words or the rhythm, pausing only to toke on a cigar-sized ganja joint when it came around. A young man with a stone sparkling in his nose passed the joint to Churston, who took a deep drag and passed it to McGuffin. When McGuffin attempted to pass it on without taking a drag, Churston jabbed him sharply in the ribs. Not wishing to offend, McGuffin inhaled deeply. It was good shit. He passed the joint to the man beside him, then followed Churston's lead.

"Are you sure we should be here?" McGuffin whispered, as they pushed through the outer circle of men and into the midst of the swirling, white-robed women.

"I want you to see Damballa," Churston said, pushing ahead.

Reluctantly, McGuffin followed, fearful of stepping on a dancing barefoot woman, apologizing once when he did. She was too stoned to notice. Not a single member of the black congregation paid any notice to the two white men pushing through their ranks. When they reached the front of the room, Churston stepped aside and motioned with his arm like a matador.

"Damballa," he said.

"My God," McGuffin breathed softly.

Damballa was the biggest snake he had ever seen, thick as a tire and possibly as long as the room. He couldn't be sure, because right now it was coiled several times around an apparently naked person, possibly a woman, but he couldn't be sure of that either, as very little of the person was showing. The identity of the voodoo doctor, however, was not in question. Bobaloa wore only a gold jockstrap and a kind of cat's mask with a cockscomb of bright feathers and furry bracelets and anklets. He was squatting down over the snake, waving his long arms in an undulating motion, as if he were trying to fly, while all the time speaking to the snake in a singsong murmur.

"What's he doing?" McGuffin exclaimed. "The snake is crushing her! Or him!"

"Just watch," Churston said, laying a calming hand on McGuffin's arm.

That was all he would do. McGuffin was a city boy. His fear of snakes was exceeded only by his ignorance of them. If anyone was going to do anything to save the girl it would have to be one of these islanders. Both fearful and fascinated, McGuffin was unable to take his eyes off the performers. Bobaloa seemed to be alternately pleading and remonstrating with the snake, hoping to remove it from the victim by the power of some mysterious voodoo song.

"Is she dead?" McGuffin whispered.

"Just watch," Churston again instructed.

McGuffin could do nothing else. Bobaloa's murmured urgings became softer now, until presently the head of the serpent swung away from its victim and McGuffin was staring directly into the dead cold eyes of the monster. Bobaloa stayed after him, pressing his lips close to the snake's ear, or whatever snakes have. The song changed; the voodoo doctor's voice now sounded more like the hiss of a snake than any human sound McGuffin had ever heard, and it caused him to shudder. Slowly the snake uncoiled, revealing its unconscious victim to McGuffin. It was Liani Carver.

Liani lay on her back, still as death, dressed only in black panties, while the snake crawled away and the voodoo doctor began his ministrations. He chanted in a strange language— only the word "Damballa" came through once in a while to McGuffin—alternately breathing in her face and waving his long hands over her body. While he did this, the snake crawled to a pile of gunnysacks under the table against the wall and coiled up for a nap.

The table was an altar, McGuffin saw, when Bobaloa got to his feet and went to it. Several lighted candles illuminated a strange collection of bottles, flowers, a machete, an egg on a bed of corn, a human skull, and an earthen jug hung with strings of snake vertebrae. The wall behind the altar was deco- rated with fanciful snakes with human heads and mysterious symbols of the kind Bobaloa wore on his dashiki. Liani, in the meantime, had not moved, and McGuffin was beginning to think she was dead—a cheap carnival trick gone wrong. What the hell was this beautiful British-educated daughter of a doc- tor doing with such primitives in the first place?

Bobaloa returned to her with a small blue jar containing a white liquid that looked to McGuffin like milk. The voodoo doctor dipped his middle finger delicately into the white liq- uid, then knelt and drew a vague symbol on her forehead. He repeated this on her lips, both breasts, her hands, and her feet. Then he returned the jar to the altar and lifted a crimson cape from a peg on the wall. With a theatrical flourish, he hung the cape from his shoulders and turned to the congrega- tion, now chanting and weaving with a gathering intensity. Did they know the girl was dead? McGuffin wondered. Did they do this every Saturday night?

When Bobaloa extended his hands in front of him, the crowd was suddenly silent. Then he raised his hands and be- gan a slow unintelligible recitation, gathering speed and energy as Damballa was invoked with greater and greater fre- quency. The others were silent; this was the voodoo doctor's big solo. A moment later Liani opened her eyes and climbed unassisted to her feet, as the crowd broke into a frenzied chant. She moved stiffly, as if drugged or hypnotized, until her eyes met McGuffin's.

The startled look had been brief—she quickly composed herself and went on as if under the magic spell of Damballa—but McGuffin had seen. It was a scam. She and Bobaloa were working the crowd. To what end he didn't know. It didn't matter.

"Let's get the fuck out of here," McGuffin said in Churston's ear.

"Wait," Churston said. "That was just the opening act."

McGuffin pulled, but Churston was a rock, seemingly as enthralled by the rites of voodoo as the white-gowned women dancing and chanting around them. When Liani whispered in Bobaloa's ear, he looked at the two white men and nodded, then turned and led her to a door beside the altar. She opened the door and stepped outside, letting it fall closed after her.

Bobaloa stood at the altar with his back to the congregation, like a red-robed priest saying Mass, but with a giant snake under the altar. When he turned he was holding the machete in his hands. The edge, newly sharpened, glinted like a diamond in the candlelight as he walked toward the two white men.

"Oh, shit," McGuffin groaned.

Churston, he saw, was smiling like an altar boy about to take Communion. Hoping that Churston knew something he didn't, McGuffin held his ground as the voodoo doctor advanced on them.

Bobaloa raised the knife in the air, and again the crowd was immediately silent. His eyes went from Churston to McGuffin and held.

"De white man has come to witness de power of Damballa!" the voodoo doctor said, lifting his cadenced voice to the assembly.

"Praise Damballa!" they replied in ragged unison.

"But de white man will feel de power of Damballa before de white man will see de power of Damballa!"

"Churston, let's go," McGuffin pleaded, smiling weakly as the congregation replied again to the voodoo doctor. Churston continued to smile as if he had no idea he was white.

"Damballa is restless!" Bobaloa cried, waving the sword in the air.

"Praise Damballa!"

"Damballa is angry!"

"Praise Damballa!"

"Damballa will drive de white debil from paradise!"

"Praise Damballa!"

"We will sacrifice our blood to Damballa!"

As the crowd replied, Bobaloa swung the blade in a downward arc toward the smiling Churston's neck. McGuffin gasped, but Churston's expression never changed when the razor-sharp blade stopped inches before his jugular vein. Frozen, McGuffin watched as the voodoo doctor dropped the knife on Churston's shoulder, then turned and walked back to the altar.

"Now can we get the fuck out of here?" McGuffin whispered.

Churston continued to smile but said nothing as the door was opened and Liani appeared, still nearly naked, pulling a bleating goat into the room. The snake moved, and the goat kicked and scratched at the wooden floor, bleating frantically as Liani pulled it toward the altar. Still carrying the machete, Bobaloa took the leash from Liani and held the struggling goat. He pointed to the floor, and Liani got down on all fours, facing the tethered goat.

"Come on," McGuffin pleaded.

But Churston wouldn't move. He didn't even seem to hear. The crowd had quieted. They were intent on the goat and the girl. Even the goat was becoming quiet. As it stared into Liani's eyes, the bleating and struggling diminished until finally the goat stood quiet as a statue.

"She's hypnotized the goat," McGuffin said in an amazed whisper.

Churston shook his head, the first sign in several minutes that he too had not been hypnotized. "They've hypnotized each other," he corrected.

"What?"

"The girl is the goat and the goat is the girl," Churston explained, not taking his eyes from either of them.

"Okay," McGuffin said, shrugging easily. He was no longer nervous. It was just a cheap carnival trick; he would relax and enjoy it. It puzzled and pained him that Liani was part of it, but show business, he decided philosophically, was her life.

Act though it was, McGuffin could almost believe that something strange was happening to Liani, something more than an act. It was ridiculous, he knew, but at this moment she seemed somehow less than human. It was what happened next, a small, scarcely noticeable gesture, that very nearly made McGuffin a convert to voodoo.

Bobaloa produced a sprig of grass from under his cloak, which he offered to the goat, while at the same time bringing the machete under the goat's neck from behind. McGuffin had been preparing himself for the inevitable bloody sacrifice—he only hoped Liani would be far enough away from the flashing blade when it happened—but he was perhaps the only one in the room who saw what happened immediately before. It was the tiniest of gestures, not designed for attention, but so distinctly the act of a grazing animal and not a human being that McGuffin could not help but notice. At the smell of grass—McGuffin was certain she hadn't seen it, so fixed on the goat's eyes was she—her lips moved over her clenched teeth in that involuntary, seemingly useless way that horses and other grazing animals have. Then as the goat nibbled at the grass, Bobaloa's knife flashed deftly across its throat.

For a split second the animal continued to chew as if nothing had happened. Then, as the goat crumpled and fell, Liani uttered a chilling, goatlike bleat, jerked violently toward the altar, and collapsed. The goat lay motionless as Bobaloa quickly stuck a bowl under its throat to collect the blood, but Liani continued to twitch until her blood-strangled bleating faded at last and died.

McGuffin stared in frozen horror. A goat had been butchered, but he had witnessed the sacrificial slaying of a human being. She was still alive, though unconscious, yet to everyone here, including Churston, judging from the look on his face, she had died. The words of his Catholic youth came suddenly to McGuffin—"As often as ye do these things, in memory of Me shall ye do them." How pale the Christian sacrifice beside this.

Two white-gowned women pushed past him, picked up the unconscious girl, and carried her out the door through which she and the goat had entered only a few minutes before. A lot had happened in those few minutes.

When Bobaloa lifted the bowl and drank the blood, the frenzied congregation surged forward, clamoring for a taste of the sacrificial blood. Another bowl was filled and another, then passed from hand to hand among the crazed voodoo worshipers. The blood was spilled and sprinkled until the white-gowned women resembled workers in a slaughterhouse. The throb of the drum intensified, and the women began dancing barefoot in the blood, and McGuffin stood staring from the edge of the crowd, both fascinated and horrified by the spectacle. That Liani Carver was a part of it was still only scarcely comprehensible. But the thought that he had gone skinny-dipping with a voodoo priestess, if that's what she was, was beginning to make him giddy. Churston noticed.

"What's so funny?" he asked, with a disapproving scowl.

"Nothing," McGuffin replied quickly. But, unable to suppress a grin, he added, "I was just thinking of something my cousin warned me about before I left San Francisco."

"What was that?"

"He told me there wouldn't be much to do here at night."

The silvery dew on the first green was still unmarked when McGuffin turned onto the drive and headed up to the clubhouse. He had already decided that love between a white private eye and a voodoo priestess was not meant to be, and was concentrating solely on the upcoming Skins game, when he saw the caddiemaster racing across the ninth fairway on his golf cart, waving frantically and calling the detective's name.

"What's wrong?" McGuffin called, halting his cart on the road.

"Dr. Kilty's dead!" Angelo shouted, bouncing the cart up onto the road and skidding to a stop.

"How?" McGuffin demanded.

Angelo shook his head and took a deep breath. "I don't know. I was just comin' to work and I seen this cart on the seventh fairway wit' clubs on it but nobody around. So I go over and there's Dr. Kilty lyin' face down in the Devil's Asshole."

"Are you sure he's dead? Did you examine him?"

"I didn't have to, man. I hollered at him and he didn't move."

"He could have passed out."

"No, man, he didn't pass out. He's dead, man. Stone cold fuckin' dead," Angelo said, jamming the reverse lever on the cart.

"Where are you going?" McGuffin shouted.

"To tell Cuppy."

"Don't tell Cuppy!" McGuffin shouted. "Don't tell anyone except Horton Ormsby about this. You understand?" Angelo nodded. "Tell Horton to get a doctor out there right away and then join me at the Devil's Asshole. But tell him not to tell anybody else what's happened. You got that?"

"Yeah, I got it," Angelo said, as he headed for the clubhouse.

McGuffin turned off the road and followed Angelo's cart tracks in the morning dew, across the ninth fairway, through the trees, and across the eighth fairway. When he came up over the hill he saw the dreaded bunkers of Normandy, and there beside the most dreaded bunker of them all, the Devil's Asshole, Byron's cart. He could see the trail left by Angelo's cart, and he could see the footprints he had left at the edge of the bunker. It was obvious that he hadn't examined the body—if Byron was indeed dead—as there were no footprints leading to the ladder. Byron's cart had left no trail in the morning dew, McGuffin noticed, indicating that it had probably been there all night. Both the cart and Byron's custom-made Peterson clubs were dripping wet with dew, he saw when he parked his cart beside Byron's and dismounted. He walked to the edge of the pot bunker, braced himself on the ladder, and looked down into the deep, steep-sided hole. There, just as Angelo had said, lay the body, face down in the Devil's Asshole. A sand wedge and a glistening white golf ball lay on the smooth sand not far from Byron's gloved hand. The body was as wet as the dew-soaked grass. There was no need to shout; Byron Kilty was as dead as you get.

Reluctantly, McGuffin lowered himself down the ladder. The rake was still leaning against the smooth clay wall under the ladder, and the sand, except for the footprints leading to the body, was smooth as the desert after a sandstorm. When he got down to examine the body, McGuffin saw that Byron's usually reposed features were now contorted and vomit-encrusted. The corpse was wet and cold and the muscles hard and knotted. McGuffin was about to rise when he noticed Byron's black Foot-Joy golf glove. The fingertips of the first two fingers were torn, while the rest of the glove, except for some dirt in the seams, looked hardly worn. And the fingernails of the bare right hand were packed with clay. He lifted the hand for a closer inspection, then dropped it and jumped to his feet.

He turned around slowly, examining the slick clay walls for any sign of fissure or other opening, but found nothing. From the bottom to the top, a height of about ten or eleven feet, the walls were smooth and straight as a newly dug grave. With the toe of his golf shoe, the detective carefully raised one leg of the corpse a few inches off the sand and let it drop. He did the same with the other leg, as well as both arms, then lifted the torso slightly from either side. Finished, he stared up at the cerulean blue sky and scratched his head, then squatted again to examine the body. He was in this position when the club president arrived.

"Is he dead?" Horton Ormsby asked.

McGuffin looked up at the big head peering over the edge of the deep hole. "Yeah, he's dead," he answered.

"Terrible, terrible," Horton said, shaking his white pompadour. "Two heart attacks in less than a month."

"This wasn't a heart attack," McGuffin said.

"It wasn't? How do you know that?" Ormsby asked.

"Muscular contractions, vomiting . . ." McGuffin said, waving a hand over the body. "Byron died from a massive dose of venom."

"Venom? You mean he was bitten by a coral snake?"

"Several coral snakes," McGuffin answered, lifting the ungloved hand. "There are several sets of puncture wounds to both hands."

"My God!" the president exclaimed. "There must be a nest of them down there! Get the hell out of there, Amos, right away!"

"There are no snakes here," McGuffin said, climbing slowly to his feet. "I've already looked."

"There must be," Ormsby insisted. "There's no way out of there."

McGuffin looked up at Ormsby, his hands resting on the sidepieces of the ladder, and suggested, "They could have climbed the ladder." Horton's hands flew from the ladder like flushed partridges. "But they didn't," the detective added.

Slowly Horton Ormsby's head reappeared over the rim of the bunker, several feet from the ladder. "How do you know?"

"Because the ladder wasn't here when Byron was bitten," McGuffin answered.

"What do you mean, the ladder wasn't here? The ladder is always here," the club president spluttered. "Where the hell else would it be?"

"Up there with you, out of Byron's reach," McGuffin answered. He pointed to a place on the wall above his head. "If you look here you'll see some furrows in the clay. And here and here," he pointed. "As well as on the wall directly across from you. Those marks were made by Byron's fingers when he tried to scrabble up the walls. There's still some clay packed under his fingernails, although most of it has been removed."

"Removed by whom?" Ormsby demanded.

"By whoever removed this ladder," McGuffin said, as he stepped on the first rung.

Horton Ormsby waited with a shocked expression while the detective hauled himself out of the hole. "You aren't implying that Byron was somehow murdered, are you?" he asked.

"Oh, I'm quite sure of it," McGuffin answered, brushing at the knees of his yellow golf slacks.

"That's ridiculous," Ormsby snapped.

"Is it?" McGuffin asked. "Look in that bunker and tell me what you see."

"What do I see? I see Byron's body. I see a golf club and a ball. And a ladder and a rake," he added with a shrug.

"What else?"

"What else? Nothing else. Just a lot of sand."

"Exactly," McGuffin said. "A lot of sand, and all of it raked as smooth as a baby's bum—except for the single trail of footprints made by Byron and me. Isn't that strange?"

"Of course not. This is the PIGC—the traps are always raked smooth," the club president answered indignantly.

"And no one was more respectful of the etiquette of the

game than Byron Kilty," McGuffin admitted. "But not even he could have raked the trap after he was dead."

"Why should he have raked the trap when he hadn't even hit his shot yet?" Horton Ormsby fairly wailed. "He climbed down the ladder and went to his ball, then he was bitten and fell over dead."

McGuffin shook his head. "He suffered violent spasms, he tried to climb the walls, and he thrashed around in the sand for some time before he finally died. And yet the sand is smooth as glass. Somebody has to have raked the trap after Byron was dead."

"It's not possible," Ormsby insisted. "A man would have to be crazy to go down into a pit full of vipers."

"It wouldn't be any problem for an experienced snake handler," McGuffin pointed out.

"But Byron wasn't an experienced snake handler. Why would he go down there if he had seen a nest of coral snakes. on the sand? And he had to have seen them—they're brightly colored little devils," Ormsby added with a shudder.

"He didn't see them because they weren't in the bunker when he went down," McGuffin answered. "Byron must have been playing alone sometime late yesterday when—"

"He was," Horton interrupted.

"How do you know?"

"Because we were sitting on the patio when he came by. He asked if anybody wanted to play a few holes before it got dark and we all said no."

"Who is we—who all was there?" McGuffin asked quickly.

"Jesus, I don't remember all of them."

"Al Balata?"

"Yes, he was there. And Cuppy and Churston and a few others—I can't remember them all. What's that got to do with it, anyway?" he asked impatiently.

"It could be very important," McGuffin answered. "After Byron went off to play by himself, did anyone on the patio get up and leave?"

"We all did."

"Shit."

"What is this, Amos? Surely you're not saying that Byron was murdered by a fellow Palm man."

"No, I'm not saying that."

"I should hope not."

"But he could have been murdered by someone hired by a Palm man. Somebody was standing here when Byron hit his blind second shot over the top of the hill. He probably didn't hit the ball in the bunker—he probably laid up short like he always does—but that's not important. Whoever was here picked up the ball and threw it into the bunker, then ran and hid in the woods, probably right over there." The detective pointed. "Then Byron came over the hill and found his ball in the Devil's Asshole. He was surprised that he'd hit it so far, but he wasn't entirely unhappy. He figured he was getting stronger, or maybe he just caught a flyer. Anyway, being a faithful practitioner of the Royal and Ancient Rules of Golf, Byron descended into the bunker and prepared to hit his shot.

"Meanwhile the murderer ran from his hiding place with a bag of coral snakes under his arm, which he dropped on the ground for a moment, while he pulled the ladder from the bunker. At first Byron probably thought it was a joke by one of his golf buddies whom he had left on the patio. Until he looked up and saw a dark cloud of snakes falling on his head. Then he knew it was no joke," McGuffin said softly. "He raised his hands to deflect the snakes—he probably fell—and that's when they got him."

"I just can't believe such a thing," Horton Ormsby said, shaking his head slowly.

McGuffin, who was by this time quite pumped up, continued. "The murderer stood here and watched Byron thrashing about, trying desperately to scale the walls, pleading for help even though he knew he was beyond help. When he was finally dead, the murderer replaced the ladder and went down into the bunker to collect his snakes. He wiped most of the clay off Byron's hands, then raked the trap smooth and climbed out."

"Horrible," Ormsby said softly. "Just horrible."

"Not a nice way to die," McGuffin agreed.

"My God!" Ormsby exclaimed suddenly.

"What is it?"

"I just remembered—Byron's grandfather died in exactly the same way."

"Not exactly," McGuffin, to whom the same thought had earlier occurred, replied. "Byron always played it as it lay."

It was a fitting epitaph for an honorable practitioner of the Royal and Ancient Game.

"For a man in the investment business, you seem rather knowledgeable about crime," Horton said, as they drove their carts, side by side, back to the clubhouse.

"It's something of a hobby," McGuffin said.

"Indeed," the club president said, staring curiously at the detective as they drove across the ninth fairway.

They slowed and bumped their carts up onto the main drive and turned for the clubhouse at the top of the hill. There were already a couple dozen players on the practice tee when they drove into the parking area in front of the pro shop, all of them blissfully unaware of the passing of one of their own. Horton caught McGuffin by the wrist as he dismounted from his cart.

"Are you going to tell me, Amos?"

"Tell you what?" McGuffin asked, glancing down at the big, sun-reddened hand on his arm.

"About your business here."

"It's golf," McGuffin said.

"Okay," the club president said, nodding slowly. "If that's the way you want it. But just tell me this. Why did you particularly want to know if Al Balata was present on the patio when Byron went out to play? Did Francis tell you of Al's connection to the Devon Corporation?"

"No," McGuffin said, shaking his head. "I told him."

"Ah, I see," Ormsby said, releasing the detective's arm. "And you think that Byron's death might have something to do with his bond and the Devon Corporation?"

"You'll know that when you find out who owns Byron's bond, won't you?"

"Yes, I'm afraid so," Ormsby answered gravely. He was staring past McGuffin, in the direction of the practice tee. McGuffin turned. Al Balata was standing at his usual place at the end of the tee, looking their way.

"Or do you already know who owns Byron's bond?" McGuffin asked.

"What? No, of course not," Ormsby answered. He took McGuffin's elbow and turned him toward the clubhouse. "I suppose we'll have to phone the local constable in a case like this."

"Of course," McGuffin said, over the sound of crunching clamshell underfoot. "Byron was murdered."

"Acording to your theory. And it's a good one," he said, before McGuffin could interrupt. "But that doesn't mean we're under any obligation to share that theory with the constable."

McGuffin stopped walking. "What are you getting at?" he asked. "Are you suggesting we let Byron's murder pass for an accident?"

"Not at all," Ormsby answered. "But be practical. Our local constable is a man who can scarcely read or write. I doubt that he's ever investigated anything bigger than assault in his entire career. Hell, he won't even recognize that a murder's been committed."

"But you and I do," McGuffin said. "Now the local cop may not be the best man to investigate the crime, but somebody's got to do it or the murderer will damn sure never be caught. Is that what you want?"

"I want the killer apprehended just as much as you do," the club president insisted. "But I have to think of the club as well. What good will it do to announce that a famous heart surgeon was murdered at his golf club, but then fail to find the murderer? Do you think the members will continue to come here, knowing there's a killer loose on the island? I want Byron's murder investigated quietly, Amos. And not by the local police," he added, again placing a hand on the detective's arm.

"Investigated by whom?"

"You did say crime was your hobby, did you not?"

"Yes."

"Then let me suggest that *you* investigate Byron's death and we keep the police out of it."

"I couldn't do that," McGuffin answered.

"Then I'm afraid you won't be able to practice your hobby at the PIGC," the president said.

"Let me get this straight," McGuffin said. "Unless I cooperate with you in concealing a felony homicide from the police, you're going to throw me off the club property?"

"I would prefer to think that I'm doing the best for this club, while at the same time doing my best to make sure that Byron's murderer is brought to justice. However, if you prefer to put it another way, I have no objection."

The options were plain. He could play by the rules, in which case probably neither Byron's nor Lyle's murderer would ever be found, and he'd be on the next plane back to San Francisco; or he could withhold evidence, no doubt a felony under British law too, and stay on the case—as well as in the Skins games.

"I'm on the case," McGuffin said.

"Good man," Ormsby said, smiling and shaking McGuffin's hand. "If I can be of any help, just let me know."

"Sure," McGuffin said, as Ormsby turned and headed to the clubhouse. His stiffness was accentuated when he walked quickly, as if his large head were too heavy for his frame. He turned at the door and smiled briefly at McGuffin before disappearing inside.

Now why is he so happy? McGuffin asked himself. Is it because the PIGC won't be compromised by a police investigation, or is it personal? It occurred to McGuffin that if Ormsby was funding Angelo and Eddie's drug business, a very personal reason, he most certainly wouldn't want the police crawling around here. When McGuffin scratched his head and glanced toward the practice tee, he saw Al Balata staring at him. McGuffin stared back, but Al didn't look away for several moments. When he finally returned to hitting balls, McGuffin turned and walked to the clubhouse.

It might be my imagination, McGuffin thought. But I think Al was challenging me to something.

18

The distinguished members of the Palm Isle Golf Club, each with a strip of black ribbon pinned to the crest of his club blazer, lined both sides of the airstrip as the plane bearing the body of their deceased member taxied slowly past them. McGuffin stood with Dr. Carver, a few paces behind the column, but short of the cluster of employees who watched as the plane came about to face the wind, then made a short dash down the grassy strip before lifting quickly into the sky. Once it was gone, the bereaved Palm men began making foursomes for the afternoon round. With the club championship scarcely a week away, the period of mourning had to be seriously curtailed.

"I wonder if Dr. Kilty will find golf in heaven," Dr. Carver mused as he and the detective watched the plane climbing into the sky.

"What would be the purpose?" McGuffin asked. "Everybody would shoot par every day."

The doctor made a clucking sound with his tongue. "Such a horrible accident."

"Yeah, a terrible accident," McGuffin said, as they turned and walked slowly across the grass to his waiting cart. "Tell me, Doctor, do you know any snake handlers on this island?"

"Snake handlers?" he repeated. "I can't say that I do."

"Funny, I thought you might."

"I'm afraid not."

"Do you think your daughter might know one?"

The old man missed a beat, then replied, "I shouldn't think so."

"The guy I'm thinking of is called Bobaloa. A tall guy with curly hair and bright shirts, kind of hard to miss. The reason I thought you might know him is because he and your daughter have a sort of dog-and-pony show they do together, only with a goat and snake. Do you know what I'm talking about, Doctor?"

Dr. Carver stopped walking and looked up at McGuffin with rheumy eyes. "Yes, I know what you're talking about, Mr. McGuffin."

"Then why did you tell me you didn't?"

"I only wanted to save everyone a lot of trouble, Mr. McGuffin—especially you."

"Thanks, but I can take of myself."

"This is not San Francisco, Mr. McGuffin. You're a stranger here."

"I'm feeling more like a native every day," McGuffin said. "I'm learning about voodoo and about the history of this island, like how the whites took the land from the blacks and killed the voodoo doctor who objected. And now there's a new voodoo doctor who fancies himself a revolutionary, but in fact he's a drug smuggler and possibly a hired killer."

"Bobaloa is no killer," the old man said.

"Spoken like a prospective father-in-law," McGuffin said.

"And a little ganja does not make him a drug smuggler."

"Not ganja, Doctor. Cocaine. Golf bags full of it."

"I don't believe you."

"Believe me, I've seen it. Bobaloa is not a good marriage prospect. He's going to go to jail for a long time. And if your daughter's involved with him she's going to get hurt."

Dr. Carver was silent while several men in blazers walked past on their way to their carts. "Why are you telling me this?" he asked, speaking more softly now. "I know Bobaloa is a charlatan, but my daughter thinks he is a—a hero of the revolution. Against such odds, what is a poor father to do?"

"You can tell me everything you know about him," McGuffin answered. "Do that and I promise I'll do my best to see that nothing happens to your daughter."

"But my daughter has nothing to do with drugs or—or murder," the old man protested. "She is a nationalist, an idealist, that is all."

"Probably," McGuffin allowed. "But without a little help from somebody like me, that's too fine a distinction to expect from the police."

Dr. Carver sighed and turned his sad eyes on the tough cop. McGuffin didn't like it—he had a daughter too. That's why he had known it would work.

"What would you like from me?"

McGuffin exhaled and lost a couple of inches. "Tell me about the cocaine. Who's Bobaloa's financial partner?"

"Until now, Mr. McGuffin, I have known nothing about the cocaine. Ganja yes, cocaine no. That is the truth, on my daughter's honor."

McGuffin frowned; the answer pained him. "Okay, tell me about Bobaloa's connection with a guy named Al Balata."

"I've never heard of this man."

"Doctor, you're not cooperating," McGuffin warned.

"I can't tell you what I don't know, Mr. McGuffin. I can tell you about his political activities. That is the extent of my daughter's involvement with Bobaloa."

"Okay, tell me about that," McGuffin said.

"May I sit?" the old man asked, indicating the golf cart.

"Of course," McGuffin said.

They walked the few yards to the golf cart, and Dr. Carver sat. The detective leaned carefully against the rough-barked palm tree near the cart and waited. Dr. Carver's story was long on local color but short on hard facts. Bobaloa was a confused and angry young man, blessed with charisma and given to mystical religion and radical politics, which he was presently amalgamating into a force for an eventual but vaguely defined revolution. His political vision was blurred, although Liani was working to correct it, and his followers were no more than the small number McGuffin had observed at the voodoo temple. The doctor insisted that the voodoo doctor did not work with coral snakes, only with the large but relatively harmless anaconda McGuffin had seen.

"And that's all?" McGuffin asked, pushing off the tree when the doctor had finished. "No violence, no homicide?"

"I'm sorry to disappoint you, Mr. McGuffin," the old man said, shaking his head. "Bobaloa is just another inept but harmless would-be revolutionary."

"Shit," McGuffin muttered, walking to the golf cart. There was more than that to the voodoo doctor, but he would get no more from the shrewd physician.

"You'll do what you can to help my daughter?" the doctor reminded him as they drove to the clubhouse.

"Just tell her to stay clear of Bobaloa's cocaine operation and she'll be all right," McGuffin answered.

The old man attempted a smile. He was pleased that his daughter was all right for the moment, but worried about her future. McGuffin knew the feeling.

"By the way, how is Mr. Dunch's chin?" the doctor asked, as they pulled around the corner of the pro shop.   *

"It's all right, I guess."

"The wound required twelve stitches, you know."

"You stitched Cuppy's chin?" McGuffin asked, stopping the cart. "He told me he cut himself shaving."

"Did he?" the doctor asked. "He told me he had fallen in his cottage. I thought it was strange that he had come all the way to the village when Dr. Kilty could have stitched him here."

"Dr. Kilty wasn't home for the last several nights," McGuffin replied, as a shipboard contretemps took shape in his mind.

"But you know, I don't think Mr. Dunch slipped and fell in his cottage at all," the doctor went on.

"Why not?" McGuffin asked.

"Because of the bloody towel he left in my office. It was a ship's towel from Mr. Boone's yacht, the *Cricket*."

"Thanks," McGuffin said, as the old man slid off the cart.

"I hope I've been of help."

"You may have been more help than you realize," McGuffin said.

19

McGuffin found a fisherman who agreed to row him out to the *Cricket* and back for five dollars. He started to make an entry in his expense book, then remembered his winnings at Skins and decided to skip it. The fisherman held the boat fast to the jack ladder while McGuffin climbed onto the platform. He thanked the boatman and started up the ladder as a young crewman appeared at the rail above him.

"May I help you, sir?" he asked.

"Yeah, I'd like to see Mrs. Boone," McGuffin grunted, as he hauled himself onto the deck. "The name is Amos McGuffin. Tell her I have some news about Byron Kilty."

"Wait here, please," the sailor instructed.

McGuffin waited while the sailor walked aft and disappeared around the corner. He wondered where she got her crew. They all looked like Santa Monica lifeguards. A moment later the tanned young man reappeared and motioned him forward.

"She's at the pool," he said, passing McGuffin on the deck.

At the pool, McGuffin repeated wordlessly. Probably just past the tennis court. There was indeed a pool, McGuffin saw when he came to the aft deck. And lying beside that pool was a long, lean, glistening woman wearing only a bikini bottom.

"Mrs. Boone?"

"Marian," she said, rolling from her stomach to her side and getting to her feet. "It's nice to see you, Amos," she said, advancing on him with outstretched hand.

"It's nice to see you," McGuffin said.

Except for the white thong at her loins she was a continuous sheet of brown, with delicately formed breasts and sharp nipples that pointed to the bridge. She sauntered across the deck with the model's practiced obliviousness to near nudity and slipped her oily hand into McGuffin's.

"Sit here," she said, tossing a damp towel from one of the two antique deck chairs beside the pool.

The name on the chair was *Lusitania*. McGuffin smiled faintly and sat. "Thanks," he said, while Marian pulled the matching chair around so as to sit facing him and the sun.

She leaned back and rested her hands on the arms of the chair and crossed her long legs at the ankles. "I sent Rick for champagne—it's getting to be that time. I'm so glad somebody came. I hate to drink alone."

"Yeah, well, I'm afraid I didn't come with good news," McGuffin said hesitantly. "Byron is dead."

"I know," she said, either squinting in the sun or smiling, McGuffin couldn't be sure. Anyway, she wasn't crying.

"You do?"

"Al Balata phoned me this morning. I was shocked. Did you know his grandfather died exactly the same way?"

"Yes," McGuffin said, deciding not to mention the difference. It would be too subtle for a nongolfer. "Is there any particular reason Al would have phoned?"

"None—except that he and Byron were good friends. He went up to New York in his private jet to fly Byron's wife and kids down to Miami to pick up the body."

"That was kind of him," McGuffin said. As well as a wonderful opportunity to get the widow's bond away from her. "I had no idea Byron was married," McGuffin lied, to get to his next area of inquiry.

"He was about to get a divorce."

"To marry you?"

"Oh God," she said, suddenly slapping her oily thighs. "Did he tell you that?"

McGuffin shook his head. "I just assumed it."

"Well, you assume too much. And so did Byron," she

added, with a hurt, pouting look. "We both agreed it was just a thing, nobody would be hurt. Byron's wife was never here and I only saw my husband when it rained, so the two of us got together and that's all it was supposed to be."

"But Byron began to take it seriously."

She sighed and stared out to sea. "I'm afraid so. I told him not to file for divorce for my sake because I had no intention of marrying him, but he wouldn't believe me. He said he had been intending to get a divorce for a long time anyway and I had nothing to do with it, but I knew better. And I felt shitty about it," she added, turning to McGuffin.

"So you began an affair with Cuppy Dunch?"

"Jesus—you're a regular fucking Liz Smith, aren't you? Who told you—that little owl Churston? After he promised Cuppy he'd never say a word? The little prick."

"It was Dr. Carver who told me," McGuffin said.

"Who?"

"The doctor who stitched up Cuppy's chin after Byron punched him when he found the two of you together here. That is what happened, isn't it?"

She looked at McGuffin and grinned. "I told Byron not to come. Tuesday night was Cuppy's night."

"Doctors aren't very good when it comes to scheduling," McGuffin said.

"You have a dry wit, Amos. I like that," she said, with an appraising look, as Rick made a warning noise somewhere behind McGuffin. "Come."

She fanned her fingers over her breasts and waited while Rick opened the champagne and poured two glasses. She uncovered one breast to take her glass, then instructed Rick to place the ice bucket on the deck beside Amos.

"To life," she toasted, as Rick disappeared around the corner.

"To life," McGuffin repeated. He made a show of drinking the wine, then placed it on the deck beside the ice bucket, practically untouched. "Are you in love with Cuppy Dunch?" McGuffin asked.

The beautiful model looked at him and shook her head condescendingly. "Amos, Amos, Amos," she said, waving a painted manicured nail in the air. "Don't you know that girls like me don't fall in love? We make contracts. With ad agencies, TV companies—and rich oil men. But we never, never, never fall in love."

"But isn't Cuppy in love with you?" he asked. "Doesn't he want to marry you, just like Byron did?"

Marian took the glass away from her lips and asked, "Is that my fault?"

McGuffin looked at her and her yacht for a moment before replying. "Yeah, it's your fault," he said. "I think a man could kill to marry a woman like you."

"Why, thank you, Amos," she smiled, raising her glass to him.

McGuffin nodded and reached for his glass. And it would be especially easy to kill one's love rival if that rival also happened to be responsible for one's imprisonment on a tropical island, McGuffin was thinking. When he looked, his glass was empty.

"Pour us another," Marian said, extending her glass to McGuffin. He filled her glass, then hesitated over his own. "Aren't you going to have another?" she asked.

"Sure," he said, filling his glass. Anything to keep her talking. He drained the glass and filled it again, but placed it on the deck, out of harm's way for the moment. "Did I tell you how much I enjoyed your performance the first time we met?"

"No, you didn't," she answered.

"Well, I did. I doubt if Horton Ormsby's been spoken to like that since he was in prep school."

"It's time someone did," she said, leaning over to place her glass on the deck beside McGuffin's. "It's a crime the way they treated Lyle. I'm not talking about Francis, you understand."

"I understand."

"And not Byron either," she added. "Byron always treated Lyle with respect." She looked at McGuffin and grinned mischievously. "Except for fucking his wife. Sorry, I couldn't resist that," she said, arranging her hands over her lap. Now she looked completely naked.

"What about Al Balata?" McGuffin asked.

"Al doesn't count. He's an outsider, like Lyle. But yeah, they were good friends," she said, closing her eyes to the sun.

"Is that why you sold him your bond?"

She opened her eyes and squinted curiously at the detective. "I didn't sell my bond to Al. I sold it to the Devon Corporation," she said.

"The same thing," McGuffin said. "Al Balata owns the Devon Corporation. I thought you knew that."

"No," she said, shaking her head slowly. "I had no idea. Why wouldn't he tell me that?"

Models make terrible actresses, McGuffin knew. Either Marian Boone was an exception or she was telling the truth. "Maybe Al thought you wouldn't sell it to him. Especially after your husband refused to sell him his bond while he was still alive. Or didn't you know that either?"

"This is the first I've heard of it," she said, squinting closely at McGuffin in the sun.

"Who made the offer to buy your bond?"

"A lawyer from Miami, a Mr. Roman."

"Before or after Lyle's death?"

"After, naturally. Why would he approach me if Lyle wasn't dead?"

"Maybe he was expecting him to die soon."

"That's ridiculous. Nobody expected Lyle to die."

With the possible exception of the person who put the poison in his drink, McGuffin said to himself. To Marian he said, "Did Mr. Roman tell you what he wanted with Lyle's bond?"

"He did, but I didn't care one way or the other, just as long as I got the money. He said the corporation was buying bonds and holding them in trust for the club. He said he had already made deals with a couple of other members of the club, so I said fine, where do I sign?"

"Did he mention the other members?"

"Your cousin, Francis Knight," she said.

"And—?"

"And Horton Ormsby."

"Ormsby! I'll be damned," McGuffin said.

"That's right," she replied, nodding firmly. "Can you imagine that hypocritical sonofabitch lecturing me for doing the same thing he did? Although it wasn't exactly the same—his was some kind of collateral for a loan or something."

"Why didn't you say something when Ormsby started lecturing you?" McGuffin asked.

"Because I didn't want to queer my deal," she answered. "All I've got so far is a contract to buy the bond, but I can't actually sell it until after the estate is closed. And the lawyer told me not to mention anything about your cousin or Horton or that could kill the deal. So please, Amos, not a word to anybody, okay?"

"Okay," McGuffin said. Not a word to anybody—except Horton Ormsby. If Al Balata's lien on Ormsby's bond provided that it automatically reverted to him in the event of Ormsby's death, Horton Ormsby had every reason to be scared. Yet when he learned that Balata might have killed Byron, Horton was as cool as the champagne Marian was now pouring.

"Would you like some more?" she asked.

"No thanks," McGuffin lied. He would like nothing more, but there was work to be done. "Have you ever heard the name Bobaloa mentioned by anybody?" he asked, reaching for his glass.

"The voodoo man!" she exclaimed, delighted.

"You know him?"

"Not personally. Someone pointed him out to me one day in the village. He's fascinating."

"Very," McGuffin said. "Who pointed him out to you?"

She shrugged. "I'm not sure who it was. Lyle and I were having a drink at the inn with some of his golfing buddies when he came by. They all seemed to know him."

"Who were you sitting with? Try to remember," McGuffin urged.

"Well, let's see," she said, staring thoughtfully over the rim of her glass. "Byron was there, I remember that. And

Cuppy—he was getting drunk. Which was annoying Horton Ormsby," she added.

"Was Al Balata there?"

"Oh yes, Al was there," she remembered. "I think he was the only one besides Lyle and me who didn't know Bobaloa. Or at least it seems that way."

"What about Churston Brown. Was he there?"

She shook her head slowly. "I don't think so."

"Did Bobaloa acknowledge any of them, or did anybody speak to him—anything like that?"

"They may have nodded or waved or something like that— I really wasn't paying any attention to *them*. The man is gorgeous, you know."

"Yeah, I know." He stole my girlfriend, McGuffin wanted to add, but didn't.

Marian continued to drink champagne while McGuffin asked a few more questions. When he was satisfied that she had told him everything she could remember, he got to his feet.

"Going already?" she asked, pouring the last of the champagne into her glass.

"I'm thinking about it," McGuffin answered, staring hard at her nearly naked body. She dripped champagne on her chest, and McGuffin watched it glide down between her breasts and through the oiled furrow of her abdomen before collecting briefly in her navel, then gliding down and disappearing under the top of her bikini bottom. She was a vulture, McGuffin knew. But dammit, she was good-looking. And available. "What do you say we go to your cabin and fuck our brains out?" McGuffin suggested.

She looked up and smiled. "You don't like me very much, do you?"

"I like you well enough," McGuffin replied. "I just don't have much respect for you."

"You're a prude, Mr. McGuffin. And I don't fuck prudes," she said, getting to her feet.

"I don't usually fuck vultures," McGuffin replied. "But I'll make an exception if you will."

McGuffin rolled with the slap, but it stung. He caught her wrist in one hand and pulled her over to the pool.

"Can you swim?" he asked.

"Yes—no!" she blurted.

"Good," McGuffin said, and threw her into the pool.

"You prick!" she shouted, when she surfaced. "Throw him off! I want him thrown off my boat!"

One of the Santa Monica beachboys appeared on the promenade deck between McGuffin and the ladder, saw his prey, and struck a karate pose.

McGuffin shook his head sadly. "Look, kid, I doubt if this job comes with much of an accident policy, so why don't you just let me pass, and then you can tell your boss whatever you want?"

"That's cool," the sailor replied, standing aside to let McGuffin pass.

McGuffin sat hunched in the stern of the boat, nursing a bruised ego, while the fisherman rowed him to shore. Just think, you're probably the only guy on Palm Isle who propositioned Marian Boone and was turned down, he said to himself. First Liani and now Marian. Face it, McGuffin, you're turning into a dog.

There was another explanation, however, one McGuffin much preferred. Maybe she wouldn't go to bed with me because she's afraid Cuppy would find out. Maybe she doesn't want another death on her hands. Or maybe she's really in love with the guy and finally ready to be faithful. I know, it's not what you'd expect of a vulture, McGuffin argued with himself. But why else would she be staying around here if it isn't to be with Cuppy? Yeah, McGuffin thought, sitting up straight in the stern. He liked this theory much better than the McGuffin-as-dog explanation.

20

McGuffin found Horton Ormsby in the president's office, sitting at his large mahogany desk, beneath a portrait of Bobby Jones. Intent though he was on bonds and homicide, McGuffin couldn't help but notice that Jones had a flying right elbow. It was no doubt a mistake by the painter, McGuffin decided. Or was it the secret of golf? he wondered, remembering vaguely that Jack Nicklaus suffered the same swing "flaw."

"The PGA was Bobby's favorite course," the club president said, in answer to McGuffin's unspoken question. "He modeled the Augusta National after it, you know."

"No, I didn't know that," McGuffin said. "But then that's only one of a few things I didn't know until today."

"Oh? And what else have you learned today, Amos?" Horton Ormsby asked, leaning back in his leather desk chair. He held a long yellow pencil in the air, as if he were about to conduct an orchestra.

"I've learned that Al Balata is holding your club bond as security for a personal loan."

"Where did you hear that—did Al tell you?" Ormsby demanded.

McGuffin shook his head. "It was a guess. And I'd also guess that your loan agreement provides that if you die before paying Al his money, he gets to keep your bond. Am I right?"

Ormsby stared at the detective. "How do you know this?"

"A lawyer friend of mine has some experience with this kind of loan."

"Francis?"

McGuffin nodded. "He had a cash-flow problem. I guess bankers get them too, huh?"

"Some," Ormsby answered. "Forgive me, Amos, but I have to ask—what is your business in all this?"

"Well," McGuffin began, stuffing his hands in his golf slacks, "as you already guessed, I'm sort of a cop, a private investigator. I was hired by Francis Knight to investigate Lyle Boone's death."

"Lyle's death? He died of natural causes, a heart attack. What is there to investigate?" Ormsby asked.

"There's at least a possibility that he was poisoned," McGuffin replied. "And now that we know Byron Kilty was murdered, it's even more likely that Lyle was too."

"And you think it has something to do with the bonds?" Ormsby asked. McGuffin nodded. "And Al Balata is responsible?"

McGuffin nodded again. "It's beginning to look that way. Al admits that he's buying up PIGC bonds, but he claims it's because he wants to preserve the club, not exploit it. He says some of the members are bro—having cash-flow problems, and he's afraid they might be tempted to sell their bonds to an outsider."

"That's preposterous," Ormsby scoffed. "The PIGC boasts some of the oldest and wealthiest families in America."

"That may be," McGuffin allowed. "But when you and Francis had a cash-flow problem, Al was there to help out."

"That's not the same thing at all," Ormsby said, shaking his gray pompadour forcefully. "Those were unusual circumstances."

"I'm sure," McGuffin agreed. "What about Byron? He didn't happen to have a cash-flow problem too, by any chance, did he?"

"Hardly," Ormsby snorted. "Byron was married to an extremely wealthy woman. Difficult but wealthy."

"Then you know her."

"Casually. She was not a golf fan."

"Could you get in touch with her and find out what happens to Byron's bond now that he's dead?"

"Yes, I suppose I could," Ormsby answered slowly. "And if we find that Byron had a loan agreement with Al, such as the one I have with him—what then?"

"Then I'd advise you to get off this island as quickly as possible," McGuffin answered.

"What?" Ormsby exclaimed. "With the club championship coming up?"

"Then you'd better pay off your loan right away," McGuffin replied, somewhat impatiently. Horton Ormsby was either very brave or very foolish.

"There's not much chance of that," Ormsby said, tossing his pencil on the desk. "Unless Al's resort should suddenly start operating."

"Al's resort?" McGuffin repeated.

"That's why I borrowed five million dollars from him. He said I'd triple my money if I invested in this Caribbean island resort he was developing. A lot of the members have invested with him and done very well, so I thought, why not? The only problem was, I didn't have five million dollars."

"So Al loaned it to you, after you agreed that the bond would pass to him if you died before paying off the loan."

"Exactly," the banker said, dropping his head.

Lawyers with cash-flow problems and bankers without money? McGuffin was rapidly losing faith in the system. "Couldn't you have borrowed it from your bank?"

"Hardly," he said, raising his sad eyes to the detective. "I've made some bad loans—that is, the bank has—to some friends of mine, and I've been covering for them. It's cost me a lot of money." When Ormsby dropped his head again, he looked to McGuffin like a bull ready for the sword.

"Why don't you foreclose on the loans?" McGuffin suggested, not unmindful of the irony of a usually broke shamus instructing a banker in matters of finance.

The banker's head snapped up. "I'm talking about friends, some of them going as far back as prep school," he informed the detective. "One doesn't foreclose on friends."

"Yeah, I see what you mean," McGuffin said, nodding slowly. "You made some illegal loans without sufficient collateral to a few of your old prep-school buddies and now you've got to cover your ass with your own money, is that it?"

"Well, I wouldn't put it quite like that," the banker said, squirming in his chair. "But yes, it's something like that."

"How much are they into you—if you don't mind my asking?"

"Over ten million," he replied glumly.

"Wow," McGuffin said softly. "So Al Balata looked like the answer to an overextended banker's prayers. He loans you five million, you invest it in his company, and you get back fifteen million. Only it didn't happen that way. What went wrong, Horton?" McGuffin asked.

"Last month the airline that was supposed to provide service to the island announced that it was pulling out," he answered in a weak voice. "I've got five million dollars invested in a half-finished hotel on an island nobody can get to."

"Bad luck," McGuffin said. "Has Al tried another airline?"

"He says nobody else is interested."

"Did it ever occur to you that Al might be keeping the airline out in order to depress the value of your stock so that you can't sell it and pay off your loan?"

"No, it hasn't," Ormsby said, getting to his feet. "Not that I think he's incapable of it. Al's a tough negotiator, I've seen that. But he's not the kind of man who could dump a bag of poisonous snakes on a fellow Palm man."

"Of course not," McGuffin agreed. "But he could have hired somebody to do the job for him. Do you know a guy named Bobaloa?"

"No," Horton answered.

"That's funny," McGuffin said, laying a hand on the back of his neck. "Because I could have sworn Marian Boone told me you knew him."

"A black fellow—?"

"Yeah, very tall."

"Oh yes, now I know who you mean."

"Forgot you knew him, huh?" McGuffin asked, a faint smile beginning to form at the corners of his mouth.

"Yes, I guess I did."

"I do that all the time myself," McGuffin said, with a now broader smile.

"Well, if you have no more questions, Amos," Ormsby said, leaning across the desk for McGuffin's hand, "I still have some paperwork to finish up."

"Sure, Horton, thanks for your time," McGuffin said, smiling and shaking the club president's hand.

Only when the detective stepped out into the hallway and closed the door after him did the smile disappear. Some people, McGuffin had to admit, in defense of Horton Ormsby, were eminently forgettable. But a Watusi in dreadlocks and hand-painted dashiki? Bobaloa was definitely not the forgettable type.

And if Horton Ormsby hadn't forgotten him, why would he have at first denied knowing him? McGuffin wondered as he walked down the carpeted corridor toward the pro shop. It was something new to think about. But first he had a few questions for the golf pro.

The palm-tree shadows were stretched far across the eighteenth fairway by the time Cuppy and the assistant pro appeared from around the corner of the dogleg. McGuffin, who had been lying on the grass waiting for almost half an hour, got to his feet and strolled down to the green as they hit their second shots. Tommy's shot fell short but hopped up to the frog hairs, while Cuppy's shot hit past the flag stick and backed up to within eight feet of the hole. Golf cheat or no, Cuppy Dunch still had a beautiful swing, McGuffin had to admit. He waited until they had putted out, then called to Cuppy, "Got a minute?"

"Sure," Cuppy said. He instructed Tommy to take the cart back to the pro shop, then ambled across the green to the waiting detective.

"How'd you play?" McGuffin asked.

"Sixty-nine," the pro answered with a shrug.

"Not bad for a guy with a bad back."

"The back's feeling a lot better lately," Cuppy said, twisting comfortably from side to side.

"I'm sure," McGuffin said. "Especially now that Byron Kilty is off it."

Cuppy froze in mid-twist. "I don't understand."

"I know the reason you're no longer playing the tour," McGuffin said.

He stared at the detective for a moment before replying. "Dr. Kilty told you?" McGuffin said nothing. "That lying bastard," the golf pro said softly. "He promised me he'd never say anything as long as I stayed at the PIGC."

"Nobody besides me knows anything about it," McGuffin informed him. "And nobody need know—if you'll answer my questions."

"What questions?" Cuppy asked, raising his putter. He held it across his body with two hands, ready to joust. "You want to know how I did it, something like that?"

McGuffin was shocked. "I'm not interested in cheating," he informed the golf pro, pointing directly at his bandaged chin. "I'm interested in why you lied to me about that."

Cuppy removed one hand from the putter and lightly stroked his chin. "To tell you the truth, I didn't think it was any of your business at the time. But now I'll tell you. Byron hit me. It was no big deal."

"Wasn't it?" McGuffin asked. "Weren't you both in love with Marian Boone? And aren't you still in love with her?"

Cuppy shrugged and scraped his spikes on the green. "I don't know what you mean."

"The truth," McGuffin demanded.

"All right, so I'm in love with her, so what?" the golf pro admitted.

"Did you ask her to marry you?"

"Yeah, I asked her to marry me."

"But she refused."

"Yeah."

"Because she was in love with Byron Kilty?"

"She wasn't in love with Kilty," Cuppy insisted, shaking his putter at McGuffin.

"But nevertheless, with him out of the way your chances are improved, am I right?"

"I hope so," the golf pro said, daring a quick smile.

"And with him out of the way you're free to leave Palm Isle and go to another club."

"Yeah, I guess so," Cuppy replied slowly, as if it were only dawning on him for the first time.

"So if you were to be entirely honest, you'd have to admit that Byron Kilty's murder doesn't fill you entirely with remorse, wouldn't you?"

"Well, you know, I feel bad for—" Cuppy began, then stopped. "What do you mean, murder?"

"Did I say murder?" McGuffin asked.

"That's exactly what you said. What is this—you trying to lay something on me?"

"Not you," McGuffin answered. "Do you know a guy named Bobaloa?"

"No, I don't," the pro answered.

"A snake handler about six and a half feet tall with curly hair and funny shirts?"

"I told you, I don't know him."

"Marian Boone says you do. She says you pointed him out to her one day in the village."

"Oh, yeah, well—maybe I know him to see."

"Then why did you tell me you didn't?"

Cuppy shrugged easily. "People forget."

McGuffin heard his name and turned toward the clubhouse. It was Horton Ormsby. "I know what you mean," McGuffin said, staring at the club president. He was standing in front of the pro shop motioning for McGuffin to join him.

"You got any more questions?" Cuppy asked.

"Not for now," McGuffin answered, starting for the clubhouse.

"You aren't going to tell anybody why I got thrown off the tour, are you?" the golf pro asked, hurrying after McGuffin. When McGuffin stopped, the golf pro bumped into him. "Sorry," he said.

McGuffin turned and studied him, saying nothing. He felt a bit sorry for this hapless professional, once a promising tour player, reduced now to giving lessons to rich old duffers. He was tempted to let him off the hook, but he couldn't. There could be more questions, and if there were, he wanted Cuppy between the rock and the hard place.

"The next time I have some questions, try not to be so forgetful," McGuffin advised.

"I will," Cuppy promised, jamming his fists in his knickerbockers.

McGuffin stared sadly after the pro as he crunched slowly across the clamshell parking lot, head down, shoulders hunched. No good can come from cheating at golf, McGuffin now knew. The few steps involved—from moving the ball in the rough to sexual promiscuity to fisticuffs and then finally to murder—are short ones indeed.

"I just got off the phone with Byron's wife," Ormsby called as McGuffin approached. "And did you know who was there holding her hand through this whole thing?"

"Al Balata?"

"How did you know that?" Horton asked.

"Just a wild guess," McGuffin answered. "Did Byron also have an outstanding loan with him?"

"No," Ormsby said, shaking his head sadly. "But Al got the bond just the same. She told me she signed an option agreement with him just this morning."

"I'm not surprised," McGuffin said.

"Well, I am," Horton grumbled. "Do you realize that man now owns thirty percent of the Palm?"

McGuffin nodded. "And if you and Francis Knight should have an accident, he'll own fifty percent."

"My God," he said, running a big hand through his white hair. "What are we going to do?"

"I told you what I'd do if I were you," McGuffin reminded the president.

"Never!" Horton Ormsby said. "I will not be driven from my golf club by anyone. Not even a murderer."

"You're a man of principle. I like that," McGuffin said.

And so will Al Balata, he added to himself, as he turned and started for his cart.

McGuffin was waiting at the airstrip when Al Balata flew in the next day. Eddie, who had successfully avoided McGuffin for several days, busied himself with the controls and avoided eye contact with the detective as he walked out to the plane.

"How was your trip?" McGuffin called, as the engine coughed its last and Al climbed down from the cockpit.

"Terrific. There's nothing I like better than flying a stiff home to his old lady," he grunted as he pulled his overnight bag from the plane.

"It was a kind and generous act of mercy," McGuffin said.

"Yeah, it was," Al said, starting across the grass to his waiting golf cart.

"I understand you were well rewarded," McGuffin added as he hurried after him.

Halfway to his cart, Al Balata stopped and turned to face the detective. "What's that supposed to mean?"

"You did get Byron's widow to give you an option on her bond, didn't you?"

"So what? I told you in the steam room and I'll tell you again," he said, jabbing a thick forefinger at the detective's chest. "What I'm doing is entirely legit and for the benefit of this club, and I'm getting a little pissed at your insinuation that it's not."

"Hey, Al, relax, I'm not insinuating anything," McGuffin protested, with a look of wide-eyed innocence. "I just came down to welcome you back and see if you'd like to play a little golf later."

"Is that all?"

"That's all."

"I'm sorry," Al said, extending his hand.

McGuffin took it. "That's okay."

"I guess I'm a little tired," Al said, as they continued to his cart beside the Quonset hut.

"Tough negotiations, huh?" Balata's sideways glance warned McGuffin to change the subject. "You know, Stymie said something very interesting to me the other night."

"What was that?" Al said, tossing his bag into the wire basket behind the cart seat.

"You told me you were standing at the back of the crowd when Lyle had his heart attack."

"Yeah?"

"But Stymie seems to think you were standing next to Lyle when he died."

Al sat on the cart and rested his hands on the wheel. "Stymie's an old man. He's got a bad memory."

"It must be something in the water," McGuffin said. "Do you now a guy named Bobaloa?" he asked, when Al reached for the key.

Balata released the key and slowly lifted his head. "What about him?"

He knows him, McGuffin decided. "I understand he sometimes does little jobs for you."

Al Balata nodded slowly. "That's right. Do you want him to do one for you?" he asked, staring curiously at the detective.

"Yeah, I might."

A faint grin broke over Al Balata's face as he studied McGuffin. "I'll be goddamned," he breathed softly. "I knew you weren't the country-club type, but I never dreamed you were into that."

"Oh yeah, I'm very heavily into it," McGuffin said, wondering if he was talking about drugs or murder or both.

"It'll cost you a hundred bucks—whenever you're ready," Al said, reaching again for the key to start the cart.

"A hundred bucks?" McGuffin repeated.

"And worth every penny of it."

"For how much?" McGuffin asked.

Al turned the key, then looked at McGuffin. "You mean how long?"

McGuffin shook his head to clear it. "Let's go back. What is it you never dreamed I was into?"

"Black pussy." Al Balata grinned.

"Bobaloa's a pimp?"

"The best one on the island," Al answered, still grinning.

"What about drugs?"

Al shrugged. "I don't know, I don't use them. But I guess you could ask."

"I don't get it," McGuffin said, stepping in front of the cart to bar Al's departure. "I know Bobaloa's running drugs through here, so why would he want to supply you with whores at a hundred dollars a trick?"

Al evidenced no surprise at learning that his pimp was also a drug smuggler. "A drug smuggler's just like everybody else, I guess. He needs a second job to make ends meet."

"Does he do any other work you know of?" McGuffin asked, placing a hand on the front of the cart.

"Like what?"

"Like murder."

A look of grave concern came over Al Balata as he studied McGuffin. "Take it from me, Amos. Don't do anything stupid."

"Me?" McGuffin exclaimed, jumping aside as Al came ahead on the cart. "Shit," he muttered, as he watched Balata disappear over the top of the hill.

When he turned he saw Eddie grinning at him from the cockpit of his plane. It was the straw that broke the detective's back.

"I want to talk to you, Eddie!" McGuffin shouted, hurrying across the grass in long strides. Eddie looked away, arrogantly, then picked up a black book and busied himself with entries. "And I don't want any excuses. You've been dodging me for too long," McGuffin warned, halting beside the open cabin door.

"Go away, I'm busy," Eddie replied.

That was his first mistake. McGuffin grabbed his leather jacket and snatched him from the plane like a Flying Wallenda. Eddie hit the ground and lay there for a moment, dazed and out of breath.

Trying not to hyperventilate, as he sometimes did when angered, McGuffin spoke in an unusually soft and calm voice. "There is still time for us to reason together."

When Eddie pulled himself up and charged like a wounded lion, that moment passed. Deft as a matador, McGuffin slipped to the side, grabbed two handfuls of leather, and drove the pilot into the side of the plane. The hollow sound of aluminum buckling was followed by Eddie's knees. When McGuffin reached down to pick him up, certain that they could now reason together, Eddie hit him a glancing blow off the side of the head. That was his last mistake.

McGuffin yanked the aviator to his feet and, in violation of his own rule—never hit anyone in the face unless it's absolutely necessary, as it can cause severe damage to the hand—snapped Eddie's head back with a short jab to the nose. Eddie hit the fuselage and went down for the third time, clutching his nose and yowling with pain. When the blood began leaking from behind Eddie's hand, McGuffin had to look away. He hated this kind of interrogation—preferred the intellectual-jousting kind—but the part had been cast; he had to play the heavy.

"My fuckin' node id broke!" Eddie wailed, spraying blood on McGuffin's canary-yellow golf slacks.

"And your fucking teeth are going to be next if you don't answer my questions," McGuffin said, waving his fist threateningly.

"You got no right—" he began. Then, "Okay, okay," he said, when the detective cocked his fist.

"That's good," McGuffin said, opening his fist. True to the rule, his hand was becoming stiff and sore. "There's no reason for you to be scared, Eddie," McGuffin assured him. "Just pretend you're on a television quiz show. As a reward for every right answer, you get nothing."

"Nothin'? What kind of reward is that?" he grumbled, digging in his pocket for a handkerchief.

"It's a blessing in disguise," McGuffin replied. "Because for every wrong answer you get another punch on that broken nose. Too many wrong answers and you're going to leave this show with nothing but a flap of meat and gristle to show for it. You get me, Eddie?"

Eddie struggled to support himself on one elbow, then looked up at his persecutor with the eyes of a trapped animal. When he nodded, blood gushed down his black leather jacket, reminding McGuffin of a gored bull.

"Now for the first question—and think carefully before answering, because your profile depends on it," McGuffin warned. "Who are your accomplices in the drug business?"

"I'm nod in—" Eddie began, until McGuffin raised his fist. "Angelo!" he blurted. "And Bobaloa."

"Who else? Who puts up the money?"

"What money? There's nobody else. Bobaloa pays the man and delivers the goods. The shit you saw on the beach cost us five grand. Me and Angelo come up with the money by ourselves, then I deliver it to a guy works at the airport and he gives us ten. But we're out of the business now, Mr. McGuffin, honest."

"Sure you are," McGuffin said. He believed that as much as he believed Eddie's figures, but he didn't have the heart to punch his already broken nose. "Was Cuppy Dunch involved in your drug business—when you were still running it?" he added.

"What—are you crazy? If Cuppy knew Angelo was back in the business he'd shit."

"Why wouldn't he just fire him?"

"He can't cuz Angelo's got somethin' on him. Don't ask, cuz I don't know—Ang won't say nothin'," he said, taking the handkerchief away from his nose. He winced at the sight of the blood. "Jeez, I'm fuckin' bleedin' to death."

"Just keep talking—you can go to the doctor when I'm finished," McGuffin said. "How did you meet Bobaloa?"

"I don't know, we just ran into him at the inn one night— the Palm Isle Inn. He got us a couple of broads and some smoke, then one thing led to another—you know."

"Yeah, I know," McGuffin said. "Did he ever supply broads to anybody else at the club?"

Eddie pointed in the direction Al had just gone. "He said he did some business with Mr. Balata, but I don't know nothin' about it."

"Whore business?"

"Sure—what else?"

"I'm the quizmaster, you're the contestant," McGuffin reminded him, closing his fist in the aviator's face.

"Sorry."

"Did Bobaloa ever say anything to you about killing anybody?"

"Hey, man, give me a break," Eddie pleaded. "If Bobaloa's into killin' people he never told me anything about it and I don't want to know. And that's the truth, Mr. McGuffin, honest to God."

"You're lying," McGuffin said.

"I'm not lyin'!" he insisted.

"I'm giving you one more chance, then I'm going to work on that nose. Tell me everything you know about Bobaloa's homicidal tendencies."

"I don't know anything about homicide, I swear on my mother's grave!" Eddie said, scooting slowly away from his interrogator. He cried out, but stopped scooting when McGuffin planted a foot on his ankle. "All right, I heard he's a bad dude, but that's all, nothin' specific!"

"Who told you?"

"His girlfriend—Liani Carver, the doctor's daughter. She told me Bobaloa's an avenging angel and he's gonna take the golf club back from the white devils. Those were her words, but that's all I can remember she said, Mr. McGuffin, honest. You're breakin' my leg," he groaned.

Slowly, McGuffin lifted his foot from Eddie's ankle. "You're a big disappointment, Eddie."

"I give you my word, I gave you everything the best way I know," Eddie assured the detective. He was rubbing his ankle with one hand while holding the handkerchief to his nose with the other. "Just don't hit my nose again, I'll tell you everything you want to know, no bullshit."

McGuffin looked at him. It wasn't much, but it was probably as much of the truth as he would get from Eddie the Aviator.

"Go on, get the hell out of here," McGuffin ordered.

"Thanks," Eddie said, scrambling to his feet.

"And if you tell anybody what happened to your nose, I'll turn you over to the narcs!" McGuffin shouted as Eddie hurried to his cart.

Eddie hollered something through his bloody handkerchief that McGuffin couldn't make out. It didn't matter. He was going to turn him in to the narcs anyway— just for not knowing anything.

When McGuffin called from his cottage later that night, Francis Knight, like the club president, was at first unable to believe that Byron Kilty's death was anything other than a tragic accident. Even after McGuffin described what he and Horton Ormsby had seen at the scene of the crime, the lawyer was still unwilling to accept the fact that Kilty had been murdered in so bizarre a fashion. It was only when he learned that Al Balata now held the option on Byron's bond that Francis Knight became a believer.

"The unmitigated gall of the man!" the lawyer exploded. "What do the police say?"

"Horton Ormsby doesn't want the police involved."

"What?"

"He says it'll make the club look bad," McGuffin said, pacing about his bedroom, phone in hand.

"Yes, I see his point," Knight said.

"I'm not sure I do," McGuffin said. "Did you know that Al Balata is also holding Ormsby's bond as security for a loan?"

"My God!" the lawyer exclaimed. "Does Horton know that he may be in grave danger?"

"He knows but it doesn't seem to bother him. He says he won't leave until after the club championship matches have been played."

"The man is a fool."

"Maybe," McGuffin said. "Or maybe Ormsby has nothing to fear from Al Balata."

"What do you mean?"

"Did you know that Ormsby and Balata are partners in a resort development project?"

"No," the lawyer answered uncertainly. "What about it?"

"Maybe Palm Isle is their next project together."

"Impossible," he snapped. "I've known Horton too long—he's a Palm man through and through."

"There are none finer," McGuffin agreed. "But Horton's bank is in serious financial trouble and he may be facing criminal charges. I know it's hard to believe, but under that kind of pressure some men might put self-interest ahead of even their golf club."

"Perhaps," the lawyer admitted. "But you'll never convince me that Horton Ormsby would condone murder, if that's what you're saying."

"I wouldn't have thought he was capable of murder either," McGuffin said. "Until he denied knowing Bobaloa."

"Bobaloa?" the lawyer questioned. "Who is Bobaloa?"

"He's some kind of religious cult figure on this island," McGuffin explained. "He practices voodoo with snakes and things and he tells his followers that he's going to take the club back from the white devils—that's you. Horton denied knowing him at first, then admitted to it later after I told him I knew otherwise. Al Balata at least admitted knowing him, even if for reasons other than murder," McGuffin added, pacing quickly now in a tight circle at the foot of the bed.

"And you think Horton and Al enlisted him to kill Byron?" the lawyer asked.

"It's possible," McGuffin said.

"It may be possible," the lawyer admitted, "but it's hardly logical. At least not from the point of view of this religious fanatic, this Bobaloo or whatever his name is. I mean, why should he help Horton and Al take control of the club if he wants it for himself?"

McGuffin halted at the window and stared out at the dark void. There was scarcely a single star visible in the cloudy sky. "Bobaloa doesn't know why they wanted Byron killed. He just knew they were willing to pay for it, and that was enough for him."

"What makes you so sure this Bobaloa isn't acting on his own account?" Francis Knight asked. "Why couldn't he have simply murdered Byron in order to frighten the members away from the island?"

"That's possible," McGuffin agreed, as a bright star appeared through a hole in the clouds. "But it doesn't explain why Horton denied knowing him."

"There is some logic to it, I'll have to admit," the lawyer said, speaking slowly. "But I just can't find it in me to admit that Horton Ormsby could have any part in the death of a fellow Palm man."

"Why not?" McGuffin asked. "You're perfectly willing to believe it of Al Balata."

"That's entirely different. The Ormsbys are an old and respected family," he snapped. "You don't intend to share your suspicions with anyone else, do you, Mr. McGuffin?"

McGuffin lifted his eyes helplessly to the dark sky. "I'll be discreet," he promised.

"I'm sure you will. I mean, even if it should turn out that Horton *is* the murderer, calling him that in the meantime doesn't really accomplish anything, does it?"

McGuffin shook his head slowly. "I'll try to find another word for it."

"Thank you. And good luck," the attorney added, before hanging up.

McGuffin dropped the receiver to his side and continued to stare at the cloudy sky. There was a soft rumble of thunder from far off, and McGuffin remembered that he hadn't seen rain since arriving on Palm Isle.

23

The rain came at dawn on a howling wind from the southeast, twisting and blowing the bedroom curtains like a kite's tail. McGuffin got out of bed and closed the window, then stood and watched the roiling sea and tossing palm trees for several minutes before returning to his warm dry bed. It seemed that he had just gone back to sleep when he was awakened a second time by a sudden terrified scream. McGuffin leaped from the bed, grabbed the gun from his suitcase, and rushed for the front door. When he burst through the front door, gun at the ready, he was confronted by Iris, his maid, pointing and shrieking uncontrollably at him. It was only then that McGuffin realized he was naked.

"What's wrong?" McGuffin shouted, clapping a gun and hand over his genitals. Iris continued to point and screamed louder. "Wait, I'll get some clothes on!" McGuffin said, turning to the door.

It was then that he saw the reason for her terror. Hanging from the blood-smeared door by a frayed rope was a horribly mutilated goat.

"Jesus!" McGuffin exclaimed, jumping away from the swinging animal. "What the hell is this?"

"Ouanga!" Iris cried. "Ouanga!" Then she turned and ran for her cart.

"Iris, wait!" McGuffin called, as she spit gravel and raced off in the direction of the clubhouse.

McGuffin turned and studied the goat. Its tongue was sticking out at him, and there was just a patch of crusted blood where its genitals should have been.

"Ouanga?" he repeated uncertainly. "What the fuck is ouanga?"

"An ouanga is a voodoo curse," Churston Brown said, peering closely at the carcass through round spectacles, perched low on his nose. "And this is a most impressive one indeed. Most victims of a voodoo curse rate nothing more than a chicken. But a goat . . ." he said, pushing his glasses up on his nose and regarding the detective with an obviously admiring look. "This is a very serious threat, Amos."

"How serious?" McGuffin asked. He was standing on the edge of the porch, as far away from the dead goat as he could decently get, while Churston performed his examination.

"Death. Or something worse," he added, as he turned his attention to the goat. He grabbed the upper and lower jaws and pulled them apart while the detective stared.

"What the hell are you doing?" McGuffin demanded, when Churston stuck his hand into the goat's open mouth.

"Looking for the ouanga," he grunted, as he pulled what appeared to be a leather pouch from the goat's throat.

"What's that? What have you got there?" McGuffin asked, bouncing nervously on the balls of his feet.

"The goat's scrotum," Churston answered.

"Jesus, put it back," McGuffin said, turning away. "You want me to be sick?"

"It's all right, the testicles have been removed," Churston said, as he stuck his fingers into the scrotum and came out with a wad of tightly folded brown paper. "And replaced by this," he added, holding the paper up for McGuffin's inspection.

"What's that?"

"The ouanga," he answered, unfolding the paper.

McGuffin edged closer for a look at the postcard-size piece of torn wrapping paper. There were several lines of uneven block letters scrawled on both sides. "It's in French," McGuffin, who had endured four years of the language with the Jesuits, recognized.

"The language of voodoo," Churston said, peering at the message.

"Do you speak it?"

"*Un peu,*" Churston answered, angling the paper at the little available light. The rain had briefly stopped, but the dark clouds remained, threatening to disgorge themselves again at any moment. "But I'm afraid I can't make much out of this."

"Let me see it," McGuffin said, reaching for the paper. They put their heads together, and McGuffin read the first line.

"*Par la force de la chèvre sanglante l'ouanga soit sur toi.*"

"*Formidable!*" Churston exclaimed.

"By the power of the goat," McGuffin translated, then stopped. "I don't know the next word."

Churston leaned in close. "Something about blood, I think. "The ouanga be on you?"

"By the power of the bloody goat may the ouanga be upon you," McGuffin corrected.

Then he went to the next line. What McGuffin lacked, Churston was able to supply, until gradually the ouanga took shape. After stumbling through it line by line, McGuffin was ready to read the note in its entirety.

By the power of the bloody goat may the ouanga be upon you. May you have no peace until you have left this island. And if you do not, may you rot slowly from within and lie helpless on the sand while birds of prey pluck out your eyes and vipers nest in your skull.

"What a beautiful ouanga!" Churston marveled. "Do you have any idea who sent it?"

"I've got a very good idea who sent it," McGuffin said, folding the paper carefully. "It was your friend Bobaloa."

"Bobaloa?" Churston repeated dubiously. "Of course!" he exclaimed, suddenly remembering. "You dated his girlfriend!"

McGuffin shook his head. "That was arranged by Bobaloa. He wants me off the island because I know Byron Kilty was murdered and he's afraid I might find out who did it."

"Murdered?" Churston questioned. "He was bitten by coral snakes—just like his grandfather."

"So it was made to appear," McGuffin replied absently. "Tell me, Churston, in your study of voodoo have you ever heard of snakes being used as murder weapons?"

"I don't believe so," he answered, regarding McGuffin strangely.

"Too bad," McGuffin said, looking out to sea. A sudden column of gold had broken through the low clouds, casting a circle of light on the churning waves. It reminded him of a ballet, each frothy wave a tutu'd dancer. "I don't suppose you'd know how one gets to be a voodoo doctor, would you?" he asked, turning back to the bespectacled anthropologist.

"It's usually passed down from father to son," Churston answered.

"Then the voodoo doctor that Byron's grandfather killed could have been Bobaloa's grandfather?"

"I hadn't thought of it, but I suppose it's possible," Churston answered, nodding slowly. "Are you suggesting that Bobaloa murdered Byron to avenge his grandfather?"

"I'm giving it some thought," McGuffin answered, staring back out to sea. The shaft of sunlight had disappeared as quickly as it had come, and now rain was falling. It appeared as a slate-gray mist pressed between a jade-green sea and a bruised-plum sky. It was both beautiful and ominous. "Could I borrow your jeep?" he asked, turning again to Churston.

"It has no roof—you'll get soaked," Churston warned.

"It can't be helped," McGuffin said. "Where does Bobaloa live?"

"At the temple. But you're not going there," Churston said, a note of alarm in his voice.

"Why shouldn't I?"

"I don't think you appreciate the seriousness of an ouanga," Churston said, eyes widening behind his wire frames. "If Bobaloa did write this ouanga, he could be very dangerous to you."

"Come on," McGuffin scoffed. "You don't really believe that voodoo shit, do you?"

"It doesn't matter whether I believe it or you believe it," Churston said, pointing from one to the other. "What matters is the fact that Bobaloa believes it. And if you defy him, he'll lose face. And if you cause him to lose face, there's no telling what he might do."

"So what do you suggest I do?" McGuffin asked. "Pack my bags and leave the island?"

"That's the safest thing," Churston answered. "But if you stay, there are certain procedures to be followed in the case of an ouanga. You have to concoct a protective ouanga that will be even more powerful than the death ouanga."

"I've already taken care of that," McGuffin said, patting the gun in his pants pocket. "Now are you going to let me use your jeep, or am I going to have to walk?"

Churston looked at the detective and shook his head sadly. "The keys are in it," he said, stepping aside for McGuffin to pass.

"Thanks," McGuffin said, stepping off the porch and hurrying to the jeep.

24

McGuffin made it to the village ahead of the rain, but when he turned the jeep onto King's Road, the sky broke and the rain fell in thick silvery sheets. He skidded to a stop in front of the voodoo temple and dashed through the puddles to the front door. He pulled the door open and walked into the dark, empty hall. The windows were shuttered against the rain, but McGuffin could hear it rattling on the roof. The only light in the place came from the open door.

"Bobaloa!" McGuffin called from the center of the room. "I want to talk to you!"

He heard a noise, either from the wind or from someone behind the door at the back of the temple, and started in that direction. He was about to call out again when the front door slammed shut behind him, leaving him in total darkness. McGuffin stopped and called again, "Bobaloa? Are you there?"

Hearing the same strange noise again, he continued slowly in the direction of the rear door beside the altar. Feeling a bit foolish, McGuffin nevertheless pulled the automatic from his wet golf slacks as he inched toward the door in the inky blackness. His blind course was true; he found the door and the handle, but found it to be locked from the outside. Then he heard the strange noise again—from behind him this time. It sounded like a human step, followed by a sliding sound, as if a man were approaching, dragging a wooden leg, or a—

"Damballa," McGuffin whispered.

He froze and listened as the giant serpent plopped and slid its way across the wooden floor. He quickly decided against shooting the snake in the dark—his chances were little better than hitting a one iron—and decided on a headlong rush in the approximate direction of the front door.

He was, he guessed, almost halfway across the room when his feet got tangled in something soft and he began to fall. He braced himself instinctively and heard his Smith & Wesson clattering across the floor as he scrambled quickly to his feet. Forgetting the gun, he lunged through the dark until he slammed against the door and spilled outside into the mud.

Cursing, McGuffin got to his feet as Liani Carver's tiny English Ford slid to a stop beside the jeep. Bobaloa, dressed in a yellow slicker, jumped out of the passenger side and hurried toward him. McGuffin could see Liani Carver, alternately clear then blurred with each sweep of the windshield wiper, behind the wheel.

"What you doin' here, mon? Don' you know you is trespassin'?" Bobaloa shouted as he advanced on the detective.

"Nobody invited you to hang a dead goat on my door either!" McGuffin shouted back.

"I don't know what yo' talkin' about! Yo' a crazy mon and I want you off my property!" he ordered. He stopped within a few feet of the detective, but within striking distance.

"Do you deny writing this ouanga?" McGuffin demanded, pulling the note from his wet pocket with some difficulty.

"Dot's bullshit," he said, pushing the note aside without a glance. "I want you out of here or dere is goin' to be trouble. You unnerstan me, mon?"

"I'm not going anywhere until you answer my questions," McGuffin said, returning the note to his pocket. "And if you don't I'm going to the police about the drug scam you and Angelo and Eddie are running."

"We not runnin' no drugs, mon, dot's bullshit."

"Then what was in those packages I saw you unloading on the beach the other night—fish?"

"Ganja, mon. Ganja's no drug, ganja is a sacrament."

"That's bullshit," McGuffin said. "There wasn't enough

marijuana in those packages to pay for your motorboat oil. You were hauling a fortune in cocaine."

"No shit, mon?" Bobaloa asked, wide-eyed. "Dey don' tell me nuttin' like dot. Dey say pick up de ganja and dey split wit' me. But dey get a million dollahs and I get nuttin' but a bag of ganja? Dot's shit, mon."

"Please," McGuffin said, waving his hands impatiently in the rain, "don't try to con me with that ganja bullshit. I know you're running coke through this island, but I don't care. I'm not a narc. Just give me some straight answers and I won't blow the whistle on you."

Bobaloa laughed. "Mon, who you tink you're talkin' to? Angelo and Eddie? You tink I don' know you goin' straight to de cops soon as you get off dis island? *If* you get off dis island," he added.

"If I'm not getting off the island you might just as well answer my questions," McGuffin replied with a shrug. "What have you got to lose?"

"Time, mon, dot's all." He glanced at Liani, then back at McGuffin. "Okay, what you want to know?"

"I want you to tell me what you know about Al Balata."

Bobaloa grinned. "He lok de girls, mon."

"You mean you pimp for him."

"Not professionally."

"What's your professional relationship? Is he involved in the cocaine smuggling?"

"I tot you wasn't interested in no cocaine."

"I'm not, I'm interested in murder," McGuffin replied.

"Mon, I sure don' know nuttin 'bout dot."

"Do you know Horton Ormsby?"

Bobaloa hesitated, then replied, "I don' know de mon."

"You're lying," McGuffin charged.

"Hey, I don' take dot shit," Bobaloa warned, taking a step toward the detective.

McGuffin held his ground. "He hired you to dump a bag of coral snakes on Dr. Kilty."

"You're full of shit!" Bobaloa replied. "Why should I do sumpin' crazy lak dot, mon?"

"For money," McGuffin answered.

"Hey, I tot I was a coke dealer. You tink a rich coke dealer gonna fuck around droppin' snakes on somebody? Shit, mon—"

"You're right, money's not the motive," McGuffin agreed. "What about vengeance?"

"Vengeance?" Bobaloa asked, interested.

"You killed Byron Kilty because his grandfather killed your grandfather," McGuffin charged.

Bobaloa's surprised expression told McGuffin that he was at least partly correct. "How do you know dot?" he asked.

"It was a guess."

"It was a lucky guess," Bobaloa said softly. "But dot don' mean I killed de doctah. Dot was a long time ago, mon. I never even knew my grandfather."

"But you want the same thing he wanted—to drive the whites from this island and reclaim the golf club. And killing a few of the members might be just the way to do it."

"We got every right to dot property!" Bobaloa shouted. "But dot don' mean wo got to kill nobody to get it. When Damballa is ready, he will give us back our land."

"Save it for your church group," McGuffin said. "I know as well as you and Liani that Damballa is nothing but a cheap fucking circus trick."

Enraged by this blasphemy, Bobaloa lunged for McGuffin's throat. McGuffin fell away from his attacker, probably avoiding a broken neck, but he was unable to completely evade the grasp of the long-limbed man. He felt himself being twisted and shaken, followed by a dizzying flight that ended with an ignominious and breathless whump in the mud. He felt himself being dragged over the wet grass and through puddles, and it seemed he caught a glimpse of Liani's laughing face behind the sweeping windshield wiper, but he couldn't be sure. He was only fully aware of what had happened when he found himself lying on the ground beside the jeep. A moment later, Liani jumped out of her car and ran into the voodoo temple with Bobaloa.

With a painful groan, McGuffin hauled himself to his feet.

Satisfied that nothing was broken, he pulled a wet handkerchief from his back pocket and began wiping the mud from his
once-white golf slacks. After only a couple of swipes, he threw
the useless muddy rag to the ground and climbed into the
jeep. It wasn't until he was more than halfway back to the club
that he remembered his gun. Why didn't Humphrey Bogart
ever have days like this? he asked himself.

The Vandal Scramble, played each year on the Sunday prior to the commencement of the PIGC championship matches, was a drunken full-handicap tournament, played in commemoration of the sack of Rome in 455 A.D. The origins of this tournament were murky, but the rules by which it was played were clear. Contestants gathered in the main bar at eight in the morning for Bloody Marys, then went in their designated foursomes to their assigned tees at noon and began play. However, unlike other scrambles, the players did not thereafter play each hole in numerical sequence.

"It works like this," Churston said, opening McGuffin's scorecard on the bar and pressing it flat. On the map of the golf course, a series of apparently random lines had been drawn across fairways, creeks, ponds, and tropical forest. "You start on the thirteenth tee with Mr. Kirkaldy, Revell, and Berwick, and you play to the first green. Then from there—"

"Wait a minute," McGuffin interrupted, speaking loudly to be heard over the drunken din in the bar. "That's all the way across the golf course."

"That's the idea," Churston said. "And the idea is also to get drunk. Don't think I haven't noticed that you aren't drinking," Churston said, pushing McGuffin's untouched drink across the bar to him. Although Churston was somewhat drunk, he was a model of sobriety beside most of the others. "Then," Churston said, tracing a second line with his finger, "you play from the first tee to the seventeenth hole, and so on and so on and so on, until you've played eighteen holes—which nobody ever does, because we've got more bars set up out on the course, just in case you don't get drunk enough in the clubhouse before you start."

"Sounds like fun," McGuffin said flatly, as he took his score-card from Churston and put it back in his pocket. Being the only one sober at the party was both a boring and unusual experience for the detective.

"It's insane," Churston said. "There'll be a hundred golfers out there hitting balls in all directions at once, cutting across fairways, wading creeks, cutting through the snake-infested forest—"

"And dangerous," McGuffin added.

Churston nodded as he drank, spilling tomato juice out of the corner of his mouth. "Golf is a blood sport," he said, as he replaced his glass on the bar. "Stymie, I'll have another!" he called. But it didn't look as if he would get it. Stymie and three temporary bartenders had more than they could handle. "Did I ever tell you my theory of golf?" Churston asked.

"No, but I'll bet you're going to;" McGuffin said, turning away from the bar to survey the crowd. Horton Ormsby, honorary marshal of the Vandal Scramble, was wearing an antique police helmet. Many of the players were wearing funny caps, including Al Balata, who was wearing a knitted tam with a large pink pompon on top. Al was looser than McGuffin had ever seen him, in fact quite drunk, probably because he now owned thirty percent of the club. And if the gentleman in the police helmet—who could not leave the island because of the upcoming club championship—should happen to be struck by a golf ball and killed in this afternoon's madness, he would then own forty percent of the club.

"That's why golf appeals to men like my father," Churston was saying. "Bankers, businessmen, lawyers . . . these are society's hunters. Golf is a metaphor for hunting, you know."

"No, I didn't know that," McGuffin answered. Someone was playing "It's a Long Way to Tipperary" on the piano while a chorus of drunks kept singing the first two lines over and over again.

"Men like my father hunt for money just as the caveman hunted for meat. But they're no longer able to form a hunting party and roam the countryside with clubs and spears. So instead they gather in a foursome on the first tee, clubs slung over their shoulder like arrows in a quiver, and set off in pursuit of their quarry, scores with such telling names as birdie and eagle. Don't you find that significant?" he asked McGuffin.

McGuffin smiled. "You don't think it could just be a game—like tennis?"

Churston shook his head. "Even the choice of verbs gives it away. One goes golfing, just as one goes hunting. But one plays tennis, he does not go tennising."

"But today most people say 'play golf,' don't they?" McGuffin argued.

"A mere euphemistic concession by the more civilized practitioners of the game," Churston said, slurring some of the words. "But the game still redounds with plenty of bloody expressions. What other game, for instance, is played with clubs? Mr. Doubleday had the good taste to call them bats when he invented baseball, even though a baseball bat looks a lot more like a club than a mashie niblick does. And why will four men shoot a round of golf together, while relegating their wives to a separate foursome?"

"Because they don't hit the ball as far as men?"

Again Churston shook his head. "Because men hunted while the women remained behind to care for the children. It's in the genes, Amos. Golf is a deadly sport played by killers."

"There may be something to that after all," McGuffin said, thinking of Lyle Boone and Byron Kilty.

Horton Ormsby was standing atop a chair, calling for order. It took some time for the word to get through to all the drunken Vandals. The Tipperary chorus was the last to get the message.

"Gentlemen—gentlemen!" the club president and honorary marshal called. "Is anyone still sober?" He was answered by a resounding no. "Then let the Vandal Scramble begin!" he cried.

True to their name, they lunged in a single drunken mass for the exit. Chanting "Rape, pillage, and burn," they plunged down the stairs and out into the cruel sun, leaving McGuffin alone at the bar. He stared at his untouched Bloody Mary for a moment, then turned and followed the last Vandal down the stairs and through the pro shop.

He became aware that the crowd had suddenly quieted down, and when he stepped outside he saw the reason for it. Bobaloa, resplendent in a gold dashiki with red lettering and symbols, stood a few yards from McGuffin, staring directly at him.

"Mistah McGuffin," he said, walking toward the detective. He stopped within arm's reach and stuck his hand under his dashiki, coming out with McGuffin's nine-millimeter automatic, which he pointed directly at McGuffin's heart. "I tink dis belongs to you."

"You know very well it does," McGuffin said, reaching slowly for the barrel. The voodoo doctor had embarrassed him on his own turf, but it wouldn't happen here, McGuffin vowed. If he was going out, he would go like Bogart.

No one breathed when McGuffin wound his fingers around the barrel of the gun. When Bobaloa released his grip and the gun came away in McGuffin's hand, there was a collective, audible sigh from the assembled golfers.

"Guns can be dangerous, Mistah McGuffin. You must try not to lose it again," Bobaloa said, followed by a deep, hollow laugh.

McGuffin said nothing as Bobaloa turned and walked away, sandals crunching on the clamshell. When he was almost to the grass, McGuffin called, "Bobaloa!"

Bobaloa stepped onto the grass, stopped, and turned slowly to the detective. "Yes?"

"Par la force de la chèvre sanglante, l'ouanga soit sur toi," McGuffin said hesitantly. The first line of the ouanga was all he could remember.

Bobaloa stared curiously at the detective for a moment, then turned and continued walking.

"What the hell was that all about?" Horton Ormsby asked,

edging through the crowd to McGuffin. "What did you say to him?"

"I said, 'By the power of the bloody goat, may the ouanga be upon you,'" McGuffin answered, before starting to his golf cart.

Ormsby too stared after McGuffin for a moment, then shook his head and started for his own cart.

A couple of hours later McGuffin was hunched wearily over the wheel of his cart at the peak of a hill near the center of the golf course, observing the maelstrom below. Golf carts, those that hadn't been abandoned in bunker, creek, or forest by their drunken drivers, crisscrossed the fairways as randomly as microbes on a slide, while golf balls whistled past from all directions. Some of the Vandals wandered aimlessly about the course in search of their comrades, while others lay passed out along the way. When Sandy Berwick, McGuffin's former cart companion, passed out after several holes, Kirkaldy and Revell laid him out beside the flagstick on the fourth green, confident that no ball would find him there.

As is bound to happen in any campaign, there were a few desertions, men who had decided to remain at one of the temporary bars where the whiskey or the barmaid was particularly to their liking. Others had forsaken golf entirely and had doffed their costumes for a swim in the ocean with a group of giggling maids, while still others had made their way back to the bivouac to fall in bed with their spikes on. Soberly, McGuffin shook his head. It was not a pretty sight.

McGuffin was waiting for Kirkaldy and Revell to emerge from the woods below, where they had gone in search of their balls some several minutes before. They had either passed out or stumbled into a nest of coral snakes, and in neither case was McGuffin going in after them. After having been twice nearly struck by a golf ball, his own was safely in his pocket. He was about to sneak back to his cottage when he saw Horton Ormsby in the fairway below, driving straight for him while waving frantically. McGuffin waved back and started down the hill in the direction of the club president.

"What's wrong?" McGuffin called, as the two carts came to a halt side by side, like highway patrol cars.

"Al Balata's been killed," Horton answered.

The body of Al Balata lay face up beside the pond on the thirteenth hole. Blood still oozed from a dimpled, concave wound over the right temple.

"It looks like he was hit with a ball," McGuffin said, looking up from one knee at the stunned, drunken Vandals gathered about the body. "Did anyone see it?" No one answered. "Who was playing with him?" the detective asked.

"I was," a pale, frightened man admitted. "But I didn't see anything. Collins and Whitley were with us for a while, but they passed out a few holes back."

"Where were you standing when he was hit?" McGuffin asked.

"Over there," he said, pointing to the trees beyond the pond. "I couldn't see through the trees. I was waiting for Al to hit his shot, and when he didn't return I went looking for him."

"How long did you wait behind the trees?" McGuffin asked.

"I'm not sure—maybe fifteen minutes. I'm afraid I dozed off," he admitted sheepishly. "I'm afraid I had rather a lot to drink, for me."

"Yeah," McGuffin said, appraising the bleary-eyed Vandals. It was scarcely a likely group of dependable witnesses. He climbed to his feet and looked around the ground. "Where's the ball that hit him?"

"We found this near the edge of the pond," Churston Brown said, lurching through the crowd, a clean white golf ball resting between his thumb and forefinger.

McGuffin took the ball and looked closely at it. "This isn't the ball that killed Al," he said.

"Why do you say that?" Horton Ormsby asked. "A few people have handled it—the blood could have been rubbed off."

"The ball that hit Al caved in his skull. It wasn't a glancing blow," McGuffin said, surveying the thirty or forty yards between the body and the pond. "It couldn't have traveled more than a few yards from the body. And this is a one hundred compression ball," he added, holding it up for Horton's inspection. "Al was probably the only player at this club strong enough to hit so resilient a ball. This is the ball Al was about to hit when he was killed."

Horton stared dubiously at the ball and shook his head. "Then what happened to the ball that hit him?"

"Somebody must have picked it up," McGuffin said. "He probably threw it in the pond."

"Don't be ridiculous," Ormsby scoffed. "Nobody had any reason to conceal the ball if Al's death was an accident."

"I know," McGuffin said.

"And if you're implying that Al was deliberately killed, that's even more ridiculous," he fumed. "I mean, do you seriously think there's any golfer in the world skillful enough to deliberately hit a man in the head with a golf ball?"

"Maybe not." McGuffin, who had some trouble hitting a target as large as a green from anywhere beyond one hundred yards, had to agree. A golf ball was a most unusual murder weapon. But then so too were coral snakes and puffer-fish toxin. "Let's call the coroner," he said.

It was a haggard group of mourners who watched from the edge of the airstrip as Al Balata's body was lifted up into the sunset and borne away from the golf club he had so dearly loved—and had very nearly owned. Club president Ormsby watched with what seemed to McGuffin a faint smile as the plane disappeared into the dusk. Then, famished after the long ordeal, the members repaired to the dining room for a funereal dinner. Al Balata, McGuffin sensed, would soon be a dim memory, just as Lyle Boone and Byron Kilty were already. But it had been a Vandal Scramble that would long be remembered.

The red message light on the phone was glowing when McGuffin got back to his cottage. He would have preferred to wait until morning before talking to his client, but he knew the damned thing would keep him awake, so he sat on the edge of his bed and picked up the receiver.

"This is Mr. McGuffin," he informed the receptionist. "You have a message for me?"

"Yas sah," she answered. McGuffin could hear the papers rustling. "Here it is, it's from Angelo, sah."

"The caddiemaster?"

"Yas sah. He says, 'I got info'mation about da golf club.'"

"Information about the . . . Is that all?" McGuffin asked.

"Yas sah, dat's all."

"Okay, hold it for me, will you?" McGuffin asked. "I'll pick it up in the morning."

"It will be here, sah," she promised, then rang off.

McGuffin replaced the receiver and yawned loudly. It had been a long day. He would talk to Angelo in the morning.

26

But McGuffin didn't get the chance to talk to Angelo the next morning. Nor did anyone else. His body was discovered by the greenskeeper early the next day, floating naked in the pond near the spot where Al Balata had been struck and killed by a golf ball only the day before. Horton Ormsby paced nervously while Dr. Carver knelt at the edge of the pond to examine the body. McGuffin stood over him, hands on his knees, watching as he studied the open eyes of the dead caddiemaster.

"I suspect the autopsy will show that Mr. Caudie was quite intoxicated when he drowned," the coroner said, looking up at McGuffin.

"What—what did he say?" Ormsby demanded.

"He thinks Angelo was drunk," McGuffin answered.

"Thank God," Ormsby said, followed by a sigh of gratitude. "I figured it was something like that. Didn't you, Amos?" McGuffin said nothing. He was staring intently at the body. "Yes, well—if you don't have anything more for me I'd like to run up to the clubhouse and get a little breakfast. God knows I could use a Bloody Mary."

"I'll tell the constable where he can find you," the coroner said.

"Thank you," the club president said, turning and hurrying to his cart.

Dr. Carver got to his feet and stared after the departing president. "I'm afraid Mr. Ormsby has little stomach for this accident."

"This was no accident," McGuffin replied.

Dr. Carver looked at him and smiled. "And what makes you think not?"

McGuffin pointed to Angelo's clothes, a pair of jeans and a Hawaiian shirt, neatly folded and resting atop his sneakers. "Take my word for it, drunks aren't that careful with their clothes."

"Perhaps Mr. Caudie was the exception," Dr. Carver replied easily.

"Maybe," McGuffin allowed. "But that doesn't explain why Angelo would want to swim in this mudhole when the ocean is only several hundred yards away."

"Drunks do not always behave rationally," the doctor replied.

"Tell me about it," McGuffin remarked absently. There was a more sober explanation, he realized. Angelo could have been diving for the ball that killed Al Balata, no doubt with blackmail in mind. It wasn't unusual for a player to mark his ball for identification before beginning a match, and some players even had their name or initials inscribed on their balls.

McGuffin was also thinking about the note from Angelo that he had picked up from the receptionist only an hour earlier: "I got information about the golf club." Could the message mean that Angelo knew who was responsible for Al Balata's death? And if so, was Al's killer then forced to kill Angelo before he could reveal his identity? It was possible, McGuffin decided.

There was also the matter of the golf pro, Cuppy Dunch. With Byron Kilty out of the way, Angelo was the last remaining source of embarrassment to the former touring pro. It would be relatively easy for Cuppy to get his caddiemaster drunk, then take him to the pond and drown him.

"Is this the extent of your evidence?" Dr. Carver asked, interrupting the detective's thoughts. "The neat pile of clothes and the place where the deceased chose to swim?"

"No, there's more," McGuffin said. "And I'm afraid you know what it is, just as well as I do."

"Indeed," the doctor replied. "And what is that?"

"This," McGuffin said, going down on one knee beside the body.

"And what is this?" the coroner asked, peering over McGuffin's shoulder.

"It's a bruise," McGuffin answered, placing his hand over the victim's shoulder. "At approximately the place a large man would have located his thumb if he was pushing Angelo's head under water." McGuffin looked up. The old man was looking at the bruise with a curiously detached expression. "You saw it before," McGuffin said, getting to his feet. "You knew that bruise was there but you weren't going to say anything."

"I must have missed it," the coroner said.

"You're lying," McGuffin said. "Why are you lying? Is it because you know your prospective son-in-law killed Angelo?"

"I'm afraid you're jumping to a desired conclusion, Mr. McGuffin," the doctor replied. "That bruise could have been caused by any of a hundred things."

"Bullshit!" McGuffin said. "That's an almost perfect thumb-print, and you know it. Why are you trying to protect Bobaloa?"

"Because I have decided that he requires protection from you, Mr. McGuffin," Dr. Carver replied stiffly. "You fancy yourself a fair man, but believe me, your suspicions are the product of a racial prejudice of which you yourself are not entirely aware."

"Aw, come on," McGuffin pleaded.

"I should tell you, Mr. McGuffin, I'm aware of the competition between you and Bobaloa over my daughter. And the result," he added.

Surprised, McGuffin replied, "That's got nothing to do with it," with little force.

"Perhaps," the old man said, gesturing helplessly with up-turned hands. "But if I cannot judge Bobaloa objectively be-cause of his relationship with my daughter—as you seem to imply—how can *you* expect to be objective, Mr. McGuffin?"

"I can afford to be objective because I have nothing to lose," McGuffin answered. "But you do. You'd like me to believe that Bobaloa is an ineffectual revolutionary with little support other than your daughter. But you were a young boy when the whites took away your land. They might even have thrown you and your family out of your own house. Why are you so goddam forgiving when your daughter and her boyfriend are mad enough to kill? I think you've been trying to con me, Doctor. But worse than that, you've been trying to get rid of me. That's why you wrote the ouanga and had Bobaloa deliver it to me. I was getting onto your revolutionary plans, so you decided to scare me off the island with a little voodoo black magic."

"Mr. McGuffin, I am truly amazed," the old man said with a trace of amusement. "Even if I were some sort of Mau Mau revolutionary, intent on terrorizing the whites from their golf club by killing a number of them, how would I, a British-educated physician, expect to frighten an obviously educated man such as yourself with a bit of primitive mumbo jumbo?"

"It wasn't exactly mumbo jumbo," McGuffin corrected. "The ouanga was written in French—the same as your zombie book, if I remember correctly. You *are* fluent in French, aren't you, Doctor?"

"Among several other languages, yes," the scholar said.

"But Bobaloa isn't. In fact, he doesn't understand a word of French. When I spoke to him it was like speaking to a wall. It was you who wrote the ouanga, Doctor," McGuffin said, softly assured. The amused smile, he noticed, had gradually disappeared from the old man's face.

"Once again you manifest your racial prejudice," the physician said curtly. "Assuming that I am at heart a Mau Mau and voodoo is my irrevocable destiny, how does that explain the death of this poor young man? If we are intent on destroying the golf club and driving the whites from Palm Isle, why should we kill the employee rather than the employer?"

"Angelo's murder could have been the result of a sour drug deal," McGuffin answered. "But more likely it has something to do with the note he wrote me last night. He said he had information about the golf club," the detective said, patting the note in his hip pocket. "I think he stumbled onto what you and Bobaloa were up to and he decided to tell somebody about it. Call it racial bias if you like," McGuffin added.

"May I see the note?" Dr. Carver asked, thrusting his hand out for it.

McGuffin hesitated, then placed his hand in his pocket and slowly drew the note out. "Okay. But if you try to eat this I'm going down your throat after it," McGuffin warned.

"Primitive though we are, we do not eat paper," he said, holding Angelo's note out to the light. He read it, looked curiously at McGuffin, and then read it again, aloud.

"This note says, 'I got information about *a* golf club.'"

"Yeah—?"

"Not *the* golf club. According to this message, Angelo had information about a single golf club, such as a putter or driver, not the Palm Isle Golf Club," the old man explained.

"Let me see that," McGuffin said, snatching the note away from him. The doctor was right, he saw. "So what?" he said. "Angelo was a caddie, not a Shakespeare scholar. What's the difference?"

"The difference, I should say, is considerable," the doctor replied. "Even a scarcely literate caddie would intuitively use the definite, not the indefinite, article, if he were speaking of the only golf club on the island. Wouldn't you say?" he asked, with a quick smile.

"'I got information about *a* golf club,'" McGuffin mused. "What the fuck did he mean by that?" he wondered aloud, as he looked up the fairway. The constable was approaching in his white jeep.

"I'm sure you'll figure it out," the coroner said, waving to the constable.

"Yeah," McGuffin replied uncertainly.

"Meanwhile I have enjoyed our philological discussion," he added, as he started toward the constable.

"Thanks," McGuffin said, stuffing the dead man's note back in his pants pocket. There were some golf courses, he knew, that were unsuitable for a certain kind of player. The Augusta National and Lee Trevino came immediately to mind. He wondered, as he walked slowly to the waiting constable, if the same was true of some cases and certain detectives.

27

On the Sunday afternoon that the club championship would be decided, Francis Knight arrived unexpectedly at the PIGC. McGuffin, who had received a call from his client from the Miami airport only a few hours before, waited at the airstrip for his arrival. McGuffin didn't have to be told—it was obvious from his client's tone that the case had come to a close. With Al Balata dead, Knight had nothing more to fear. That plus the fact that McGuffin was no closer to a solution now than he ever had been was more than sufficient grounds for the lawyer to terminate their agreement.

It's too bad, McGuffin thought, as he watched the plane land and taxi to a stop near the Quonset hut. He hated more than anything else to leave a case unresolved. But what the hell, he said to himself as he started across the runway, with Al and Byron both gone there's not much Skins money to be had anymore anyway.

Francis Knight stood on the grass with a small bag in one hand, as Eddie gunned the engine and made a turn around McGuffin. With his bandaged nose and blackened eyes, the pilot looked like an exotic bird perched in the cockpit.

"Good afternoon, Mr. McGuffin," Francis Knight said, as McGuffin halted the cart beside him.

"Good afternoon," McGuffin replied, as his client slid onto the seat beside him.

"Let's go straight to the clubhouse," Knight said, when they approached the turn to his cottage. "I'd like to see the scores."

McGuffin drove in silence to the yellow-and-white-striped scorer's tent beside the eighteenth green. He would say nothing about the investigation until his client asked, McGuffin had decided. If he was going to be terminated, let Knight bring it up by himself.

McGuffin stopped the cart outside the tent and followed his client inside. The place was empty, as virtually all of the members were out on the course, playing the final round of the tournament. It was a seventy-two-hole affair, eighteen on Friday, which was also qualifying day, eighteen on Saturday, and the final thirty-six on Sunday. The twenty low scores played without handicap for the club championship, while the rest of the field was divided into four flights according to their qualifying score and allowed full handicap. The level of play was not keen, but the intensity was feverish, and even as a spectator sport it ranked right up there with the Super Bowl as far as the men of the Palm were concerned.

"Do you know this is the first club championship I've missed since joining the Palm?" Francis Knight asked, peering at the scoreboard.

"I'm sorry you had to miss it," McGuffin said.

"It was that damned trial," the lawyer mumbled.

McGuffin nodded. He knew it was Al Balata who had interfered with his client's plans, but he said nothing.

"Just look at those scores," Knight exclaimed. "They're awful. Hell, I might even have qualified for the championship flight if I had been here on Friday."

"All you had to do was break ninety," McGuffin said, studying the scores. Preoccupied until now with an investigation that was going nowhere, McGuffin had paid little attention to the tournament. Churston Brown's eighty-one was the lowest of the three rounds posted to date, followed by Horton Ormsby's eighty-three.

"If I had known the play was going to be this bad, I might have stayed in San Francisco. However," Knight said, turning to the detective, "it's probably just as well that I did come. Always best to do something like this in person, don't you think?"

"To do what in person?" McGuffin asked, fixing Knight with his innocent altar-boy expression.

"Well, surely you must see, Amos. The case is closed." It was the first time he had used the detective's first name. "Balata is dead—it doesn't matter anymore if he killed Lyle and Byron or if he didn't."

"I suppose not," McGuffin agreed. "But what if someone else killed all three of them? And Angelo too. Aren't you interested in catching the murderer then?"

"Really, Amos, you can't believe that. Angelo's death was an accident. Even the Miami medical examiner said those bruises were there prior to his drowning."

"He said they *could* have been there prior to his drowning," McGuffin corrected.

"Either way, who'd want to kill the caddiemaster?" the lawyer asked.

"At least three people that I know of so far," McGuffin answered. "Either Bobaloa or Eddie, if they thought he was going to pull out of the drug business and testify against them. Or Cuppy Dunch," he added.

"Preposterous," the lawyer scoffed.

"Is it? After Byron's death, Angelo was one of the few people remaining who knew that Cuppy was thrown off the pro tour for cheating. If Angelo had been blackmailing Cuppy—if that's why he was caddiemaster here—I'd say Cuppy had good reason for wanting to be rid of him."

"Many people have reason to kill, but fortunately for society, few have the will," Francis Knight said in a patronizing tone. "Believe me, Cuppy Dunch is no more capable of murder than I am."

"I wish I had your gift," McGuffin said. "It would save me a lot of legwork."

"I am saving you a lot of legwork, Amos. I'm taking you off the case. You're flying back tonight," Francis Knight said.

"Okay," McGuffin said, nodding slowly. "You're the boss. When you say it's over, it's over."

"Thank you," the lawyer said, then turned and started out of the tent. When McGuffin called his name, he stopped and turned. "Yes?"

"Did Horton Ormsby ask you to take me off the case?"

"Horton has nothing to do with it," the lawyer snapped.

"Who stood to gain the most by Al Balata's death?" McGuffin snapped back.

Francis Knight stared evenly at McGuffin for a moment, then took two steps forward. "Surely you aren't implying that I had something to do with Al Balata's death, are you, Mr. McGuffin?"

"Of course not," McGuffin replied. "You gained very little by Al's death. You still have to pay off your debt to his estate, and so does Horton Ormsby. But Ormsby has an additional interest. He and Balata were partners in a resort development. Now just as a general principle of law, what ordinarily happens to a partner's share of the business when he dies?"

The lawyer shrugged. "Ordinarily it passes to the surviving partner. However—"

"Exactly," McGuffin interrupted, before the lawyer could get to the exceptions to the rule. "And if it turns out that Ormsby now owns all of Al's resort instead of half, I'd say he has a good reason for wanting me off the case, wouldn't you?"

"No, I would not," Knight answered. "I've told you before and I'll tell you again, for the last time, Horton Ormsby is not a murderer."

"And I'll tell you something," McGuffin said, pointing a finger at his client. "Byron Kilty was murdered. I don't know about the others, but I know Byron was murdered, and so does Ormsby. First he forced me to suppress evidence and now he wants me off the island. There's something wrong here."

"Not that I can see," Francis Knight replied, then turned and walked out of the tent.

"Fuck!" McGuffin exclaimed, slamming his fist into the scoreboard and knocking it off its pedestal. The hand hurt like a sonofabitch but it no longer mattered. He had played his last round of golf at the PIGC.

He picked up the scoreboard and replaced it on the pedestal, then turned and started out of the tent. When he stepped outside he saw Cuppy Dunch approaching with an

enormous trophy, glinting like a polished mirror in the tropical sun.

"That's the ugliest trophy I've ever seen in my life,"
McGuffin growled as the pro hoisted it up onto a table beside
the eighteenth green.

"Isn't it," Cuppy agreed. "But you know, there isn't a
player out there today who wouldn't give his left nut to see his
name inscribed on this ugly cup."

McGuffin stepped closer to examine the gem-studded gold-
and-silver cup. An etched golfer in plus fours was striking a
pearl golf ball to a diamond flag in the center of an emerald
green. The first name, inscribed in 1921, was Jonathan Kilty,
Byron's grandfather, a man who had founded an industrial
empire and amassed millions only to die from a snake's bite
while illegally moving his ball in a bunker. Life is full of surprises, McGuffin thought. There were no great golfers among
the names that followed, but it was an illustrious group nonetheless, many of them famous for their strokes on Wall Street
if not on the golf course. The last name on the cup, immediately above the blank space for the current year, was that of
Lyle Boone. The club champion prior to him was Dr. Byron
Kilty, who had ironically died as his grandfather had died, and
the champion before him was Al Balata.

"Lyle Boone, Byron Kilty, and Al Balata," McGuffin read
aloud. All past champions and all dead. "Maybe golf really is a
curse."

"It was for me," Cuppy said.

"You brought that on yourself," McGuffin said.

"Yeah, I blew it," the pro agreed.

"We both blew it," the detective said, as he turned and
headed for the clubhouse.

"Where are you going?" Cuppy called.

"To get a drink," McGuffin replied. "I'm off the case."

Except for Stymie and a few waitresses, the bar was empty
when McGuffin stepped inside. Stymie was standing in front
of the window overlooking the ninth green, watching a couple
of corporate presidents battling for the third-flight cham-

pionship. Neither of them could break ninety if their stock option plan depended on it, but right now each man was studying his putt more carefully than any proposed corporate merger.

"How are they doing?" McGuffin asked, as he slid, unnoticed, onto a bar stool.

"Oh, hello, sah," Stymie said, turning away from the golfers. "Dose men are not doin' so good, I don' tink. But Mistah Ormsby shot tirty-nine on de front side, I heard."

"Is that right?" McGuffin said. "Let me have a Paddy's and soda."

"Yas sah," Stymie said, reaching for the bottle.

When Stymie put his drink in front of him, McGuffin picked it up and walked silently into the oak-paneled anteroom. He didn't feel like talking to anybody. He slumped heavily to the leather couch in front of the great fireplace and raised his glass to the PIGC coat of arms.

"*Golf ad mortem*," he said.

He finished the drink quickly, then laid his head on the back of the couch and waited for the alcohol to absolve him of defeat. Nothing happened; he still felt shitty. He was about to get up and return to the bar for another drink when he was arrested by something on the wall in front of him. He didn't know what it was, but something seemed vaguely amiss.

Then he saw it—or rather didn't see it. Instead of a pair of crossed golf clubs joined by a knotted metal ribbon under the golden palm tree on the coat of arms, there was only a single club lying diagonally across the shield. The iron club with the steel golf ball attached to its face was missing.

McGuffin jumped off the couch and dragged the coffee table to the hearth. He had thought those steel clubs were welded to the face of the shield. But when he climbed up on the table and touched the remaining club, a wood, he saw that this was not the case. The clubhead rested on a metal peg, from which it could be lifted and slid through the hole in the knotted metal ribbon. It was molded from a single piece of cast iron (which explained why it hadn't been welded) and painted to resemble an antique driver, and it weighed,

McGuffin guessed, at least ten pounds—more than enough to cave in a cranium. The missing club was the one that had been used to kill Al Balata, he realized. And they hadn't been able to find the ball simply because it was still attached to the club.

Someone had concealed the club in his bag on the day of the Vandal Scramble, McGuffin decided. Then he had removed it while Al was concentrating on his shot, and struck him on the head with it. Drunk as everyone was, it was nevertheless unlikely that Bobaloa could have done it and gotten away unnoticed. The murderer has to be a Palm man, McGuffin decided.

Then he remembered Angelo's note, still in his pocket—"I got information about *a* golf club." It was the caddiemaster's responsibility to clean the clubs and return them to the storage room following the match. No doubt the murderer had intended to return the club to the coat of arms, but he wasn't able to remove it from his bag before Angelo saw it. Dr. Carver was right—Angelo did have information about a particular club, and the murderer knew it. Whoever killed Al Balata had to kill Angelo to shut him up.

"McGuffin, what are you doing up there?" Francis Knight demanded, as he stepped into the anteroom.

"I know how Al Balata was killed," McGuffin said, jumping down from the coffee table.

"Of course you do," the lawyer agreed. "We all do. He was struck on the head by an errant golf ball."

"Not exactly," McGuffin said, pointing to the coat of arms. "Look up there. What do you see?"

"What do I see? I see the coat of arms. What am I supposed—" He stopped suddenly and glared accusingly at the detective. "What have you done with the other club?"

"I haven't done anything with it."

"Then where is it?"

"With Al Balata's murderer," McGuffin answered.

"Mr. McGuffin, please—"

"Listen to me," McGuffin ordered. Then he carefully explained the conclusion he had just come to, watching as the lawyer's expression changed gradually from resistance to amazement.

"But—all those people—surely someone would have seen it," the lawyer said uncertainly.

"Obviously no one did," McGuffin answered. "But unfortunately for the murderer, Angelo happened to see the club before the killer was able to get it back to the shield." The lawyer nodded with quickening interest as McGuffin went on to explain the contents of Angelo's note.

"But who did Angelo see with the club?" the lawyer wailed, helpless and frustrated.

McGuffin stared past his client but didn't answer. He was pushing possibilities through his mind, but nothing was coming out.

"Horton?" Knight asked, fearfully.

"Possibly," McGuffin said, beginning to pace slowly. "He and Balata were already in the resort business together, but somewhere else. Maybe they were trying to take over the Palm to convert it to a resort as well. So Ormsby killed Balata in order to get it all for himself—that would make sense," McGuffin said, thinking aloud. "But why would he have killed Lyle and Byron?"

"Maybe those were just accidents," the lawyer ventured.

McGuffin shook his head. "Byron's death was no accident," he said. He clamped his hand over the back of his neck and began walking faster, in a tight circle. "Al killed Byron? He hired his pimp to dump the snakes on him?"

"Pimp?" Francis Knight repeated.

"Al was into black women," McGuffin answered. "Anybody could have poisoned Lyle. Balata, Ormsby—everybody was there—"

"For his bond," the lawyer put in. He was warming to the idea of murder.

"As well as to make Horton club president," McGuffin added, continuing to circle beneath the shield with its ominous message, *Golf ad Mortem.*

"Why should he wish to be club president?" Knight asked.

"For at least two reasons," McGuffin answered. "To be in a position of influence in case the disposition of the club should come to a vote. From what I know of your friend Lyle, he would have fought tooth and nail to oppose any sale of the Palm."

"That's true," the lawyer said. "What's the second reason?"

"To be in a position to control any later homicide investigation—which he did," McGuffin explained.

"So I see," the lawyer said softly. "You were right, of course—it was Ormsby who asked me to take you off the case. He was afraid your investigation would embarrass the club. And so it will. I owe you an apology, Amos," Francis Knight said, extending his hand. McGuffin didn't hear. He was standing stock still, staring into the blackened fireplace. "Amos—?"

"What?"

"I'm sorry I doubted you. I just couldn't believe that Horton was capable of murder, but I realize now that I was wrong. Under certain circumstances I suppose anyone is capable of murder, even me."

"Yeah, even you," McGuffin said, as Knight pumped his hand.

"It's all very clear, isn't it?" he asked, releasing the detective's hand. "It was Balata who dropped the strychnine into Lyle's drink. He and Ormsby were already partners, but I'm sure Ormsby didn't yet have the stomach for murder. He only came to it later."

"Probably," McGuffin said.

"Then one or both of them hired this Bobaloa fellow to kill poor Byron in the terrible way they did, which resulted in their owning two bonds."

"Plus their own two," McGuffin reminded him.

"Exactly. They were getting very close to control of the Palm. Then Horton, who had by now grown accustomed to murder, became greedy. He decided to kill his partner and keep all the profit for himself. And he would have succeeded had it not been for Angelo's watchful eye. Is that how you see it, Amos?"

"I couldn't have said it better myself," McGuffin answered.

"Yes, I do seem to have a knack for this business, don't I? Not to take anything away from you, Amos. You've done a commendable job."

"Thanks," McGuffin said.

"Horton Ormsby," the lawyer said, shaking his head. "I couldn't be more surprised if it had been Churston Brown."

"Why do you say that?" McGuffin asked. "I thought anyone was capable of murder—even you."

"But not Churston," the lawyer replied with a short laugh. "Churston can't do anything. Except play golf," he added. "He tried working in his father's bank, but quit after a few weeks because he didn't like New York. There are no golf courses on Wall Street, you know. He thought he'd like Paris, so his daddy made him manager of the Paris branch, but that didn't last long either. I'm afraid that boy is a bitter disappointment to his father," he said, as McGuffin brushed past him. "Amos—?"

"Stymie!" McGuffin called, hurrying to the bar.

"Yas sah, Paddy's and soda," Stymie said, turning away from the window. He had been watching the golfers on the ninth green.

"Amos, you're not going to start drinking now!" Francis Knight said, following McGuffin to the bar. "We have to find that club."

"We will," McGuffin assured him. "Forget the drink, Stymie. Who is Mr. Ormsby playing with?"

"Mistah Brown, sah. Dey made de turn about fifteen minutes ago, I should tink."

"Find them," McGuffin said, turning to Francis Knight. "And when you do, don't let either one of them out of your sight."

"Where are you going?" the lawyer called, as McGuffin started out.

"To find the missing golf club!" McGuffin called, as he disappeared around the corner and down the stairs.

28

Churston Brown's cottage lay in a jungle clearing not far from the Devil's Asshole, where Byron Kilty had met his herpetological end. Little more than a door at the end of a tunnel of overgrown foliage was visible to the detective as he skidded his cart to a halt at the head of the path. It was, McGuffin observed as he plunged into the tunnel, stooping under elephant-ear leaves that hung like useless fans in the still air, as if man and nature had conspired together to cloak the cottage in secrecy.

The door was locked, but McGuffin was able to open it quickly with his American Express card. It occurred to him as he pushed the door open to the living room that it was the first time he had used the card since its revocation, several weeks before. The room, McGuffin saw, was an incredible mess. Except for a clearing on the carpet where a putting cup and three balls lay, the room was strewn with papers and books. He waded through the papers and picked up two of the books on the coffee table in front of the couch. One was an English translation of *Tristes tropiques*, by Claude Lévi-Strauss; the other *The Psychic Side of Golf*, by Dr. William Hickock of the Institute for Dynamic Consciousness. The last sounded familiar. Probably one of those loony farms in Marin County, he decided, dropping the books on the table. He went quickly through the living room and kitchen, looking under the couch and behind the refrigerator, and any other place the missing golf club might be hidden, but he found nothing. He looked behind the curtains, went through the china and linen cabinets, and then got down on his knees to examine the underside of the dining table. Nothing, he said to himself as he got to his feet.

He started for the bedroom, then stopped and returned to the dining table. There was a typewriter on the table, along with a thin pile of manuscript and a single book. No doubt this was the scholarly study of the peoples of these islands that was keeping Churston so busy, McGuffin thought, as he picked up the manuscript. He leafed through it, found nothing interesting, then dropped it onto the table. Judging from the dust that billowed up, Churston hadn't worked on the manuscript in months. McGuffin picked up the bound volume lying beside the manuscript and turned it over. It was another book by Lévi-Strauss, entitled *Les Structures élémentaires de la parenté*. This one, however, was not translated from the original French.

"*Voilà*," McGuffin said softly.

He dropped the book on the table and walked toward the bedroom. The nose was working. He was, finally, onto something. It was apparent that the guest bedroom hadn't been used in a long time. It took only a few minutes to tear the bed apart and go through the chest of drawers and closet.

"Nothing," McGuffin said. Undismayed, the nose still working, he went on to the next room.

The master bedroom was being used as still another study. There was a desk and typewriter beside the bed and a neat row of books along an overhead shelf, all of them on golf. The pile of manuscript pages beside the typewriter was much thicker than the pile on the dining-room table and not nearly as dusty. McGuffin picked up the manuscript and plopped it over.

"'*The Secret of Golf*, by Churston Brown,'" he read aloud.

The audacity! Churston Brown, who could barely break eighty, was writing a book, not on anthropology, but on the far more complex subject of golf? The unmitigated, presumptuous gall.

But McGuffin was even more shocked by the next page.

Beneath a photograph of the author swinging a golf club was the heading:

ABOUT THE AUTHOR
Churston Brown is the reigning club champion of the exclusive Palm Isle Golf Club . . .

"Jesus," McGuffin breathed. I just hope Knight finds them before Ormsby wins the match, he thought.

McGuffin turned to the first page:

Golf is a blood sport . . .

the book began. It was the same theme McGuffin had heard from Churston in the bar, but this time he had strained the metaphor even further.

Golf is war! Your opponent is your enemy! And all is fair in love and war! The most important thing in war, as in life, is winning! Win, win, win! Don't be a loser! No one loves a loser! Fathers hate losers, mothers hate losers! All the world hates a loser!!!!!!!

"My God," McGuffin said softly, as he leafed ahead. It was more of the same. Page after page, the delusions and rantings of a deranged golfer driven to madness by the most frustrating game of them all. Perhaps, like the capacity for murder, this madness lurked in all golfers. The less afflicted might throw clubs or abuse caddies, but it was only a matter of degree, McGuffin knew. And this sudden realization caused him to shudder.

McGuffin dropped the manuscript onto the desk and continued to look for the murderous golf club. He discovered bizarre bits of golf paraphernalia hidden away in drawers like marital aids. There was an ugly brace worn to keep the wrist stiff and a steel headband on a stand to hold the head in place during the swing. There was a putter with a bubble in the head and another with a telescopic sight. There was a mat with a crazy-quilt pattern that only a Karsten Solheim could decipher, as well as a drawer filled with doughnut weights, straps, harnesses, chains, pulleys, and unfamiliar things whose function McGuffin could only guess. But nowhere in the room could he find the lethal golf club he was looking for.

In the closet he found shirts and slacks and a few umbrellas standing in the corner, but no golf club. The back of the closet was concealed by a wall of shoe boxes, which McGuffin, on hands and knees, began throwing out into the room. When he heard a light tapping sound that seemed to be coming from outside the house, he assumed it was a bird pecking at the roof. But when his hand brushed against a plate of glass as he cleared the last shoe box away, he saw in an alarming instant that it was not birds on the roof, but snakes in a terrarium making the tapping sound.

He scrambled backward into the shoe boxes, then lay motionless, staring at the striking coral snakes as they hurled themselves repeatedly at the glass, trying to get at him as they had poor Byron Kilty. There were several of them, less than a foot in length and eerily beautiful with their bright bands of red, yellow, and black.

When he could move, McGuffin got to his feet, kicked the shoe boxes out of the way, and slammed the closet door on the agitated snakes. He no longer needed the golf club to prove that Churston had murdered Al Balata. The snakes were more than enough to convict him of the murder of Byron Kilty.

And anyway, he said to himself as he started out of the house, I know now where I'll find that golf club.

Pushing the accelerator to the floor, McGuffin labored past the Devil's Asshole and the drowning pond, then on to the last few holes, where Churston Brown and Horton Ormsby were fighting the duel of their lives—even if Ormsby was unaware of it. Seeing Sandy Berwick and his partner on the sixteenth green, McGuffin veered sharply in that direction and hollered, "Sandy!"

Startled, Berwick knocked a short putt twenty feet past the

hole and threw his putter into the air. "What the hell do you think you're doing?" he shouted.

"Sorry. Have you seen Brown and Ormsby?" the detective asked.

"They're on fifteen. Is it so goddam important that you've got to shout when I'm putting?"

"You can take it over," McGuffin said, backing his cart away from the green.

"By what authority?" Berwick's opponent demanded.

"Rule Fourteen dash Seven, subparagraph C!" McGuffin called over his shoulder. It had an authoritative ring to it.

He found them on the fifteenth hole. Horton, looking relaxed, was standing on the green beside his ball, while Churston was preparing to hit from a greenside bunker. Francis Knight, looking a bit apprehensive, stood between them. The lawyer was obviously relieved to see the detective roll up just as Churston hit out of the bunker. Distracted possibly by the detective's appearance, Churston hit it thin, and it shot low across the green. A great grin appeared on Horton's face, until the ball struck the wheel of McGuffin's cart and bounced back onto the green, to within eighteen inches of the hole.

"What the hell is that cart doing there?" Ormsby bellowed, as he started across the green toward Churston's ball.

"Don't touch that ball!" Churston shouted.

"The hell I won't! That ball would have rolled fifty yards down the fairway if it hadn't hit that goddam cart!"

As Ormsby stooped to pick up the ball, Churston dived on his back, knocking him to the green. Cursing and thrashing wildly, both men rolled about on the green while Knight and McGuffin hurried to pull them apart. McGuffin pulled the larger man off the top only a moment before he was about to do some serious damage, while Knight wrestled the smaller man away.

"He's crazy!" Ormsby shouted, trying to pull free of his captor. "He's stark raving mad!"

"You don't know the half of it!" McGuffin grunted.

"It's the rub of the green!" Churston shouted, squirming in the lawyer's grip.

"Hold still—he's liable to kill you!" Knight said, pulling Churston away from Ormsby's loose hand.

"It's not him!" McGuffin shouted. "It's him!"

"Who?"

"Churston!"

Francis Knight dropped him like a coral snake. "Churston is the murderer?"

"Yes!"

"You're all crazy! Let me go!" Ormsby demanded.

"Okay, but no more fighting," McGuffin said, releasing the club president. Ormsby shook himself like a wet dog and glared at Churston, poised defensively over his ball. "And no more golf," McGuffin added.

"What do you mean, no more golf?" Ormsby demanded. "We've got three more holes to play and I'm one stroke up."

"You won't be after I tap this one in," Churston said.

"Oh yeah?" Ormsby said, starting across the green.

McGuffin grabbed him from behind as Churston quickly knocked his putt in with the edge of his sand wedge.

"Par!" Churston exclaimed.

"I want a ruling!" Ormsby howled.

"I'm trying to give you a ruling!" McGuffin shouted, as he continued to struggle with the president. "Churston Brown is a murderer!"

"Don't you mean Horton?" Francis Knight inquired uncertainly.

"I'm gonna kill him if he doesn't put that ball back where it belongs!" Ormsby threatened.

"Horton, will you stop thinking about golf for a minute and listen to me?" McGuffin demanded, shaking the club president violently.

"All right, I'm listening! Let go of me."

McGuffin released him for the second time and backed slowly away. "Please, just keep quiet and listen," he urged. Then he turned and walked slowly across the green toward the murderer. Churston regarded the detective warily as he approached. "That was a nice putt," McGuffin said.

Churston smiled faintly. "It counts, doesn't it?"

"Sure it counts."

"Like hell it does!" Ormsby said.

"Horton!" Francis Knight warned, bringing his finger to his lips.

"That makes us even," Churston informed the detective. "If Horton two-putts I'll be one stroke up."

"He could easily three-putt from there," McGuffin said, stopping just out of range of the sand wedge in Churston's hand. "Then you'd almost certainly be the club champ. Just like it says in your book."

"You saw my book?"

McGuffin nodded. "I also saw your little pets in the closet. The ones you dropped on Byron?" Churston's eyes followed as McGuffin moved, circling closer. "It's all right, we understand," he said soothingly. "You had to do what you did so Byron wouldn't win the club championship. That is why you dropped the snakes on Byron, isn't it, Churston?"

"No," Churston replied. "I'm as good as Byron. Even better. He's just luckier than me. I just wanted to be sure he didn't get lucky."

"You made sure of that," McGuffin said.

"What the hell—?" Ormsby asked.

"Keep still," Francis Knight said.

"And what about Lyle Boone?" McGuffin asked. "He used to get lucky too, didn't he?"

"All the time," Churston answered.

"Except the night he drank the poison. What did you give him, Churston? Was it snake venom, or just plain old strychnine?"

Churston shook his head. "Castrix."

"Castrix," McGuffin repeated. "Rat poison." The means was no less banal than the motive.

"I don't believe it," Horton said.

"Just listen," Francis instructed.

"Now tell us why you drowned Angelo," McGuffin urged.

"I had to. He saw me take the club out of my bag. I parked my cart around the corner by the side entrance so I could take the club back upstairs, but Angelo saw me coming, and he followed me around the corner to get my clubs. He shouldn't have been so efficient."

"What club?" Horton asked.

"Sssh!"

"Did he say anything about the club when he saw it?" McGuffin asked.

"No. He pretended he hadn't seen it, but I knew he had, and I knew I had to do something about it. So I went to his cottage that night and I offered to give him a lot of money if he wouldn't tell anybody. He agreed, and then I took him to my cottage. I told him we were going to get the money, but instead I got him drunk. Then when he passed out I took him out to the pond. I took his clothes off and piled them on the shore so it would look like he had gone for a swim. Then I pulled him into the water and held him under until he drowned. I didn't want to kill Angelo, but I had to," he said, turning a sad face to McGuffin.

"It couldn't be helped," McGuffin said. "Now tell Horton how you killed Al Balata."

"I hit him with the ball," Churston answered.

"Bullshit!" Horton exclaimed. "You can't even come out of a bunker, let alone hit a man in the head with a golf ball!"

"Have a look in Churston's bag," McGuffin instructed.

"You know, there are people behind us," Horton said, as he walked to the cart.

"They'll have to wait," McGuffin answered.

"Hey, he's got fifteen clubs in the bag. That's illegal," Horton charged. "And this one's got a golf—I'll be goddamned! It's the club from the coat of arms!"

"It's also the club that killed Al Balata," Francis Knight said. "Put it back in the bag, Horton. It's evidence."

Horton dropped the club back into the bag as McGuffin reached for the club in Churston's hand. "Give me the wedge, Churston."

Churston clutched the club to his chest. "I need it to finish the match."

"I'm sure Horton will concede the match," McGuffin said.

"What—?"

"Horton, shut up," Francis ordered.

"Tell Churston that you concede," McGuffin instructed.

"I will like hell."

"Horton!"

"All right, I concede," he grumbled.

A big smile crossed Churston's face. "Does that mean I'm the club champ?"

"You're the champ, all right," McGuffin said, prying the club from his fingers.

29

Late on a Friday afternoon, McGuffin was seated at his usual place at the end of the bar at Goody's, anxiously watching the door for prospects of employment. There were a couple of judges at the bar, several lawyers, a claims manager, and a smattering of civil servants, cops, and members of the fourth estate, all of them good for a lead now and then, but not today. Things were slow in the PI business. He was thinking of moving on to another joint when he looked up and saw a familiar though unexpected figure coming through the doorway, nattily attired in a gray homburg and slim fitting chesterfield with a velvet collar. Judges and lawyers nodded respectfully as Francis Knight made his way diffidently down the bar, deeper and deeper into the unfamiliar smoke-filled room.

"Good afternoon, Amos," he said, stopping in front of McGuffin.

"Francis," McGuffin said, sliding off his stool to shake the lawyer's hand. "It's good to see you."

"Your answering service suggested I might find you here," Knight said, glancing appraisingly about the bar.

"Yeah, I come here occasionally," McGuffin said. "In the line of business. Can I buy you a drink?"

"Thank you, I'll have a cassis and soda," the lawyer said, removing his homburg.

"Goody?" McGuffin called, catching the hat before Knight could place it on the bar in a beer puddle. He placed it on the shelf above the coat hooks, then turned to the lawyer and asked, "Do you want to hang your coat up?"

"I'll keep it," Francis said, sliding onto the bar stool next to McGuffin's.

Goody waddled down the bar, regarding his new customer warily. "Yeah?"

"Goody, this is Francis Knight," McGuffin said.

"Glad to know you," Goody said, wiping his knobby hand on his apron and sticking it over the bar.

"How do you do?" the lawyer said, shaking hands hesitantly with the bartender.

"You got another one of them golf-course jobs for Amos, or somethin' like that?"

"I'm afraid not," the lawyer replied.

"Cuz he could use it," Goody said. "How much you say you won playin' golf down there, Amos? Several thousand dollars?"

"Hundred," McGuffin said. "Several hundred."

"Funny, I thought you told me five or six grand. Oh well, what do you want to drink, Mr. Knight?"

"Cassis and soda," McGuffin said.

"What?"

"Any kind of brandy will be fine," Knight said.

"Right," Goody said, turning and heading for his meager store.

"So, several thousand dollars," the lawyer said, turning to McGuffin.

"A gross exaggeration," McGuffin said. In the excitement following Churston's arrest, they had forgotten to split up McGuffin's Skins winnings, as they had agreed. Or at least Knight had forgotten. "I'll tally it up and send you your check." The lawyer made a dismissive gesture but said nothing. "How are things at the Palm?" McGuffin asked.

"Changed," Francis answered. "The caliber of play has fallen off drastically now that our top four players are gone."

"That's too bad."

"In a way," the golfer answered, enigmatically. "And Cuppy is moving to Hawaii with Marian."

"No!"

"Yes. You knew they were married, didn't you?"

"No."

"Yes, they were married shortly after you left. In Bobaloo's church, by the way."

"Bobaloa," McGuffin corrected. He wondered if the snake had been there.

Goody returned with a wineglass filled with brandy. "We don't get much call for snifters here," he said, placing the drink in front of Francis.

"That's quite all right," Knight said. He raised the glass to McGuffin and toasted, "To golf!"

McGuffin nodded unenthusiastically and sipped his whiskey. After witnessing Churston Brown's madness, he had taken the pledge—he would never play golf again.

"What do you hear from Churston?" McGuffin asked, replacing his glass on the bar.

"I understand Churston is getting along just fine," Francis gasped, after swallowing Goody's brandy. "He's confined to an institution near Palm Beach, but he's allowed to play golf every day with his doctor."

"I hope he's not allowed to play for the club championship," McGuffin said.

Francis smiled. "I think not."

"The brandy's not so hot, huh?" Goody said, pointing to Knight's drink.

"It's hot enough," Francis answered. Satisfied, Goody returned to the far end of the bar as Francis Knight turned a questioning look to McGuffin. "You know, I never did fully understand, Amos . . . in the clubhouse you had me convinced that Horton Ormsby was the murderer, but when you got to the fifteenth green you told me it was Churston. What happened in the interim?"

"Nothing," McGuffin answered. "I knew that winning was important to Churston—the most important thing in life. He was willing to betray a confidence and call a friend a cuckold in order to win, and I had listened to his crazy theory about golf being a blood sport. But I just never thought he was crazy enough to kill. Until you reminded me that he had worked in Paris."

"And that makes him crazy?" Francis asked.

McGuffin shook his head. "Ever since the ouanga there was something nagging me about Churston, but I never could put my finger on it."

"What's the ouanga?" Knight asked.

McGuffin explained briefly and then went on. "Churston pretended that his French was no better than mine, yet he was the one who translated all the more unusual words. If I had remembered then that he had mentioned working in Paris while we were playing golf, I might have been suspicious. But I wasn't thinking about that at the time. I was thinking that Bobaloa had reason to want me off the island because I was threatening to break up his drug operation, just as Churston knew I would."

"You mean he was making a red herring of Lobaloa," the lawyer interjected.

"And doing a masterful job of it," McGuffin said. "He told me how Byron's grandfather died just so I'd think Bobaloa killed Byron in the same way, as an act of vengeance. And then to get a rise out of Bobaloa, Churston told him I might be a CIA operative intent on thwarting Bobaloa's revolution. That's why Bobaloa's girlfriend took me skinny-dipping."

"Pardon me?"

"She used her body to get information out of me," McGuffin explained.

"I see."

"Only I didn't have any to give. And anyway we were interrupted by Bobaloa in his motorboat, which I'm sure neither of them had counted on."

"I don't understand," Francis interrupted.

"It's not important," McGuffin answered. "Churston had me chasing my tail, and I might still be if you hadn't reminded me that he had worked in Paris as a bank manager. That's when I realized that Churston was faking the extent of his fluency in French. Suddenly everything else—the bonds, the drugs, the love triangle—none of it mattered anymore. Because at that moment I also remembered something that Cuppy had said less than an hour before, when he was carrying the trophy out to the eighteenth green. He said, 'You know, there isn't a golfer out there today who wouldn't give his left nut to see his name inscribed on this ugly cup.' And then it dawned on me. The same thing is true in every country club in America. Every weekend thousands of ordinarily decent, peaceful middle-class gentlemen take up their golf clubs and try to figuratively beat one another to death. None of them are really that much different from Churston Brown. Churston just went a little too far. He mixed his metaphors insanely, if you will," McGuffin said, suddenly snatching his glass from the bar.

Francis Knight stared as the detective gulped his drink. He wore a worried look, concerned perhaps that McGuffin might soon be joining Churston's golf club. But McGuffin put an end to this speculation.

"That's why I've given up golf," the detective said, replacing his empty glass on the bar.

"What? You've quit golf?" Francis asked.

"I'll never go near a golf club again for as long as I live," McGuffin vowed.

"No," Francis gasped. "You can't do that."

"Why can't I?"

"Because I need you."

McGuffin turned to his former client. "Don't tell me there's been another murder at the PIGC."

"Not yet," Francis answered, shaking his head. "But there soon will be."

"Who?"

"Horton Ormsby. I intend to kill him in the member-guest tournament at the Palm next week. I'm speaking figuratively, of course, but listen to me, Amos," the lawyer said, clutching at McGuffin's sleeve. "Horton's guest partner is a banker from Texas who claims to be a six, but I happen to know that he's a ten with a big ego—although Horton doesn't. So knowing this, I've made a rather sizable wager with Horton that my guest and I will beat him and his guest. That's why you have to come out of retirement, Amos. I've told him that you'll be my partner and he's agreed to give you eleven strokes."

"Eleven!" McGuffin wailed. "I'm no more than a seven!"

"I know, I know," the lawyer chortled. "And I'm playing much better than my eighteen handicap. That means we get twenty-nine strokes, Amos. We can't lose!"

"Assuming there are no sandbaggers in the field," McGuffin reminded him. A sandbagger was a player who artificially inflated his handicap.

"There are no sandbaggers at the Palm," the lawyer said, drawing himself stiffly erect on the stool.

Twenty-nine strokes, McGuffin thought. Francis was right, it would be hard to lose with such an advantage. But golf was no less dangerous than alcohol, McGuffin knew. One game leads to another, then another and another—until I end up like this wild-eyed, greedy WASP sitting next to me. Or worse, like Churston.

"No," McGuffin said. "I can't do it."

"You can't—" the lawyer repeated dully. "Amos, are you crazy? This is not a sporting event I'm proposing, this is a sure thing."

McGuffin nodded. "I know."

"Then what's wrong? You're offended, aren't you?"

"No, I'm not offended."

"Because it's not cheating—I earned that eighteen," the lawyer assured him.

"I'm sure."

"Okay, we'll knock a stroke off yours."

"I'm sorry," McGuffin said. "I've played my last round of golf."

Francis stared at McGuffin for a moment, then sighed. "You really have, haven't you?" McGuffin nodded. "And there's nothing I can say to change your mind?"

McGuffin shook his head. "Nothing."

"What if I said I'd be willing to forget my half of the Skins winnings?"

"It wouldn't make any difference," McGuffin answered.

"You're a tough case, Amos," the lawyer said, getting to his feet. "But, no hard feelings," he added, extending his hand to the detective.

"Thanks," McGuffin said, shaking hands.

Francis went to the shelf for his hat, then returned to the bar. "By the way, there's also a small cash prize to the winning team," he added, adjusting his homburg as he peered into the yellowing mirror behind the bar.

"How much?" McGuffin asked.

"About twenty thousand dollars, I should think."

"Have you got a car here?" McGuffin asked.

"Yes—"

McGuffin slid off the bar stool and stood facing the lawyer.

"Let's go to the driving range," he said.